i

The Butcher Princess

Louise Furley

Stand-alone

Jezábel and the Assassin

Solitar

Halo Valley

Isle of Orainn

Anastasia

The Kissing Number

The Poser

Wrath of Wolf

Auction Block

Jace's Elusive Woman

Rogan's Treasure

Shawn's Prisoner

The Butcher Princess

ISBN- 978-1-7378341-0-6 (Paperback)
ISBN- 978-1-7369376-9-3 (eBook)

Cover design by Pixel Mischief Design

The characters and events portrayed in this book are fictitious. Any similarity to real persons, living or dead, is coincidental and not intended by the author.

The

Butcher

Princess

Chapter One

*L*iving up to his notorious title as one of the most ruthless warlords in the land, King Jashar D'Avenant raced ahead of his men roaring, "*Ionsaí a dhéanamh!* Attack the marauders!"

His league of bellowing warriors quickly encompassed the band of combatants that charged at them with swords raised in aggressive fervor.

The king didn't have time to reflect on why these scurrilous insurgents were on the border of the Black Frost Forest, part of region of *Thuas sa Spéir's* property, he just gave the order to engage, and a hail of chopping, lancing, battering and roars of hell ensued.

Amongst the chaos and noise of steel-on-steel clashing, shouts of victory rose above agonized screams of fallen invaders and wailing cries of defeat.

Jashar's attention was drawn to the peripheral of the fighting, where it appeared a group of men were chasing a boy through the tall grass.

With a rapier in each hand, Jashar slashed at several soldiers, earning his savage moniker, the *Daigéar Láidir,* the Bloody Dagger.

Killing two and critically wounding the third, not waiting to see them fall to the ground, he changed direction and ran after the men chasing the boy along the skirt of the woods.

Hearing the thumping boots of his brothers, Kaermon and Daron stomping the earth like thunderous giants behind him, a partial wry grin nicked the corner of his mouth

The half-grin compressed to deadly concentration as he neared the pursued gang. He wondered if the boy had committed a criminal act and they were trying to catch him and take him for punishment, or just going to kill him right there for his misdeeds.

Regardless, Jashar wanted to find out why they were trespassing on his lands.

Unfortunately, one of the men turned and saw him. The warrior whistled a shrill warning and the lot of them dodged instantly into the thick of the woods where within seconds the pounding of horse hooves roared through the forest.

Kaer and Daron raced after them on foot, unfortunately, they had all left their steeds across the field when they had engaged in combat.

Something peculiar about the fleeing boy peeked Jashar's interest.

The boy ran oddly, his long thin legs almost knock-kneed like a newborn calf, sloughing through the knee-high grass with arms raised in wussy flails in his awkward frantic attempt at escape.

Jashar's eyes were drawn to the boy's rump. "*Damnú!*" he spat a curse at the surprise shock of heat that struck his groin like a branding iron.

Sickened at the flush of weird desire strumming through him at the sight of the oddly appealing behind, he spat another curse. Yet, his eyes stayed glued to the small round globes bobbling in the tight pants as the boy tripped and flailed across the uneven field.

His shoulder length hair streaming behind him, Jashar upped his speed in pursuit of the boy. It took little effort on the part of the swift warlord to catch up to the child.

Nearing him, the king reached out, grabbed the boy around the neck and hoisted him up in the air.

The boy shrieked then kicked and punched his hands out uselessly.

Close to a half a dozen inches over six feet, Jashar outweighed the boy by well over 100 pounds, and most of that was muscle cordoned upon steel muscle. Not just workout muscles, but blocks of sinewy strength built by real time fighting with swords, knives, hand-to-hand battle, and endless rounds of training.

An overlarge hat clung to the boy's head hiding his hair. As he fought his capture, the jacket he wore started sliding down his thin arms.

Jashar's huge hand encircled his neck holding him up in the air. The boy choked and gagged, kicked frantically and twisted.

The king caught a glimpse of his eyes, and felt that strange flush of lust again. Twin auroras, a blend of the lightest indigo and brilliant blue, fringed with long, curled lashes, gleamed in abject terror at him.

Stifling the uncomfortable feeling that kept striking Jashar's loins, after all, he clearly was only attracted to women, his eyes dipped to the tiny plush lips that the boy was biting the hell out of in his panic.

Another lustful stab hardened his manhood, and Jashar had enough. No boy should have such pink pouty- he yanked the boy's hat off, absently dropping it when a yard of thick, wavy, warm cinnamon laced with ribbons of bright flax tumbled down.

"What the *fujon* is this-" Jashar froze in bewildered shock.

The boy jerked and gasped, his small slender fingers grasped at Jashar's hand trying to pry it off his neck.

Jashar grabbed the jacket, yanked it off and tossed it aside, his eyes popped when they lowered to the boy's chest.

Under a shirt that had several buttons torn off in their scrabbling, a pair of the supplest, most comely breasts Jashar could ever remember seeing, and he'd seen more than his fair share of them, were partially exposed.

Perfect pearlescent globes mounding over cloth bindings threatened to spill out with any more violent movement on the part of the- obviously not a boy-

Jashar released the female like she was on fire. She dropped hard to her feet, stumbling backwards, he lashed out his hand and caught her arm to steady her, then instantly let her go again.

Repeating, he barked, "What the *fujon* is this?"

The girl blinked those indigo eyes, so big and gleaming, Jashar felt like he was face to face with a woodland fairy. Then she spun on her heel and ran.

It took a second to recapture his equilibrium, then Jashar burst a few long-legged strides and snatched his hand around her arm halting her in her tracks.

She shrieked, "Let go of me!" and turned on him swinging. The king easily caught her delicate wrists holding them with no effort while she struggled futilely for all she was worth to break away.

"Stop it, stop fighting right now!" Jashar ordered in his commander's voice.

Ignoring him, she writhed and pulled from him so violently she was obviously hurting herself.

"That is enough!" he barked, shaking her so hard her teeth rattled.

She looked up at him.

It was like looking in twin mirrors. He could see his own dark orbs reflected in her big eyes, his were brutal pits of black ice, chilling and pitiless.

Her gaze skittered over the scar at his temple, down his noble nose to the harsh, chiseled full lips, the strong jaw covered with a few days' worth of scrub, and back to his remorseless gaze that echoed her doom.

Then, her eyes rolled back in her head, her knees buckled, and she fainted.

"Shit- woman-" Jashar threw his hands under her and lifted her into his arms. She weighed but a feather. Although curvy as hell, she was as slender as a willow.

He looked down at her. The woman's slim neck arched over his arm, her head hung, that lustrous hair flowed and swayed.

His attention drew to those unbelievable breasts rounding full and lush- in one movement he maneuvered her to drape on her belly over his shoulder, his arm clasped below her knees.

Striding across the field, Jashar passed dead bodies littering the grass. In short shift his brothers were beside him.

"What in the hell did you get yourself there, *mi bráthair,* my brother?" Kaer asked with a peeked laugh.

"Aye, *dearbh bráthair, mi* blood brother," Daron piped in, jostling around his brothers to get a better look. A lewd grin erupted across his handsome face at her rounded ass propped over Jashar's wide shoulder.

Daron chuckled, "A woodland nymph, I see. Looks like you've got yourself an after dinner treat! You gonna share with your beloved *bráthairens?*"

5

Never slowing his stride, Jashar shot his brother an annoyed frown. "I don't know who she is. There were insurgents chasing her. She was disguised as a boy, she is not one of us-"

"Oh shit, here comes bad news," Kaer grumbled, nodding to the figure approaching.

Another young man, in his own lighter way, was as handsome as the three rugged D'Avenant brothers, but dissatisfaction, dissipation and deceit pitted his face distorting his good looks,.

He hurried up to the brothers. Fine, light blond hair on the thin side swept to the side off his wide forehead. A longish narrow nose, more a nobleman and less a warrior, he had pale skin, light eyes, and was tall but not even close to the brothers' massive builds.

As usual, perpetual irritation pinched his full mouth, pulling it down at the corners. "What the *fujon* is going on? Hamish said you were all to be in the north practicing with the youths, why are you here?"

His pale blue eyes narrowed at the woman slung over Jashar's shoulder. "Who the hell is that?"

Kaer shook his head, dark floppy hair swiveled around his dome. Near as tall and broad and thickly built as his brother, King Jashar, he said, "We dannae know yet. Jash saw a gang of interlopers chasing her and he grabbed her up. The others quickly dispersed into the forest. We gave pursuit but they had horses hidden and made off."

A smug brow lofted. "Oh? The famed perfect warriors allowed intruders to get away?" The pale man shook his head with a sarcastic tsk tsk. "I fear tis you that needs the practice, not the young."

The youngest of the three brothers, Daron, growled, "Why don't you shut the *fujon* up and piss off, Fainge, dear half-*bráthair*?"

The other man scowled his annoyance at Daron. "Your mother has instructed you to stop calling me that," he sniffed. "Fainge, or Fang is no longer funny. You will address me by my correct title, Lord Aran." His long nose in the air, he haughtily ignored Kaer and Daron's mocking laughter.

"Sure Fainge," Daron said, "we-"

The woman stirred over Jashar's shoulder.

Jashar splayed a big hand across her slender back and carefully set her on her feet. She swayed, dizzy, a small hand swept her hair from her face.

"Oh, *mi Dias dhílis!*" Aran slammed a hand to his heart and recoiled in horror. "Tis she, the *Búistér!*" He slugged in a ragged shocking breath and stepped back.

Jashar shoved his long hair back behind his ears and wound both hands around the young woman's upper arms holding her immobile.

His dark brows, angry slashes over black as night eyes, he said, "What the hell are you talking about? Butcher?" He watched his brothers and his half-brother Aran stare at the girl.

Kaer and Daron's eyes lit, their pupils dilated at the sight of her breasts about to plummet out of the torn blouse. But, his half-brother's repulsed gaze never left her frightened face.

Aran made the sign of the cross over his heart. "Aye, she is the *Búistér Striapach.*" He took a labored breath continuing, "*Iníon rí, Principessa Búistér Striapach.*"

Daron's brows lifted to his hairline. His eyes bounced in disbelief from Aran's pallid crass face back to the breathtaking young woman quaking in fear in his brother's steely grasp. "You are crazy, foolish Fang, the Princess Butcher? You're saying that she is the infamous Princess Butcher-Whore?"

Shaking his head, Kaer's gaze heated over her exposed bosom. "Nay, there is no way this slip of a girl is the infamous Butcher of Ailanthus? The Princess Butcher?"

Seeing the men eyeing her décolletage, Jashar let go of one of her arms and tugged the lapels of her blouse together to cover her exposed flesh.

Feeling his hands at her chest, the woman flinched, tried to slap at his hands and push away from him. He wrapped both of his huge arms across the front of her and yanked her against his torso.

Big mistake. He didn't know why he kept reacting to this foreigner like he was, but his manhood again instantly firmed. He jerked his pelvis away from where her rounded buttocks suddenly pressed against him.

She struggled in his arms but it was like a kitten fighting an ox. He exhibited very little exertion to contain her.

Jashar unhooked a small length of rope from his belt, pulled her hands behind her back and tied her wrists together then flipped her long hair over the front of her torn blouse.

To the other men, he asked, "What are you fools talking about? Who is the Princess Butcher?"

Making another quick sign of the cross, Aran snarled at the woman and answered, "She is the killer, the one who abducted our children. Those twenty young girls that were first flogged, imagine, girls as young as three, their tender backs whipped until no flesh was left." He drew in a harsh breath, his narrow eyes putrid with disgust glared at the woman.

"After they were barely clinging to life from the torture," he exhaled, "she had them raped, brutally gang-raped by half her village's men."

He watched the three brothers' expressions blanch aghast at his words. "Then, after more torture," Aran paused for effect, "she had them killed. Beheaded. Murdered. Our precious babies." His mean eyes like sharp flint speared at the girl.

A corner of Aran's wicked lip curled at the bewildered look on her lovely face. "Not only that," he added with dark glee, "tis told that she whores herself to her servants, and," he sucked in a lewd breath, "apparently to any male of her choosing.

"The word is that her father, King Lanaris, has labored to marry her off, but," he sighed again, "to no avail. No honorable man would sully himself with a whore that butchers young children."

"What?" Kaer blurted. His eyes bugged out, taking in the young woman, from the top of her cinnamon hair that waved with its flaxen ribbons down almost to her waist, over the sheer brilliance of her indigo eyes, the pouted lips, down her insane curves, to the tiny waist, the slender flare of her slightly rounded hips.

"Nay, she would not be capable of such atrocities, she is too young. She is but a wee *cailín* herself." His gaze scrolled her young body. Shaking his head in disbelief, he said, "A renowned whore? She can't be but 16? 18 tops?"

"Aye," Daron agreed. "She has the face of a bleatin' *aingeal*." He studied her face and figure with interest, and desire. Confirming his thoughts, "Nay, she is too fresh, too soft, too," he looked at her clear, bright, terrified eyes and finished, "innocent."

The men could tell by the bewildered look on the female's face that she wasn't understanding their language. They switched to mostly English.

Aran sneered at the fearful look on her face. "Aye, she may be a young girl, but she is known as the most brutal, vicious, bloodthirsty woman in all the lands."

He nodded, his eyes slanted up at her under hooded lids. "Aye, tis she, the woman who tore our children from their mothers' bosoms and tortured then killed them, tossing their bodies one by one as they were spent into the ravine where we found them. Not only six months ago it was that we found the latest one. Aye," he nodded again, "tis she, the Butcher Princess."

Her round eyes popped at hearing his words. "No," her head shaking vehemently, she declared, "I am not-"

"Shut up," Jashar snapped at her. He was confused. When confused, he did no action, he always waited until the cloud cleared and the truth rose to the surface.

"We will take her to the tribunal and find the truth. Come." He started walking, jerking her along with him. His strides so long she tripped and stumbled beside him, held up only by the iron grasp he kept around her arm.

Seeing her difficulty, he slowed his steps. His brothers trod beside him sending shocked, and admiring, glances at the girl every step of the way, watching her breasts jostle, waiting for them to escape her torn blouse.

They finally reached their horses. Jashar climbed on his steed and had Kaer hand the girl up to him.

He sat her in front of him with his arm wound tightly across her. She had to be greatly uncomfortable with her hands bound behind her. He noticed she seemed awkward sitting on the horse, like she wasn't used to it.

Aran rode ahead to announce the tale that they had captured the notorious Princess Butcher-Whore.

Chapter Two

By the time the brothers reached the castle, *Caisleán a Chéile,* Castle of Each Other, the tribunal was already gathering.

The higher echelon of the enclave, males only, were there, as was Jashar's father, King Allon D'Avenant.

King Allon had long passed his crown and his reigning monarchy to his eldest son, Jashar, yet he was still called King. And, although it was rarely needed, Jashar respectfully deferred to Allon's rulings when he proffered them.

The group was bunched around King Allon, eager with morbid anticipation awaiting Jashar's arrival with his prisoner.

Aran had gleefully and loudly made no bones about who the infamous prisoner was that Jashar was hauling to the castle.

Kaer and Daron moved ahead, pushing the 12-foot high double doors apart, solid inches of thick wood enhanced with iron, and led the way inside.

Jashar followed with the captured female. His heavy boots clomping, he brought her across the room, aware every male eye was on her. He walked slowly, but still her curvy attributes moved sensuously, even under the curtain of luxuriant hair. Her arm quivered in his grip.

Without seeing her eyes, he could feel her shaking body, limbs stiff with fright. Still, she held her head elegantly high with royal dignity, but her lids were lowered, he could tell she was terrified out of her skin.

Jashar brought her to stand in front of his father. Then he put his big hands on her slim shoulders and forced her to her knees. Her wrists tied behind her, she lowered her head.

Jashar looked to his father.

Allon nodded imperially to him.

Jashar thrust his hand in her thick hair winding it around his fist and pulled her head back so her face was tilted up towards the ceiling. Her neck bending back hard caused her small but plush lips to part in fear and pain with a gasp, tears sprung in the gleaming eyes.

Her spine arched exposing her throat. Jashar drew a rapier from his side and put it against the tender neck. He saw her blink back fresh tears, she swallowed hard.

Looking down, he thought how white and slender her young neck was. Her lustrous hair a soft thick rope lashed around his huge fist, her beautiful eyes awash with sheer terror.

Jashar didn't hear the unusual silence in the room; his gaze had dropped to where her blouse spread open revealing a good measure of her bosom. He could feel the heat roll up the back of his neck to the tips of his ears.

His eyes devoured the rounded globes, as smooth alabaster as the rest of her creamy skin. Fresh and full, sitting high and firm on her delicate chest as if asking for a man's hands to claim them.

Jashar's palms itched. He couldn't take his eyes off her breasts, then realized neither could his brothers who bookended him.

He glanced up and cursed silently. There were no other women present. Clearly by the gawking stares, every cock in the room was as hard and at attention as was Jashar's.

He lowered his knife and shoved it in its sheath. This bit of a girl wasn't going anywhere or hurting anyone. He was about to loosen his grip to at least allow the woman's hair to cover her bounty when his father stepped forward, stopping mere inches from her.

"Son," he said in partial English to Jashar, glaring with unconcealed hatred at the female. "They tell me this is the infamous *Iníon rí, Principessaé Búistéir Stríapach*, The Princess Butcher-Whore."

Her head still drawn back tightly, the woman cried, "No! I am Princess Maratia Madrilena Araminte of Ailanthus, I-"

Whack!

Allon slapped her across the face. "Shut up!" he roared at her.

Beside him, Aran grinned nastily. His gaze slipping oily from her red face down to her breasts, he muttered vulgar obscenities under his breath.

Allon whispered something to him. Aran's face crimped angrily and without a word he stepped back into the crowd.

Jashar was shocked at the slap but didn't move.

Twitters sprung up around the room.

He shot sidelong glances at his brothers. Both Kaer and Daron were grim, surprise hovered in their eyes as well. Jashar's eyes fell to the girl he held.

A red handprint shone against her fair skin, she was biting the inside of her cheek to keep the tears at bay.

Leaning over to get closer to her, his voice riddled with hate and hostility, King Allon declared, "You will pay for what you did to our children. You stole twenty of our young girls, had them beaten, whipped, viciously raped and then you took their heads. The rumor is that you wielded the sword to each of them yourself and chortled in glee as their heads rolled."

Blinking rapidly, the young woman gasped, "No, I would never do such a thing!"

Holding her hair, Jashar's dark brows slew down over the low ridge of his brow. He took in the woman's youth, her slight build, small dainty hands. It would have been impossible for her to have lifted a heavy sword much less behead the captured girls.

He remembered a few of the young women were in their late teens and outweighed this princessa by many stones. "Father-"

"Nay," Allon held up a hand. "What she did was indefensible and unforgivable."

He leaned over further, his enraged red face sputtered vilely at her, "You will suffer the same fate you gave each of our babies. For each one of the twenty murdered, you will be raped like they were, twenty times."

He sucked in a furious breath and went on, "Then you will be flogged like you did to them. You will be tortured for twenty days the same way you befouled our citizens. At the end of that time, if you still live, we will cheerfully take your head, as you took each of theirs. I only wish we could do that to you twenty times as well."

If possible, her face paled further. The last of the color fled her rounded cheeks, lips parted with a quiver. Her voice a frightened rasp, she cried, "But Sire, I did not, I am not-"

Whack!

He slapped her again so hard her head snapped. She would have hurled to the side if Jashar didn't have such a strong grip on her hair. He loosened his grasp slightly and her head fell forward, Allon had hit her so hard she was stunned, almost into unconsciousness.

Jashar let her head drop further then released her hair, discreetly flicking the locks to cover her half exposed breasts, and moved to stand partially in front of her, subtly placing himself between her and his infuriated, vengeful father. Out of the corner of his eye he caught both his brothers smirking at him.

King Allon straightened and turned to his son. "Jashar, as I said, I order her to be raped, whipped, beaten, and beheaded. You will personally inflict each and every punishment as I pronounced them."

Jashar stared unblinking at his father. He cleared his throat. "I will see to the investigation, Sire. At the moment there is only speculation and rumors. We-"

Allon frowned at Jashar's not immediately, without hesitation, blindly agreeing to his command. He said, "I have made myself clear." Eyes dark like Jashar's but without the same rich pure blackness, narrowed at his son.

No one ever denied or questioned Allon's orders. Ever. No one. He may have passed on the crown, but he was still Jashar's sovereign patriarch.

Hearing the murmurs growing loud in the audience, offers to rape her here and now, and others shouting for her head, "Of course, Father," Jashar said quickly, bowing his head, his long hair swished over his face.

He would figure out what to do when the immediate heat died down. To refuse right now, he could not prevent the crowd of enraged and lustful, men from taking her. There were too many for Jashar to fight, and he didn't dare kill the echelon of their society to stop them. A rock and a hard place.

"Good," King Allon remarked with a nod. "As I said, you will of course dispatch the punishment yourself."

Jashar's eyebrows shot up his forehead, he shoved his hair back. "Me?" The girl knelt at his feet, her head bowed. She didn't move. He stared down at the top of her quivering head.

At his son's obvious reluctance, Allon's eyes turned to steel, he grated, "Aye. You are king. It is your duty to set the example. It is your duty to fulfill the sentencing punishment of any foreign royalty captured, no matter the degree of scum." He levered a glower of vitriolic repugnance at the female.

Jashar stepped from the girl, straightened his already ramrod shoulders, and inclined his mouth to his father's ear. He said quietly, "She is a female, Sire, I do not murder women. Or children. Or commit rape. I will conduct a thorough investigation-"

Allon's face hardened. "It is your duty."

"Sire-"

Allon cut him off again, "You think about the girls, Jashar. You knew little Felicity quite well. One of your best warrior's daughter. Remember when they found what was left of her body. She'd been raped until her little body was almost split in two, she'd been beaten so badly her face was unrecognizable, then stabbed thirty times."

He shook his head. "Thirty times a knife slashed that child's innocent body, before her head was removed," his skin took on a hint of grey.

Continuing his gritted discourse, King Allon's eyes tapered fiercely to slits. "You think of her when you are meting out the punishment to the Butcher Princess Whore.

She is to be fucked and whipped every night for twenty nights, then take her head."

He jabbed an unmerciful look to the girl then to Jashar who had moved back in front of her. Allon's enraged glare at her was so fierce it seemed to physically push her back.

"I want her fucking head on a pole and stationed outside the compound's gates in twenty days." Allon pivoted on his heel and left the room. He didn't see the female's face wither further as she struggled to keep from fainting.

Jashar glanced at her then stared after his father. Then he turned and set his gaze back on the woman.

She still knelt, sitting back on her heels, hands tied behind her back, her eyes rolled weakly up at him. When she saw his chilling expression, even with the side of her face bright red from his father's slaps, she blanched further and lowered her frightened eyes.

Jashar looked for a specific guard in the crowd. Finding him, he raised his chin indicating for the guard to come to him.

A tall, strongly built man with dark blond hair and dark blue eyes, classically handsome in an olive green uniform with red tie came directly to Jashar, bowing briefly when he stood in front of him.

Jashar said to the guard, "McGee, take the prisoner to the dungeon."

Robbie McGee clicked his heels together with a snapped bow and reached down to the girl. He grasped her shoulders and with no effort lifted her to her feet. Holding her arm, he walked her towards the door.

"Ah, *mi bráthair*," Kaer sidled up to Jashar. Teasing him about covering her breasts with her hair he nudged him, "You saving the view for yourself alone? I will cover them with my hands for you, yet they may not be big enough for all of her precious gifts."

"Shut up, Kaer," Jashar growled with a scowl, his eyes on the girl being led across the room. The crowd of men parted for her like the red sea.

Her head high, spine rigid, her eyes were aimed straight ahead. McGee half-shielded her from the men with his body as he walked with her.

Jashar frowned. Was McGee being safety minded or personally protective of the beautiful prisoner?

To his grinning brothers he muttered, "I was trying to avoid any kind of fight over her. After Father's declaration of punishment, I was afraid chaos would arise and the men who volunteered for the job of assaulting her would tear her apart in a tug-of-war."

Daron shrugged without pity. "So what? She deserves at least that after what she had done to our little girls."

The three brothers stared at her trying to reconcile the petite, soft, slim yet curvy young woman with the thick wavy hair and big frightened blue eyes with that of a vile rapist and murderer of young children.

"Well, she obviously did not commit the rapes, but it was said that it was she who had ordered them done," Daron commented.

Jashar called the guard McGee back over. "Daron," he said to his brother, "go stand guard with the girl for a moment."

McGee standing with the girl placed against the wall away from the fray, waited until Daron reached them before going to see what Jashar required.

When McGee reached the king, Jashar said quietly to him, "I will be the only one punishing her. I don't want to see a bruise or a cut or a whip or a grope or a fuck to her that

I didn't do. I chose you specifically to guard her. I find out anyone but me touched her and it will be your head. Hear me?"

McGee bowed sharply, his dark blond hair bounced once. "Of course, Sire, as you wish. I admit even I felt a stirring at her munificent attributes, even so, you are aware of my predilections when it comes to the flesh."

Jashar's head was lowered, hands clasped behind his back, he looked up at the guard and the side of his mouth tugged in. "Aye, you prefer the stronger sex."

McGee smiled. "I will keep the other randy ones that lust after the fairer sex away from your female."

Jashar frowned. "She is not my female."

McGee's smile turned dryly sardonic. "Aye, tell me how you feel after you've fucked her, flogged her and removed her head. Am I dismissed?"

His face a dark scowl, Jashar muttered, "Take her to the dungeon, have the maids bathe her, and," he voice dropped, "see to any injuries she has…ah…incurred," referring to his father's strikes, and even Jashar's own rough treatment of her. "See that there are sufficient blankets. The dungeon is dark earth cold and damp."

The guard's golden brow rose over a slightly sarcastic blue eye. "You care, Sire?'

His mouth compressed in a frown, Jashar replied annoyed at the question, "Nay. I want her in the best of condition to take the wretched punishment that will be dispensed to her."

His eyes shifted briefly to her then back to the guard. "Find her an appropriate dress," his gaze swept the torn blouse, the weathered breeches, "and get her, uh, under, uh, garments."

He cleared his throat, continued stronger, "And then bring her to my chambers after the evening prayers." He nodded curtly.

McGee bowed then marched back to the girl, pushing through the men that were slowly gathering around her.

Jashar could see her brilliant eyes burning with fear roiling around the room at the men stalking closer and closer to her, hate and lust vivid on their faces.

He didn't realize he had been holding his breath with his hand on his sword until the guard had led her out of the castle.

Chapter Three

Hours later, she was brought to him.

McGee rapped hard on the door then opened it. He brought her inside, took her through the living area to Jashar's sleeping chambers.

Standing behind her, the guard untied the new rope binds he had put on her for the walk from the dungeon. He dropped his hand gently on her shoulder with a light pat, then left the chamber.

Jashar was standing by the window. Big and powerfully built, he turned like a dark nemesis, his expression blank, icy eyes chips of obsidian.

She was clean and dainty, attired in a soft dress with tiny flowers, a low collar and long full skirt. Still a bit of red glowed on one cheek from his father's slap.

He could see her visibly quaking, but she stood without cowering. *Ah, brave bitch,* Jashar thought, then shook his head slightly. *Of course, she is the butcher whore.*

He held a whip in his hand. Snapping it twice, watching her eyes pop, his voice dark and quietly low he said, "First, will be the flogging," he snapped it again.

The whip rolled out in an upward loop coiling towards her then cracked sharply without striking her then returned to him.

The female stood defiantly, but the terror fairly screamed in her young eyes. Jashar hardened his heart that was already often pronounced as being cold and hard as a black glacier.

Cursing the young woman, he took a step towards her, said with harsh rancor, "You are a proud, heinous creature. You ordered twenty young girls raped, over and over until they were shredded, then had them beaten, tortured without mercy before you yourself took their heads."

His gaze unwavering, he observed her so frightened of him she labored to stay on her feet. He could see her chest rising with rapid, shallow, panicked breaths. She should be afraid, he thought, she'd been caught and was now about to endure her own horrible torture.

"Therefore," Jashar slapped the whip's handle against his palm as he moved closer to her. Her shaking doubled, her eyes on the whip, she still didn't flinch. "You will suffer their same agony. What you did to them will be done to you. Beginning right now."

What was left of her color drained, making her skin so white it appeared translucent. She looked about to toss her cookies. Swaying slightly, her brave gaze did not waver from his.

"Princessa," a sardonic twist of distaste curled his lip at the title, "remove your clothes, all of them, and get on the bed. Lie down and spread your legs, make ready for me. The less work for me the less indignity for you, *Stríapach*, whore."

He waited.

She didn't move, a muscle. Her panicked eyes did not falter from his resolute, merciless gaze.

Jashar felt uncomfortable, he'd never been in this position before. Women fell at his feet, begging him to choose them for the night, for the moment. He was pissed he was being forced to force this woman.

He looked at the trembling guileless indigo eyes. This *girl*, he was to force his cock into her- his gaze swept her form, his stomach dropped. She was petite, on the delicate side, almost too thin, and he was a big man, all over.

The females he used, and that was unfortunately the word for it, he had neither the time nor the inclination to dally, with any of them, he got his rocks off and moved on.

The women he spent time with tended to be very experienced, and, yes, tough. Not fragile like- her. He shook his head. Doesn't matter, he has a job to do.

Still, she did not move.

Irritation at the whole thing and for her making it all that much harder by not complying, burned his neck and scraped at his craw.

Snapping the whip, he barked, "I said get on the fucking bed and make ready for me. You are a whore, it shouldn't be such a big fucking deal."

She took a step away from him.

His brow hardened, eyes narrowed. Snapping the whip, the cord cracked right next to her head. She flinched, tears sprung but didn't fall.

Her face flamed red over the petrified paleness. But, she stood like a carved statue, like an alabaster goddess, breathtakingly perfect.

Glaring at her, Jashar hesitated. He'd never had to deal with a willful woman before. Everyone, including his family, his brothers, mother and sisters do as he commands. A sigh slid out.

Except his father who although only a figurehead now, Jashar always did as the elder king ordered. He studied the princessa from head to toe and back. She looked at him then dropped her eyes.

He realized that she was too stubborn, at the moment anyway, to do as he instructed. He will wait on the flogging, he will have to work on that with her. She will learn who her liege is and obey his every word.

But, right now, he could tell that she will stand there and let him flog her, strip every shred of skin off her and die before doing as he commands. Is it pure stubbornness, or was it *cróga*- bravery?

His ire grew, pinching his insides. Well, she will see that he will be obeyed. He threw the whip to the side and stalked to her.

Now she moved, she swiveled and ran to the door. Yanking desperately on the handle, she wrenched the door open- behind her he slammed his hand on the door over her head and shut it.

He moved his other hand down in front of her and locked it. Her rigid shoulders rose to her ears, her back shook.

"*Sáith*, enough of this." He bent, picked her up with one movement and carried her to the bed.

As soon as he set her down, she immediately rolled to the other side of the bed to get up and run again, although there was nowhere she could go- quickly he knelt on the bed. Grabbing her waist he dragged her back, pushed her down and straddled her.

With a shriek, she punched at him, screaming, "Get off of me you heathen beast!"

Jashar clinched her wrists staking them beside her head. Her defiance fueled his wrath. Snarling, he seethed through his teeth, "Beg me little butcher whore, beg me to stop like the little girls did as they were being ripped apart."

Her eyes filled but she blinked to keep the tears from falling. Struggling to free her wrists, her voice breathy and girlish, she cried, "I am not that person! I have never harmed anyone or given orders to hurt anyone much less a child in my whole life! Stop this, Sire-"

"Nay, little whore, beg me to stop, beg me!" He gripped her wrists tightly but mindful he could easily snap them they were so thin.

Seeing he would never believe her, she closed her mouth and turned her head from him.

This only angered him further. He gripped her jaw, forcing her to face him. "I said beg me," he growled huskily.

He could see her chest heaving with heavy frightened breaths. Her breasts straining against the soft material, spilling out of the top, blue eyes vibrant with salty tears. Porcelain white teeth bit down on her perfect yet tiny bow mouth to staunch its trembling.

His thought, *why couldn't she be fat or old or ugly?*

He glanced down at her freed hand that went to his arm to fend him off. The slim hand appeared even smaller against his huge bicep bulging under his shirt, the long sleeves rolled up revealing brawny forearms covered with dark hair. To him it looked like he was a raging immense beast attacking a fragile, defenseless fairy.

Her shaking voice belied the conviction of her words, "Go to hell," she uttered and turned her head from him.

He forced her chin back and held her still. "Aye, and that is where you will be going in twenty days. If you live that long." He watched her expression go full fright again.

But she whispered, "No, my Lord and Savior will take me with him."

Jashar was taken aback at her words, a tingle surged up his spine. "How is it that a butcher of young children can believe that? Say those words?" He watched her pink lips as they opened.

"I am not-"

"Shut up! I've had enough of your lies, enough *sáith!*" He suddenly bent and without thought, seized her mouth with his. Forcing her lips apart he thrust in, violating her with his tongue, tasting her until he was driven to madness.

Thrashing under him, trying to move her head, her frantic whimpers pulsed against his mouth. He had forgotten to tie his hair back; it slashed at her face with his wanton aggression.

Guilt was already scrolling down his back, he shook it off, he had to stay true to his duty. He reached down and grasped the hem of her dress yanking it up to above her waist.

She jerked her mouth free of his and cried out punching him in the chest. It was like a butterfly striking out at an ox. Her legs kicked frantically.

Jashar moved to lie beside her and threw a leg over one of hers halting her flailing, and grabbed her undergarment. He hesitated only a second before ripping the sheer swath off and throwing it aside then quickly rolled between her legs.

Screaming hoarse protests, she bucked her hips trying to get him off her, but he held her immobile with his weight.

"Stop fighting me, Princessa, just be the fucking whore we all know you are and make it easy on us both. Let's get this first part done and behind us."

Jashar grasped both her wrists again staking them to the mattress and glared at her. His stomach cringed at the utter terror in her big eyes, they watered, her lips parted letting out hysterical pants.

Again he faltered. Again he compared the enormity of his body, the bulk, the strength, the raw power compared to the delicate grace of hers. Knowing even if she were a whore, he was too big for her, he would still without a doubt hurt her.

He could feel his cock straining in his pants; it didn't care about anything except getting at her. He hadn't even touched her sexually, and he was so turned on by the girl his body felt on the edge of exploding. But he couldn't thrust his girth into her small body.

Then he remembered seeing little Felicity's body. What was left of it after she'd been horribly attacked by vicious men.

He moved between her legs, lifted his hips and jerked his belt open, released his pants and pulled his throbbing, rock-hard erection out.

Holding it in his fist, he couldn't believe how turned on he was. Not over his threat of rape, but, his eyes devoured her from her shining eyes to those lush lips to her plump breasts molding over the low collar of her feminine dress.

He nudged her thighs apart and pressed the head of his iron club against her opening. She cried out in surging panic and struggled for all she was worth.

Her slim, almost too thin, thighs so smooth against his muscled legs reminded him how small she was, then he pictured Felicity, she'd been small too. When they'd found her, she'd been so damaged, so destroyed, there was so little left of her.

Roughly shoving her thighs apart, with one violent thrust King Jashar plunged into Maratia Madrilena's tender, chaste body.

A sharp suck of an airless gasp, her mouth froze open in shocked pain. Her eyes widened, then an agonizing scream ripped from her throat as he brutally burst through her hymen, tearing her young flesh apart-

Oh mi Dias- she is a virgin

Her woman's channel was too tight, too small, this girl has never known a man. Not even halfway inside her Jashar came to a dead stop.

Her neck arched, her mouth open in graphic agony. Jashar watched tremors of hoarse screams rasp in her strained throat, then she was gasping as if she couldn't catch her breath. Her chest rippled with cutting, weak inhalations.

He withdrew, knowing it was just as agonizing for her but could do nothing about it, and rolled off her.

As she fought for breath, her body shook like she had the chills. She pushed her skirt down and crossed her arms down over herself in a protective V with her hands over her pelvis, her eyes crushed in pain.

Jashar was stunned. For the first time in his life he didn't know what to do. Helpless to know what to do for her, do to her, say.

She continued gasping her pain, writhing slightly, the tears pushed out of the corners of her closed eyes.

Fuck- he moved off the bed to his feet. Fixing his pants he strode to the door.

He could not comfort her, she was the butcher, the whore. He blinked, the virgin actually, well, not exactly any more. He shook his head in confusion- *what the fuck-*

Yanking the door open Jashar stepped outside and closed it. Pausing to catch his own crazed breath, he could hear her wrenching sobs.

She'd kept them bottled inside until he was gone before releasing them. Jashar dragged a miserable hand through his thick dark hair.

What a night for firsts. His first rape, his first virgin, the first woman he made cry. Great. He was a real man. At least he hadn't given a woman his first whipping- yet.

The wretched sobs were tormenting his ears. He trod quickly down the hall and up several flights of stairs to the servants' quarters.

Chapter Four

*J*asper sought out the woman who raised him.

Anna looked up in surprise as he strode into her room without knocking at the open door.

Her slightly plump cheerful face welcomed him with a warm smile. On the far side of sixty, Anna Pakina's family had been servants to the Royal D'Avenants for generations.

Everyone had a role in Thuas sa Spéir, the Land up in the Sky, the name of their region portion of the land.

The D'Avenants had been the royal family from as far back as there were records, and the Pakinas were their servants from the beginning of time. Of course there are other servants, but the Pakinas were the closest to Jashar's family.

Anna had been his *mahmen,* not his blood mother. His biological mother bore him and then went on with her queenly duties while Anna raised him and his other siblings. Therefore, in Jashar's heart, Anna was his true mother.

Besides Kaermon and Daron, Jashar has another brother, Makir the youngest at 16 and a sister, Sheera who had just passed 21.

"Darling Jasha," calling him by his childhood pet name, Anna swept her long skirts up and moved to him, her arms out in greeting. "What are you doing here?"

He was always welcome of course, but it was not often the liege set foot in the servants' area. Jashar wanted them to feel that their rooms were theirs and would not be under imperial scrutiny.

Anna's face wrinkled more so than normal at the disturbed look on Jashar's customarily stoic face.

"Ah, *Mahmen*," guilt and shame threatened to overwhelm Jashar's noble impassive countenance. He closed the door. Firming his voice, strengthening the tone, he said, "I, uh, I need your assistance."

Concerned, Anna took his hand and pulled him to a chair but he refused to sit. "Nay, I need swift aid."

"Of course, my Jasha, whatever you need, speak and I will make it happen." Twining her fingers in front of her frilly apron, Anna smiled but it was edged with worry. She waited patiently, her face kind and compassionate.

Jashar looked at her. The light blue eyes circled by fine wrinkles, laugh lines mostly, lips that almost always turned up, an ample bosom she'd rocked Jashar and all his siblings on.

Shame flushed his regal face. He coughed, "Ah, you have heard of course, of our…prisoner."

She nodded, brown hair shot with grey bobbled. "Aye, aye, they said it was a young woman. Something about she is a- a- horrible murderess, that it was she that ordered the- the- assault on our children?" The curly hair shook back and forth in her renunciation of the horrendous atrocities.

"I cannot believe it of a woman, they say she may be only in her teens herself she is so young. I just refuse to believe it, Jasha."

She peered at him through round glasses. "I hear she is breathtaking, an indescribable beauty, foreign, not from here, is this true?"

Jashar stuffed his hands in his pockets. "Aye." His head down, he peered up at her. "Did you also hear my father's decree? His command? My duty?"

Anna stiffened, eyed him warily. "Aye, Jasha, the men were full of gossip and rumors. They said you were to- to flog and then, um, assault her, then kill the woman, that King Allon ordered it. But that was all just- just- gossip? Made up?" Her head cocked at him. "Wasn't it?"

He shook his head miserably. "Nay. Tis all true. Father commanded me, I could not defy him in front of the entire tribunal. I had to do- as he ordered."

Her grey brows jumped in disbelief, her hands flew to cover her mouth. "Nay, say it isn't true, my Jasha, you did not- not-"

He nodded. "I, ah, did not strike her, but I did..."

Anna's mouth turned into an aghast O. Her head went from side-to-side in denial. "Nay, Jasha, you did not...you did not *rape* that child?"

Jashar pushed the shame and guilt down and out. He turned cold empty eyes to his *mahmen* and admitted, "I did."

Her shock was palpable; it filled the room like tainted cotton wool. Time stalled, she stared at him, he glared at her. Her mouth opened but no words fell out.

"Anyway," he said gruffly, "why I am here. It turns out she was a..." he didn't blink, "a virgin. I took her roughly, without, ah, preparation. She is quite...small. I may have injured her."

Ignoring her shocked gasp, he went on, "I need you to see to her. Help her, cleanse her, then I will have McGee waiting outside to return her to the dungeon." Not caring for the stark accusation and condemnation in her kind eyes, he turned to the door.

His hand on the handle, his head down, he said, "Don't look at me like that, she is the butcher whore. Tis my duty to punish her for her monstrous actions perpetrated on our children." He drew a deep breath. "And change the sheets, there is blood."

"*Mi Dias*, Jashar, you assaulted her? You- *raped* that girl?" Anna's voice rang with disbelief and revulsion. "Nay," she shook her head even as she watched the guilt cross his implacable face, "not my Jasha. Nay, you would never attack a woman in that way-"

"*Sáith!*" he barked, "*enough*, tis not up for discussion. She is not a goddamned child; she is a grown woman, a killer. Just clean her up, see to any…wounds. Remove the bloody sheets and let the guard take her."

"Uh huh," Anna grunted with a withering glare. "Clearly she is not a whore, maybe she is also not the butcher?"

He raised his head and glared at her but didn't respond.

"The dungeon, Jasha? She is but a child herself, a young woman you just violently assaulted, she will be in pain. You cannot-"

He said bluntly, "See to what I commanded," and stalked from the room.

With a sigh so heavy the next village could hear it, Anna followed him down the hall, down the stairs and to his chambers.

He carefully opened the door unsure of what to expect, and strode inside.

At his heels, disturbed at his callousness and stunned by his violent actions, Anna said, "Sire, really,"

He held a hand up stopping her. Standing inside the door he stared at the bed.

The girl had rolled into a ball facing away, clutching herself, her body wracked with silent sobs. The lustrous hair waved over the bed behind her. Her ruined underwear was lying on the floor by the bed.

Jashar cleared his throat of the lump, then said to the girl, his voice as harsh as a hail storm, "Princessa, you will be brought here every night for the next 19 days for the same thing, with flogging. Prepare yourself."

Ignoring the maid's gasp and angry scalding look, as he passed by her to the door he mumbled, "See to her."

As he reached the door, Anna said with quiet sarcasm, "What about her beating? Are you forgetting tonight's whipping?"

He stormed out slamming the door.

Hurrying down the stairs, Jashar made his way to his father's den where he knew he'd find him enjoying a late liquor and smoke. He rapped his knuckles on the open door.

His father looked over the reading glasses perched on his nose and set the book he was reading down in his lap and the glass on the table beside the chair. In the ashtray sat a half-smoked cigar. "Come in, son."

He waited while Jashar stepped inside, he gestured for him to sit, but Jashar stood.

The room was dark browns and deep mahogany wood. Animal furs lined the walls and floor, thick cushioned heavy chairs and a sofa filled the room.

Bookshelves lined with books braced a wall, another wall was taken up by a floor to ceiling window. The windows were real glass made from melting the sand of the shore.

Louise Furley

Heavy brown drapes were pulled. Paintings of mostly hunts with horses and dogs hung on the walls. It was a deeply masculine room. A fire crackled in the stone fireplace that anchored a third wall.

"So," through wire-rimmed glasses, the elder king's eyes swept his son taking in the frozen mask the hard planes of his face had hewn into, "it would appear by your grim mien that the deed has been fulfilled. Is she alive? Did she suffer?" He patiently, dispassionately, watched emotions flicker across Jashar's hard face.

Jashar's midnight eyes narrowed at him. "Aye. I raped her." He watched the satisfaction soften his father's coarse features.

"Good, good. The flogging? Did you whip her or just beat her? I hope you didn't break all her bones, left some for the next few weeks."

"She was a virgin, Father. I stopped the second I realized."

Allon's wiry grey eyebrows rose, then dropped. He pulled off the glasses as if they were distorting the truth. "How could that be?" Before Jashar could answer, shaking his head, he said, "Nay, it must have been a trick, she tricked you."

If possible Jashar's cold eyes hardened even more. "Nay, twas no trick. She was a virgin. Clearly not a whore."

At his father's skeptical surprised look, Jashar repeated Anna's words, "Could it be possible she is also not the person accused of those deplorable crimes? I need to instigate an investigation-"

Not hiding his annoyance, Allon moved his book from his lap to set it beside the glass of liquor on the table then uncrossed his long legs to lean forward.

He spoke over his son's words, "Grow up, Jashar," he snapped coldly. "One can be a whore and still be a virgin. There are other ways to perform sexual acts than just with her vagina. You of all people are aware of that."

Allon's eyes slit with his annoyance. His voice heavy with contempt, he said, "Do not be an infant, Jashar. You have a duty; you have been given a…task. You must fulfill the task. Act like the king that you were born to, do your job like a man with his guts intact."

His father's words struck him as they were supposed to, as slaps against his heritage and his manhood. Still, Allon hadn't felt her agony, heard her scream. He started his protest again, "Father-"

"Dammit Jashar!" Allon's voice lashed viciously like Jashar's whip had. "Stop this childish whining." He inclined his head towards his son. His dark eyes even more chilling, more deadly, contained more pitiless cruelty than Jashar's own enigmatic sooty orbs.

"You only witnessed the last of the victims. While you were away last season warring in the north region with the Forálachas against their enemy, that Butcher-Whore had her people sneak onto our land and take our daughters, twenty of them. One-by-one they used their tender bodies, tearing them asunder from inside, ignoring their cries of mercy, then they beat them and slaughtered them."

"I know Father, I have men investigating those-"

Allon slammed his hand on the chair arm and bellowed, "Stop it! Stop with the damned detective-fucking-work! It has brought no fruit, and it will not bring the children back!"

He jammed a finger at Jashar spouting, "Now tis the time for payback, revenge. You," he pointed rigidly at him, "you will avenge our people."

Allon slanted his head closer to his son, fury brought dark color into his weathered face. "I don't give a fuck if she's a child herself. She, the *Principessaé Búistér Stríapach,* the Princessa Butcher Whore, ordered the attack, she did the beheading herself. She is the one to pay, to be punished for her heinous sins. She is guilty, do not feel sorry for her."

Jashar stood with his hands clasped behind his back, his boots planted firmly on the rug over the planked floor. Warrior shoulders rigid, head high, eyes straight at his father, he accepted the tongue lashing in silence.

"Now," Allon took a beleaguered breath, exhaled sharply. "Buck the fuck up. Stop being frightened of a little girl, a mere *mici cailín,* be the *laoch,* the warrior hero that you are and go finish the deed." He plunked his glasses back on his noble nose, same as his son's yet longer, coarser, and snatched up his book and glass.

Then he pointed his commanding gaze like a longbow at Jashar and said, "Do not speak to me of this again until 19 days from now when you present her head to me on a stake." He dismissed his son with a flip of a page and a sip.

Jashar stood, his legs wooden, heart hammering, anger suffusing his brain. He pivoted on his heels and left the den.

Chapter Five

The next day, Jashar threw himself into his war practice, parrying with swords for hours. He worked furiously hard at swordplay with his brothers, and wrestling other warriors until his clothes were drenched in sweat.

He removed his shirt and ran miles in just his breeches, returned and practiced for more long hours with his bow and arrows. He'd worked so hard he'd had to frequently stop and retie his hair so it stayed out of his face. Now he was exhausted.

He had hoped keeping his mind and body busy he could forget about her. Push her out of his brain. But no such luck. Even without responding to the constant questions and comments from his brothers and the other men about the princessa, he could still hear her piercing scream of agony as he thrust into her virgin body.

He also could not forget the feel of her; soft, tender, tight, she smelled fresh. His legs pressing against her silken thighs- *argghh*- gritting his teeth he clomped across the field to the castle to bathe, change and eat. He had to prepare himself for the evening.

McGee brought her after evening prayers, same as last night. The guard knocked, opened the door, ushered her in.

Waiting calmly in breeches and a long-sleeved shirt, Jashar had tied his hair back in a tight ponytail.

He watched McGee set his hand on her shoulder and give it a gentle squeeze. Huh. She had culled McGee's sympathy. Not an easy thing to do.

"That will do, Guard," he said coldly to McGee indicating for him to leave.

McGee gave him an odd look, patted the girl again then left.

She stared at the floor. Apparently she had just been bathed. The thick hair waved in damp curls down her back, tendrils swirled around the frightened heart-shaped face.

Her hands folded tightly in front of the dress she wore, different from last night, fingers clutched so tightly they were white.

The dress was too big for her, it hung on her trim frame but clung more tightly to her curves. Whoever's garment it was, was bigger than the girl yet less kindly endowed.

It did Jashar no good to study her attributes, except it did make him ready to take her again. His man's sword was already hard and straining at his breeches.

He did not say a word to her, just pointed to his bed. She stood as still as a statue, her arms now wrapping protectively around her body, as if that could keep him from doing as he wished with her.

The big shiny eyes glazed a frightened hop at him before darting back to stare at the floor.

His mouth pulled in wryly, the little witch had learned nothing from last night. It was futile to disobey him.

Stifling his aggravation, Jashar thought, *why does she have to make this harder than is has to be*? He stomped over to her, ignoring her baleful cringe from him, grabbed her up in his arms walked her over and deposited her on the bed.

As she moved to scuttle away, he dropped down beside her. Laying his bulky arm across her was sufficient to hold her from even attempting to flee.

Reaching for the buttons on her dress, his tone cold and low, he said gruffly, "Make this easier on yourself, woman, yield to me, it will be over more quickly and less painfully for you."

He told the truth about the quickness of the act ending, he could already feel himself ready to release; his body now touching hers was like lighting a match.

But he lied about it being less painful for her. Without preparing her to take him in her, and that would entail touching her, fondling and...licking...sucking...even kissing parts of her, he grunted back his thoughts, trying to cool his desire.

Nay, he would make it as quick as last night. A few thrusts, he would shoot his seed and be done with her. His gaze fell to the trembling lips. Aye, it would hurt, probably as badly as it had last night because she had to be sore, already in raw pain.

Bah- enough with his concerns. Deciding it would be best if he did not see, or touch her naked flesh, he stopped unbuttoning her dress. Already her breasts mounded, glistening their sweet paleness at him. Instead, he reached down and grasped the hem of her dress like he had the evening before and tugged it up.

She smothered her screams in her throat and silently fought him. Her panic and fear was tangible in the flailing of her arms, the kicking of her legs, the frantic twisting of her body, and the crying terror in the innocent blue eyes.

Jashar grasped her wrists. Holding them taut, he tore his gaze from her frightened face. He growled, "I can't stand to look at you, you make me sick." In truth, what he couldn't stand was to look at her while he's hurting and humiliating her.

"Then leave me alone!" she cried, trying to twist from his grasp.

Grabbing her shoulders, Jashar flipped her over, thinking, *I'll take her from behind, then I won't have to scar my soul with sight of the dreaded alarm, pain, and misery on her face.*

Suddenly lying on her stomach, the girl lay stunned for a second. When Jashar lifted her skirt, she threw herself into renewed fighting.

His big hand splayed on her back to hold her still, Jashar leaned over, his mouth close to her ear and said, "Just fucking stop resisting me, let me do what I need to and it will be over."

Her scent curled from her dampened skin and hair up into his nostrils. Without intending to, he inhaled deeply. She smelled…fresh…pure…like young female and springtime. *Fuck*- this was not helping-

He slid his palm under her pelvis and lifted her butt up high and put his other hand on the back of her shoulders shoving her face into the mattress. Her gasping whimpers scraped out her throat, closed in fright, into the bed.

Tuning out the torturous cries, she sounded like a mewling kitten trapped in a hole; he pushed her skirt up further. Her behind propped up, it rounded so perfectly.

Jashar saw the tiny undergarment Anna had found for her, barely covering the fine little ass. Ahh, his entire body shuddered with a scorching bolt of lust.

Gingerly, he slipped his big fingers under the delicate underpants and pulled them down, exposing her naked rump. *Mi Dias*, he groaned. He couldn't take his eyes from her perfect globes. Without conscious thought, he lifted his hand and palmed one, squeezing it in his long fingers, then the other, relishing the ungodly satiny, juicy plump feel of them.

She squirmed and cried out, "Please! Sire, I beg you! Don't do this!"

Before he could stop himself, Jashar grasped both globes in his hands. Kneading them, he bent over and pressed the side of his face against them, feeling the smooth flesh, the fragrance of her skin wafting in his nose.

He stroked her creamy skin relishing the pure softness of her. He took handfuls of her small bottom and squeezed her flesh, kneading them harder as the lust fired up like a burning torch inside him.

Rubbing his face over each soft cheek, he put his mouth against her skin and licked. She tasted like fucking sweet nectar, and he sucked hard on one globe until a red mark grew, he about came in his breeches.

Thinking to himself, *all I have to do is open my pants and shove into her. From behind, I won't have to look at that beautiful, terrified face as she screams in torment-*

Her voice a tiny whimper begged, "Please."

Last night he had commanded her to beg and she had refused. Now, she did as he had asked, she begged. But it brought him no satisfaction.

Releasing her luscious flesh, Jashar dropped his hands and sat back on his heels. He stared at the graceful length of her back.

Mi Dias, he groaned, the god's tempting curve of her ass, and down, for as small as she was she had long legs, sensuously shaped but still on the thin side, like she had just completed her transformation from child to woman. They shook with her fear.

His scrutiny drew up to the amber hair waving over the mattress, the slight shoulders quaking with suppressed sobs. She was managing to stifle her whimpering cries by shoving her face into the blankets.

He dragged his sleeve across his face wiping the perspiration from his eyes. *Gah*, when had he become the defiler of women? How the fuck had this bloody task fallen upon his shoulders?

His father's words were sharp in his ears, "It is your duty to avenge our children, our people." His eyes dropped to her quivering form trapped under his iron hold, the thoughts hurtled through him, *if only she were fat and coarse, more mature, rougher, thicker, older- uglier- anything but the young innocent beauty that she was*!

Shaking his head ruefully, nay, he just couldn't fucking force himself inside her again. She was still a virgin in concept. He rubbed between his eyes, his gaze on her quivering stunning bottom.

His cock was hard enough to break rocks, but he couldn't make himself fuck her, not at this moment anyway.

But he was still duty bound to mete out her punishment.

Chapter Six

$\mathcal{E}$arlier in the morning Maratia had thought about last night. Even with the blankets the heathen Satan King had ordered she have, and the additional ones McGee had added, Maratia lay huddled, shivering, her body wracking with pain and despair.

After McGee had closed the cell door, Maratia could feel his sympathetic eyes on her.

The guard was the only one of the males that didn't look at her way the other men did, with greedy piggish lust, like each swine wanted to take a big vile bite out of her.

Although she had little experience with men, she could tell that McGee did not lust after her like the others, he looked at her almost kindly as he would a little sister.

He must be one of those...she thought of her cousin Garald who preferred the intimate company of men to women. It made no difference to her; at least she didn't need to fear his attacking her like the Satan King, the horrid King Jashar D'Avenant.

McGee murmured words of comfort, then he left.

She was left alone, in the dark. The guard had put a small lantern near her cell but was unaware when he closed the outer door the draft blew the flame out. He was to stand guard outside the dungeon all night.

It didn't matter. Now that there was no one to see, Maratia let the tears fall. Tears of hopelessness and desperation of her captivity. Tears of pain as her insides burned and bled from the beast's brutal assault from last night, and tears for the loss of her maidenhood, her innocence.

He'd torn her very femaleness from inside her like a rutting animal. "Ohh," she sobbed in lonely anguish, and they called *her* the monster.

The heathen's assault was still vivid in her mind. Her mortification as he climbed on top of her, pushed up her dress, ripped off her undergarment and shoved his ugliness into her like a wild dog.

The intense burning, stinging, she never expected the sudden excruciating pain, the physical, and mental violation. Then, as soon as he'd driven into her, he'd stopped, as if...he was confused. What on earth could the ogre have been confused about?

She was surprised when he stopped after only one thrust. But then, she sniffed back her sobs trying to get control of them, rape was rape.

She had been paraded in front of hordes of horny fierce warriors on her way to the dungeon. They had cat-called and whistled, shouted out what they'd like to do to her, some yelled for her head.

She had noticed two of the men standing beside the ogre. They looked so much like him they must have been brothers. All had dark hair and eyes, but none as black and shiny as King Satan's.

The heathen's hair fell thickly past his shoulders, the other two brothers had shorter hair. Maratia remembered hearing that every warlord king was to wear his hair long as a sign of virility and leadership.

All three were enormous brutes, each one bigger than the last; the ogre was the hugest of all. So tall with massive muscles, he was built like a formidable bull, huge and powerful on top but his hips were as lean as a young sapling's.

His thighs were muscular, his arms like blocks of cement. She'd seen a hint of kindness in one of his brother's eyes, but there was zero pity or kindness or remorse in Satan's black and cold, hard as cinder eyes.

She had hoped and prayed that he would have forgotten about her. Done his dirty deed and moved on. But no, he'd had her hauled back to his lair, ignominiously tossed her on his bed and climbed on her again.

This time, he crudely pushed her face into the mattress and was going to take her from behind like the base dog that he was.

Maratia bit back her cries, and her pleas, but she couldn't stop her whimpers as she felt his huge heathenish paw slide under her pelvis and lift up her hips, push up her dress, pull her underwear down and expose her bare behind to his gloating view.

Oh my God in heaven, will it never end? The humiliation- Then, *oh God please,* he put his big filthy hands on her nude bottom!

Maratia struggled for all she was worth, smashing her face into the bed, wriggling her butt to push his calloused hands off her body, but, he just kept feeling her, stroking, squeezing her flesh, then-

Oh my God- his face, he put his face and now his mouth on her bareness and was- licking her flesh, what on earth? In her innocence she had never known any of this kind of behavior, was this normal? His mouth- he was sucking her skin!

His big hard hands clutched her bottom and he was licking- and sucking her body! She let out a deafening scream and tried to thrust out of his hands- to no avail- the abominable monster was too huge, too strong.

Jashar contemplated his duty. He was still under his father's instructions, and the law of his people, to punish her. He tried to pull his heated gaze from her nakedness, but his eyes were drawn back to her plump behind like bees to lustrous flowers.

His hands itched to grind her flesh in his fingers again, and then explore the rest of her womanly curves and hollows. Search every inch of her tender skin, between her legs- he swallowed hard.

Nay, get a grip Jashar, he scolded himself. He felt like a young teen with his lust out of control.

He'd had far too many women in his short lifetime to be this on the edge, so about to lose it without even being inside the female. Yet, as turned on as he was, he still couldn't force himself into her. His ears could not bear that agonized scream again.

She jerked and twisted her hips trying to shake loose of him. Jashar watched her firm flesh tremor with her struggles. He felt a pull in his groin; his damned loins were on fucking fire.

Before he gave it a second though, Jashar suddenly snapped his hand out and slapped her on her nude bottom.

"Oh!" she burst with the pain and shock of it.

He spanked her again.

She writhed and cried out. It twisted his gut, but he didn't know what else to do. He couldn't fuck her, he couldn't whip her, he wasn't about to punch or slap her. A few harsh spanks wouldn't hurt her too badly. Her pride maybe, but then if she did what she was accused of she had no pride.

The picture of little Felicity all torn up and battered came to his mind and made him strike her harder, several more times. When he started thinking about doing this with the female but in willing sexual games, Jashar knew it was time to stop.

Her cries hurt his ears. The ivory skin of her perfect ass turning bright red hurt his eyes. He yanked her underwear up and jerked her skirt back down to cover her nudity.

Jashar sat glaring at the back of her head. He was a cowardly wimp. He still had not fulfilled his duty of the night- to violate her body with his. She must serve the same abominable assault that was perpetrated on the young girls that she herself had condemned.

The spanking would only, and barely, suffice in lieu of the beating he was to instigate on her, the beating he was supposed to have commenced last night, but again, he'd been too cowardly to strike the young female.

But, the spanking did not cover the sexual assault his father had deemed necessary to avenge the horror done to the children.

Furious with his own cowardice, he wondered what happened to his normal cold, fearless bravery in the face of any adversity no matter how deadly. All he had to do was force himself on a wee slight woman-

Arghh, he rolled off the bed to his feet, bent, grabbed her above the waist and hauled her off the bed. He pushed her to her knees on the floor and abruptly released her.

She threw her arms out to gain her balance, and her equilibrium. He was so strong and fast, he'd lifted her like she was nothing but a doll and pushed her to the floor.

Jashar didn't wait for her to catch her breath. He moved to stand directly in front of her. She didn't raise her head to look at him. He could see her lashes flutter with uncertainty and apprehension.

He unbuckled his belt and unbuttoned his pants. Now he had her attention. He could see her eyeballs glued to his groin.

Her lashes were raised in alarm, his erection was obvious. He was so hard the bulge in his breeches was rigidly apparent, and big. And growing bigger. She inched away from him on her knees.

"Nay," he grabbed the back of her hair to hold her. Pushing open his pants, he took out his phallus, so engorged already it looked about to burst.

Holding it in his fist, he shoved it at her and demanded, "Take it in your mouth, *mici striapach,* little whore, you must at least be experienced with that."

Tears glistened, her neck wobbled from her hard swallow. She turned her head and tried to scuttle away from him.

Clutching her hair, he held her head immobile and pushed his bulging cock against her closed lips. "I said," his voice coarse and threatening, "take me in your mouth, *now female-*"

Her mouth stayed clamped, her eyes stared at the floor.

"Goddammit," he cursed, ordered harshly, "do it." Grinding his teeth, he pulled her head back by her hair trying to force her lips to part.

Her body was shaking like a blade of grass in a storm, her teeth chattered, tears gleamed but didn't fall.

He pushed his cock against her lips but they only quivered. Her soft lips trembling against the head of his throbbing erection almost made him embarrass himself by shooting his seed without even being in her mouth.

His own body shaking with fury, he suddenly released her, jerked his pants closed and stomped from the room. The door crashed closed behind him.

Buckling his belt over his straining cock, he moved to a door next to his room and slipped inside. The chamber was barely bigger than a closet. But inside was a tiny hole in the wall.

He had to see her behavior. He had to know if she was acting the frightened innocent with him, or something else, an evil, clever actress. He peered through the hole.

Maratia had slid from her knees to her bottom. She'd pulled her knees up and buried her face in them. Her shoulders hitched with her helpless sobs.

Jashar stood watching her pour her distress into her arms. He was astounded that she'd been able to hold back the tears, waiting until she was alone, or thought she was alone, to release them.

The woman had a spine, and pride, he couldn't help but admire her for her will power. She'd fought him at every turn. Turned her chin up defiantly at his whip, and refused to obey anything he commanded. She was definitely made of princess material, she'd make a fine queen.

What the hell was he damned dreaming about? She was a coldblooded, ruthless killer of children. He would do well to remember that.

Nonetheless, he watched her cry, for several long minutes until she lifted her head, then that little pointed chin stuck resolutely up in the air. She rubbed her palms angrily over her eyes, as if ashamed and angry at her weak tears.

Jashar waited, curious to see what she would do next. His brows arched in surprise as she rolled back onto her knees, twined her fingers together holding them in front of her chest then bowed her head. He could just barely see the tiny pillows of pink lips moving.

She was praying. By the living gods- the Butcher Whore was praying. Incomprehension roiled all over his body. It was too much of a contradiction, too incongruent, a soulless murderer- praying. He shook his head.

She stayed like that for a long time. So long Jashar's feet tired of standing.

Sighing heavily in bafflement, he left the room to get McGee to return her to the dungeon.

Pushing aside the image of the girl's slight body shivering under thin blankets in the icy dank cell, Jashar quickened his pace.

Chapter Seven

After a long day like the preceding one of hours of hard, back-breaking training and work, Jashar slid into his seat at the head of the table, his hair still damp from his recent bath. The long locks were tied back in a low ponytail.

His father, King Allon resided at the foot. The table was made up of many connected together, big enough to seat fifty people. And all of the seats were filled tonight.

Many of his relatives that resided in the castle were there, as well as many of his top warriors, chiefs, head castle personnel, and all of their eyes bounced around the room always coming back to land on him.

They whispered behind their hands, seldom looking away from the fierce young king.

Jashar kept his countenance inscrutable, harsh and blank. Nothing could be read in the grim turn of his mouth or his flinty eyes. He let his gaze drift around the room lowering it when all he saw was sick curiosity, and brazenly wanton invitations from many of the women, single as well as married.

Way down at the end of the table, way down, thank the Lord, was Thandie. Her golden cat eyes boldly trying to caress him across the distance.

Gorgeous Thandie had long ago contrived designs on making Jashar her husband. She constantly brought up how lovely, 'Queen Thandie' sounded. Tall and quite voluptuous, the woman clung to him whenever she was in the castle, which lately, thanks to his interfering cupid mother, was frequent.

His mother, Queen Vashana has made no bones about how she felt about the combining of Thandie Mahli's aristocratic family and the D'Avenants.

Even now Thandie leaned over slightly so that her huge breasts could spill over even further out of the extremely low-cut bodice.

The dress was so tight over her full-blown figure that was just on the edge of going plump, it cut into her skin just above her areoles causing her flesh to mound over the bodice.

It looked damned uncomfortable to Jashar. His nose twitched, and she had sort of large ass. Flat-ish and wide, not small and sweet and round...as he was realizing he preferred.

Now that she had his attention, she ran one manicured finger around the curve of her bodice, over the swells of her breasts, teasingly dipping it in and out of the top. Her tongue travelled around her cloying thick lips copying its trail.

He could smell her ambrosia perfume from where he sat.

She had so many overpowering different scents, mixed with her bath oil and her shampoo and her soap and whatever else she doused herself in, he felt like he'd fallen into a vat of decomposing flowers, and he wasn't even near her.

Jashar couldn't believe her father, who was sitting near Allon, would allow his daughter to dress that... provocatively, no, it was downright slatternly. The man that married that woman would have his hands full trying to keep her from straying.

Although Thandie was woman enough, strong and mature enough to handle Jashar's strength, and large...body, he'd never had any desire to bed her.

Of course that never stopped the brazen woman from throwing herself at him at every opportunity. Even now she raised one sleek black brow over a golden chatoyant eye in pure invitation.

Jashar looked away from her slightly slanted eyes, letting his gaze continue its travel around the room.

Peripherally, he could see Thandie steam in her seat at his indifference to her and his cold dismissal. She snapped her head angrily, flipping the arrow straight black hair to swish across her shoulders.

The room was opulent red velvet walls gilded with gold trim. Oil-fueled chandeliers made of crystal prisms showered rainbows over the room, and the people were seated on handsomely carved chairs with red velvet cushions.

The lavish glassware sparkled, the gold plates shone and the silver gleamed. The rich wood planked floor was so highly waxed the guests could see their reflections on it.

The ornate room wasn't all that pleasant to Jashar. He felt more comfortable in his own office and sitting rooms. He preferred the darker heavier woods, plain chairs sturdy enough not to squeak and protest his bulk, and arched doorways he didn't have to bend his head to move under.

He liked the comfort of his wealth, but was not into the gaudy frills, lace and gild. He had no paintings on his chamber walls, only stuffed bookcases and a desk filled with research.

His rooms were on a corner so he had many big windows. His living quarters contained besides his bedroom, an office, bathing room, and a relaxing den with animal furs to warm the sofa, and a stone fireplace, and three more bedrooms that were empty.

A league of windows stretched across the front of his sleeping chamber making the room bright. There were dark blue woven curtains; the braided rugs and the comforter on his bed matched the curtains.

He liked his bed, it was big enough to accommodate him. Preferring to keep his privacy, he'd never brought a woman to his chambers, at least, not before…her.

Unbidden, the princessa came to his mind. He pictured her lying on her back in the middle of his bed with her dress pushed up, legs spread, him between her soft thighs-superseding that image was the picture of just before he'd left her the second night.

After he fondled and sucked her flesh, he'd spanked her like an ignominious brute, then forced her to her knees shaking like a leaf with him standing with his cock in his fist trying to shove it down her trembling throat while watching the tears gather in her mortified eyes.

His head bowed as the shameful color rolled up his neck. He tried to suppress the gall that climbed up his throat threatening to choke him by superimposing a different picture over it.

An image of the two of them in the same pose, but her with that exceptional long, thick hair the color of amber and gold waving down her lissome back. Willingly wrapping her slender fingers around his shaft while she slipped her smiling lips over the blunt tip. Those beautiful eyes looking up alluringly at him through the long lashes-

"Well?" Kaer jabbed him in the side. He sat to his brother's left.

Their mother struggled in vain to make people sit boy-girl but they always ignored her and sat where they pleased. And tonight, Kaer was pleased to sit close to Jashar where he could needle him endlessly.

"Well what?' Jashar muttered shifting in his seat, he discreetly reached down to adjust his breeches over his sudden boner. He grabbed a roll and fiercely buttered it then shoved it whole into his mouth.

"Come on, then, dear *bráthair,* everyone knows what Father ordered you to do. Everyone knows, well," his voice lowered, "most of us know that you fulfilled a portion of your duty. Although Anna tried to hide it, the bloodstained sheet was discovered." He stabbed a portion of beef and bit it off the knife with his teeth.

Chewing loudly, Kaer said coolly, "Tell me, *bráthair,* how the fuck does a whore bleed? Better yet," he added with a derisive lift of one brow, "how does it feel to rape a defenseless virgin? You feeling manly now?" He didn't hide his sarcastic contempt of his brother's actions with an acidic grin.

Kaer loved and respected his older brother, but hell, he couldn't believe Jashar would assault a helpless woman, no matter what they claimed she'd done.

Both brothers could feel their mother's furious gaze on them. Both ignored her.

Jashar muttered fiercely, "How about you just shut the fuck up little *bráthair?"* His shoulders twigged at his brother's caustic chuckle.

Kaer shook his head in disapproval of his brother's rumored actions against the woman, but the disapproval morphed into doubt that Jashar had actually done such a shameful hideous deed.

"But seriously, Jash, what the hell is going on? It's incredulous to believe that especially you, of all people, the big hero warrior, the *cróga*, the protector of the people of Thuas sa Spéir, especially its women and children, raped a young woman. Just a wee slip of a girl, almost a child herself, a virgin-"

"*Sáith!* Enough!" Jashar bellowed slamming his fist on the table.

Many at the table jumped, Kaer did not. His accusing tapered eyes did not change. He could believe such behavior from his stone-cold heartless father, but his prized brother? He shook his head again as if to disperse the charge.

That Jashar didn't deny it lent truth to the rumor. They would speak in private later, the siblings kept no secrets from each other

"Jashar, really," their mother, Vashana, was glaring daggers at her eldest son.

Few people ever attempted to reproach Jashar, only Vashana, and his other *mahmen* Anna. His father of course did it all the time, as well as his brothers Kaer and Daron thought they could. Alas, his younger sister, Sheera did it too, and was at this moment winking annoyingly at him.

All of the siblings rejoiced when they could provoke Mother and set her off, especially in public. The only member of his immediate family that never tried to admonish Jashar was his youngest brother, Makir.

Even now, the sixteen-year-old stared in wide-eyed admiration at his big brother the king.

Makir, Mak, worshipped Jashar, emulated him. He couldn't wait to grow up big and brave and as bleeding strong as his warlord brother, and earn his own moniker like Jashar's *Daigéar Láidir,* the Bloody Dagger.

In truth, no one truly ever rebuked or questioned Jashar, not even his mother, he only allowed his father that privilege. His brothers and sister teased, but they knew whose fist ruled the kingdom, and that included them. But, they were loyal to a fault so they truly obeyed him out of love and trust.

Jashar's eyes slid to his father, the elder king at the other end of the table.

Allon still carried himself with warrior regality. Most of his hair was still thick and mostly dark, and the canny and cunning, and trace of icy cruelty had never left his dark eyes.

The five siblings all got their dark hair and dark eyes from their father. The boys had his big build and easy strength.

Jashar's eyes settled affectionately on his mischievous sister, Sheera.

Sheera, with her deep chocolate hair waving down her back was tall and willowy like her mother. Tanned from a lot of time spent outdoors, fine-boned and slender, yet taller and sturdier than the fair-skinned, delicate Princessa Maratia- *dammit-*

Jashar scowled turning his attention back to his father.

Allon was speaking quietly to the senior chief beside him. He had glanced up briefly at Jashar's outburst of temper; he frowned at him then turned his attention back to the chief.

"Hey, moon to Jashar, come in *bráthair,"* Kaer teased. "What's going on in that overly serious skull of yours?"

All of the siblings chided Jashar for being exceedingly stern, strict and serious much of the time. But then again, a kingdom weighed on his young shoulders. The oldest at 27, a shade over a year or two separated each of the children except for teen Mak.

Allon had started Jashar's training at the tender age of three.

He'd placed a small, but real, sword in his tiny hands and sent him out into the woods, alone, to battle a wild, feral tiger-like animal that had been terrorizing the village.

The deadly cat was described as 'black as the velvet night, a savage killing beast that silently stalked and pounced, tearing its prey apart with fangs as big and sharp as daggers.'

Another reason, besides his adeptness with knives, that Jashar was called the *Daigéar Láidir,* the Bloody Dagger was his battle with the voracious animal.

Jashar doesn't remember much of it. He was told he'd managed to climb a tree and wait for the big cat to go by. When it did, Jashar had launched himself from the tree, landing blade down on the cat.

Judging by the bloody gouges and claw marks on his small body it had taken more than one blade thrust to kill the cat. He still carries the scars, one crosses from his forehead in a curve down his temple.

The tale told that because of his kill, the animal's soul had morphed into Jashar, giving him his feral grace, his icy, fearless calm in warfare.

They say that he metaphorically stole the panther's eyes, his own orbs mutated from dark as the deepest soil brown to glittering black and formidable as diamonds.

Jashar had walked out of the woods with pride, triumphant, bloody, and scared out of his mind. It was only the beginning of Allon's harsh, brutal training.

Allowed little contact with the females in his family, including Anna, Allon felt they would soften his young heir, Jashar had no choice but to grow up fast, hard, strong, fearless, the scant softness and kind feelings had been stunted in his heart.

Being the testosterone-ridden male that he was, he required sex, robust, and often rough sex. He chose women tough enough to handle his powerful, big body. Fortunately, those kinds of women did not require any vow of commitment on his part.

He had a kingdom to run, he didn't need some female fawning all over him, trying to trap him into marriage and incurring a lifetime of her endlessly complaining and telling him what to do.

He tried to recall the last durably aggressive woman he'd been with. It was Blair, no, Hazel, no that was last month, the latest had been...funny, they all seemed to blend into one another.

A picture of the female, the Princess Butcher, floated into his vision. The huge indigo eyes teeming with tears she refused to let him see fall. So proud, the sensuous trembling lips, the delicate, fine body, her breasts heaving under the clinging dress, that perfectly round ass- shit- he needed a drink.

Ignoring his brother's attempts to engage him in discussion of the girl, Jashar motioned to a servant to bring him a drink.

"Seriously, Jash, tell me about her. That dainty hot piece you have stashed in that cold dark dungeon, all alone. Wait," Kaer snapped his fingers, his disapproving tone snide, "she won't be too alone, I'm sure there are plenty of rats-"

Jashar slammed both palms on the table and shoved his chair back. All eyes flew to him as he got to his feet. He bowed respectfully to his mother then to his father, saw his father glance deliberately at the clock, evening prayer would be soon.

He quickly strode out of the room.

Chapter Eight

Jashar's skin tingled with anticipation, and abhorrence. He had a job to do, and all he could think about while bathing and shaving was that soon she would be brought to him.

He was tempted to take care of his erection in the shower so he could handle her coolly, the situation, with more composed ease. But, nay, he was a king, a warrior, a man, he could control himself.

After all, she was just a girl, a female. He'd been with plenty of them and he'd never had this fucking lack of control issue before. What the hell was it about the *mici,* the little chit that stirred his blood, heating it until his cock had a mind of its own?

Standing in front of the looking glass, Jashar scrubbed his fingers down his face and took a slow, deep breath and held it, he would control his body dammit. He did the breathing technique many times before he felt his body cool and his erection diminish.

Splashing water on his face, he combed his hair and went to his sleeping chambers as before to wait for her to be brought to him.

By the time McGee rapped on the door and then opened it, Jashar was sitting calmly on the floor by the large fireplace with his back resting against the stones.

He wore brown breeches, a white shirt, his long hair hung straight past his shoulders. Before he'd waited for her in his stocking feet, this time he had his boots on.

As usual, McGee brought her in and when he released her she stood as if made of the same stone as the fireplace.

Jashar's dark gaze fell on the princessa, blazed with slicing heat, then shifted to the guard.

McGee bowed and as before keeping his expression blank, gently patted the woman on her shoulder and left the room closing the door behind him.

She stood unmoving. Jashar could see visibly that she immediately felt bereft at the guard's leaving.

Her shoulders stiffened, her nipples hardened, he could see them pressing against the thin dress. Her fair skin paled and she pulled her plush lips in to keep them from trembling.

Jashar stared at her for a long time. She kept her eyes down and did not move. He nodded to the space near and in front of him on the floor and said without affect, "Come and sit."

Letting out his held breath, he kept his expression impassive as for once she did as he said. Good, things were starting out with less animosity.

He watched her slowly, elegantly move towards him, gracefully sink to her knees then sit in front of him, crossing her legs. She folded her hands primly in her lap. Her eyes rolled up briefly to his then quickly lowered.

Jashar had considered how he would discreetly interrogate her, see if he could discern the truth. His gaze scrolled from her shiny hair down the front of her to her legs crossed under her dress and back up to wait for those dazzling eyes to rise to his. They did not. He sighed.

"So, ah, Miss…Princessa **Araminte,** let me ask you, do your parents live?"

Surprised at the question, she looked up at him and nodded. "Yes, both my mother and father are well."

He already knew that. "I see," he nodded in return. "Do you have siblings?"

Confused at his interest, she answered carefully, "Yes, a younger brother and an older sister."

"Hmm." He regarded her impassively. "I have of course heard of your land, your people, the uh, *Saorghlanadhs.* You are from the land of *Saorghlanadh*, the Land of Catharsis?"

She inclined her head with a faint nod. "Yes."

He stretched out his long legs and crossed his ankles. Settling his bulky torso more comfortably against the stones, he said, "My experience with your people is that you are fairly nonviolent, nonaggressive.

"You mind your own business and avoid warring unless it is brought to your doorstep, unfortunately not like us where so many factions draw us into fighting for our land. It is prized as it is a large region with the coast on one side and cradled by the mountains to the far east."

She nodded mutely.

"The, ah, day I captured you, you were running from…some men, it appeared from one man in particular." He watched the pink in her cheeks fade. Averting her eyes, she said nothing.

"May I ask, *cad*? Uh, I mean why? And, *cé,* that is, who,` who was this man and why were you running from him?" He had to remember to speak only English with her.

Jashar watched her skin pale further, her eyes dashed around the room, landing on the door. He waited patiently, for what seemed a very long time.

Finally, she inhaled deeply then let out the breath. "He, um, is, was," she took another breath looking pained, "my fiancé."

Jashar could not stop the shock of surprise that flooded his face. "Your- fiancé?" For some reason his stomach pitched. He had not considered she had a- man. She seemed so terribly…young…and dammed innocent.

Personally, if he were her fiancé, he would come after Jashar with sword raised for his head for what he'd done to her. Jashar would if a man did what he had to his sister, or any other woman actually.

She nodded wearily. "Yes. My fiancé."

"But- you were running *from* him? I don't understand?"

Her eyes flit back to the door. "Yes. It was a planned, shall I say forced," her mouth twisted wryly, "engagement. Our parents, and unfortunately he as well, wanted us to marry. I did not."

His brows rose, he was perturbed at the odd feeling in the pit of his stomach that she was attached, planning to marry.

"But, why not? I saw him, he was fairly young and," Jashar was not used to talking about other men to women, "uh, handsome I guess, I mean as far as I could tell. We were all running that day."

She snorted elegantly. "Sure. He is fair looking and rich, and as blue-blooded and titled as they come, but…"

"But?" he prompted when she paused.

Her face colored slightly. "Other than the fact that I did not love him, he could be…cruel…violent. He is much older than me. Besides groping me since I was quite young," her mouth twisted in repugnance, "he has...struck me, pinched me. He liked to dig his fingers into my...skin until I couldn't help but cry out. And, he did...other things on the occasions I couldn't get away from him."

His dark brows knit low disgruntled over his tapered eyes. "Your parents, ah, didn't you tell your parents?"

One shoulder shrugged glumly, her lips pulled in. Slightly embarrassed, slightly sad, she replied, "They, uh, my parents told me they thought I was...exaggerating because they knew I didn't want to marry him. They told me to grow up, accept what is best for everyone, meaning them and him," her voice scraped bitterly.

His face a stony pillar, Jashar stared blankly at her, but his mind was angry. He waited for her to continue.

Her lackluster sigh and pained expression tugged at the back of his mind where, if he had actual feelings, would have made him feel sorry for her.

His mouth tightened. He was not there to feel emotional towards her, he pushed aside the unfamiliar feelings of compassion that tried to eke in.

Eyes still on the floor, she said, "Anyway, the day I was fleeing, he had cornered me in a room. He wanted..." she glared at him, "the same thing most men want, to have his way with me. I refused. He slapped me. I still refused, he punched me in..."

Her lowered eyes chilled over. Voice bleak with a shade of anger, she continued, "My stomach. He hit me hard enough to knock me down, and then he attacked me. He tore my dress, I-" Her eyes flicked up to his. "I got away from him and ran."

Her glare at him rueful, she said, "It would appear I only jumped from the skillet into the fire. You succeeded where he failed." She shot him a bitter accusing glower.

He said nothing, his expression remained blank.

She looked away, still sad, but thoughtful. Her voice soft and wistful she said, "Maybe now that I am no longer a..." her eyes flickered to him then away, "a, uh, virgin, I can go back home. He may not want me now that I am," her voice caught, throat tightened, "damaged, used, ruined." She suddenly climbed to her feet.

"Sit. Down." His command was harsh and he meant it. He was pissed she threw his rape of her in his face on the tail of explaining her own fiancé's assault on her.

Added to that, he felt inexplicable rage at that man, for forcing his engagement on her, for forcing himself on her, for hurting her, just for being engaged to her. Unfamiliar guilt, and possessiveness crawled up his insides, he didn't like it.

He needed to stop hearing her lovely lilting voice; he needed to put his strange feelings back to status quo. To do that he had to remind himself of his duty.

Earlier in the day his father had taken him to task for leaving the girl relatively unharmed. He reminded Jashar of his duty to punish the villainous woman. He called Jashar a weak coward for failing to follow through with scourging her.

Jashar had not told him about the spanking, it sounded so...well, he knew his father would not consider it severe enough punishment.

Maratia hadn't moved but she looked towards the door. Softly under her breath she murmured, "You have ruined me. My life."

"I said sit down," his tone ringing angry. He growled, "If you do not, I will make you." He did not like what she was saying to him.

Jashar was king; he could have any woman he wanted. It wasn't right for her to not want to lie with him. It wasn't his fault she had horror attached to her name and he had been tasked with dispatching her punishment, as barbaric as it was. He was feeling too soft towards her.

Sáith. Enough. He fumed; he will act like a king and do his job.

She stood for a moment, her legs visibly shaking. She sank nervously to her knees then slid down onto her butt, her legs curled to the side.

His eyes scarcely visible under his hooded lids, Jashar contemplated the female. He needed to think of her as a criminal. Not used to throwing women around and raping them, and knowing that it was necessary to do it again, right now, he paused.

The thought of assaulting her again sickened him so much that for once he was not hard in her presence. But this was the time he needed to be. Maybe if he saw her nude, touched her intimately, he could force himself on her again.

He ordered roughly, "Get on your knees." He didn't need to look at her eyes to know that she was filled again with terror of him. Her shaking fear was so discernible he could literally feel it in the currents in the room.

Very slowly she moved to her knees. Her eyes stayed staring at the floor.

"Sit back on your heels."

Like she was being taken to the gallows, about to be beheaded, she complied.

"Undo your bodice," he commanded, his voice roughly edged.

He saw her entire body go rigid, the color drain completely from her face. Of course she did not move.

His deep voice low, coarse, he ordered, "Do it or I will, and the dress will be in shreds and you have little else to wear. Do it."

Allon's words sifted in his ears, that she was the Butcher; she could be a whore and still be a virgin. There were other parts of her body she could use to-

Instead of doing as he said, blinking rapidly but not looking at him, Maratia crossed her arms over her chest in a protective cross, with her hands clinging to opposite shoulders.

He moved closer to her with his hands out with the obvious intent that he was going to rip her dress off her.

Now she looked directly at him. Her eyes so big and fluid. Like before, he could see himself in them, his own dark discs were blank, devoid of humanity.

Before he touched her, she put her fingers to the buttons on her dress. Her trembling fingers fumbling, it took a long time before she managed to undo her bodice. Her head lowered, she peered up at him, her expression begged for him to stop, to let her go.

But his eyes, white lightning flamed in the thunderous black, were leveled at her chest. His unpleasantly rough voice lowered further like from a gravel pit, he said unequivocally, "Open it."

He intensely watched her small hands clutching the sides of her unbuttoned blouse. She wore no bindings under the dress. "You have two seconds before I do it, and it will not be gently."

Biting her lips to keep them still, and to keep the gathering tears from falling, with quivering fingers she pulled the blouse open, then stopped.

Seeing the partial creamy swells of her breasts, there was no problem with his desire now, he was no longer soft.

His erection pushed at his pants, he resisted the urge to rub it, rearrange it.

He growled, "Pull the blouse back off your shoulders and pull the sleeves down your arms." His gaze never wavered, it blazed at her like he was touching her with graphic fingers.

She froze. Shaking her head, her eyes pleading with him to stop, her long hair fell over her front, covering her.

Jashar's body was on fire, his pants were tight and uncomfortable, his color deepened as did his voice. He barked, "*Do it.*"

When she didn't comply, he started moving towards her again, the threat clear in the smoldering onyx eyes.

Maratia took a deep breath, she could no longer control any of the quaking that struck her body. He made another move towards her. She had no chance against the huge, powerfully built man.

Staring at him, she slowly pulled the top down baring her breasts but covered them with her hands. "Sire, please, don't do this," she struggled to hold back the tears and the tremor in her voice. She spoke so softly it was a wonder he could hear her.

The pleas made no difference. Images of the murdered girls floated behind his eyes. "Put your hands behind your back."

Her eyes wide and pleading, he deliberately kept his gaze off her pleading eyes stark with fear and humiliation, keeping it straight on her chest.

He told her, "Move your hair behind your shoulders and put your hands behind your back or I will bind them and you will not be able to move at all."

The tears threatened to fall, the indigo orbs were awash with them. She blinked them back, swallowed hard, and didn't move.

He leaned towards her, whispered harshly, "Last chance to follow my orders, I will strip you naked and tie your wrists behind you."

She squirmed back from him a little.

His anger heated up with his desire, he snapped, "Do not move from that spot, and do as I say."

She still didn't do what he said. "*Bine*, all right," he stood up. "I'll get rope."

With a small cry, sitting back on her heels, Maratia pushed her heavy hair back behind her shoulders then slowly put her hands behind her back.

Defenseless, naked to the waist, her body quaking, she closed her eyes; her bared breasts were forced to thrust out and up for his perusal.

He sat back down and was quiet for so long, she thought maybe he had left the room. She cracked her eyes open and blanched again seeing his manhood big, hard, straining at his breeches for release. His midnight eyes turned white hot as he just stared at her breasts.

Jashar had had hundreds of women but he didn't ever recall becoming this hot just staring at a pair of luscious breasts. Keeping his eyes off her face, he didn't care to see the panic, fear and mortification he knew was there, he looked only at her bare flesh.

Her breasts were full, they sat up high and round and firm, pure cream with soft pink areoles and darker pink nipples that pebbled as he stared at them.

She didn't move. Just knelt with her hands behind her back and her proud eyes piercing across the small space between them as if she could cut him to pieces with them.

He looked at her ravishing breasts for a long time, his mouth dry, his gaze like a physical trace over her flesh. Like he could actually feel their weight, crush their softness in his hands.

Picturing himself kneading her globes with his long fingers, his thumbs brushing over the little pink nipples, he started to give her another order, then made the mistake of raising his gaze to hers.

He felt the anguish and suffering in them like a punch in the gut. His eyes fell to the floor. Self-disgust rose like bile in his throat.

Feeling sick to the end of death, without looking at her again he murmured, "Princessa-"

A knock was heard at the door.

He cursed, then ordered brusquely, "Fix yourself."

He started to get to his feet when she said, "You are a despicable, horrible man, no," she shook her head. "No, you are not a man, not even a human being. You are less than an animal, you are- are- Satan."

She swept him with a virulent hateful look. "You are a disgrace of a person, a vile pig." Her soft beautiful lips were twisted with loathing, unadulterated hate.

He had to stop himself from nodding in agreement with her. Feeling every bit the piece of garbage she called him, he stood up and went to the door, opened it and closed it as he stepped outside.

A guard was there to only ask a quick question.

"Sire," he bowed. "I apologize for coming to your chambers but your brother Kaermon advised me to. We need to know what time practice is in the morning?"

Jashar answered him then decided to not rub salt in the princessa's wounds, he didn't return to his room. The desire to see how she was reacting was too irresistible to deny.

He still had to keep in mind she might be the Butcher Princess after all and a damned good actress, he would find out for sure. But he didn't think she was faking the tears he saw her shed the last time when she was unaware he secretly watched her, or the acute despair on her face just now.

As the guard left, Jashar slipped into the side room and observed her through the hole in the wall.

She had pulled her knees up and buried her face in her arms. Her slight shoulders rocked with great sobs.

Jashar couldn't tear himself away from the spyhole. His own stomach twisted and turned with her distress. She could not be faking this.

He dragged his hands through his hair and wiped his mouth. *Dias*, if he were her father or brother or husband, he would kill him for what he's done to her.

He closed his eyes; her pain was too intense for him to bear. But he had a duty to perform- he scowled bitterly, fuck the duty. He'd had enough of soiling this poor girl. Even without this display of emotion, he had felt it in his gut that she was innocent of the charges against her.

It was clear in those big pure eyes, the sweet lilt of her voice, and the soft innocence of her lips that she didn't have an evil bone in her body. But he did. He sure as hell did.

His eyes opened slowly, hating to see further pain on her face.

She struggled awkwardly to her feet, slightly off-balance as if her crying episode had weakened her. *Ah shit-* her blouse was still undone, still down. Those tits- those fucking beautiful bare- he looked away, at the door, the floor, anything but her bosom.

She drew the blouse back up over her shoulders, and still wracked with cries, she dashed at the falling tears while buttoning the dress.

Jashar left the room and went down the hall until he found a guard. "Officer Debennett," he said catching his attention, "get Officer McGee. Tell him I require his presence to return the prisoner to the dungeon."

The guard bowed and left immediately to do his bidding.

With a deprecating sigh, Jashar went back to the little room with the hole in the wall.

She was dressed now. He could look at her all he desired without degrading her further. He was done with the punishment. Done with this abusing of this female. He didn't care what his father said, Jashar was the king of Thuas sa Spéir.

He, and only he can make the ultimate, the final decisions. And he made one now. The abuse was stopping as of this minute. But for now, he needed to take another shower, he felt so dirty. He wondered if he'd ever feel clean again after what he's done to Maratia.

Then there was that fucking dungeon. He was required by their laws to keep her there. But, picturing her all rolled up in a ball in the dark, cold, lonely cell, rats circling her, *arggh*, he spat, what could he do about it?

Why in *Dias'* name was he there that day to see her fleeing and decide to capture her? He remembered, he'd thought she was a boy. Huh.

Grunting at that ridiculous thought of the time he pushed aside the image of her fine ass as she was running. There was nothing remotely boyish about her.

At the time he'd thought she, or he, had committed a criminal act and was perhaps fleeing the law, and he'd felt it was his duty- bah- there was that damned word again- he thought he should stop her- him and look into the matter. And look where it's led. Shit.

Unfortunately, he could not return her to her people. She still had charges against her regardless of what he thought about her innocence. He had to keep her in custody.

Her people may not war, but his did for preservation of their clan and their land. In the meantime, he would see what he could do to clear her name.

Jashar pushed away the thought that he had no desire to send her back to that thug of a fiancé, or her family that chose not to believe her, or that he just did not want to return her at all, at least for now.

He wasn't about to explore why he felt that way, it was enough that it prodded at him like an annoying bee buzzing around the back of his brain.

Deciding he would take a last quick look at her then go take the shower, a freezing one, he peered through the hole. His brows drew down in puzzlement.

She was pulling the sheets off the bed. As she pulled one sheet off, she tied it to the other one.

What the hell?

She took the sheets and tied them to the end of the bedpost then dropped the linen rope out the window and climbed up on the sill.

"Oh shit!" Jashar raced out of the room and into his.

She was climbing over the sill as he burst in and was already starting to climb down with one hand on the sheets and the other on the sill.

Her hand on the sill started slipping as she dropped further.

Shouting, "Maratia!" Jashar ran to her.

Leaning over, he grasped her wrists. Her body was hanging, her legs kicking out at open air.

She screamed at him, "Let me go!"

He huffed, "Goddammit-"

Fearing he would snap her fragile wrists with his strength, he carefully hauled her back through the window. Grasping her around the waist, he lifted her out of the window and set her carefully on her feet.

Releasing his grip on her waist, he grabbed her upper arms and shook her.

The long wavy hair fluttered and bounced against her back, brushing the top of her small waist.

"You stupid fool," he cursed at her, shaking her. "You could have fallen to your death!"

She wrenched at his grip, said with hopelessness strangling her throat, "What difference does it make? I would have welcomed it."

His mouth dropped open. His fingers digging into her arms, Jashar just stared at her aghast that she would even attempt such an escape much less be uncaring whether or not she died.

The light in her eyes dimmed bleakly.

"Ah, Maratia," he groaned, so sad to see her beauty shadowed with his attacks and her incarceration hanging over her, at least he could put part of her mind at peace.

"Listen," he was unaware he rubbed her arms with his thumbs while he talked. "I, uh, I promise you, Princessa, that I am done with my, uh, assault of you."

He watched her eyes widen with hope, then quickly darken with disbelief.

"A trick, Sire? To get my hopes up and then rape me again, adding the whipping perhaps to make it even better? Just to punish me further by giving me hope then throwing it cruelly in my face."

Her tone indicated such a man, or monster as she'd called him, would be quite capable of setting her up for a nasty fall. She looked down at his hands twining around her arms tightly, his thumbs brushing soft circles over her skin.

Realizing what he was doing, he released her and forked his fingers through his long hair.

"Ah, Princessa," his voice filled with disconcertment. "I swear to you, on my honor as a king, and as a man, and," he sighed rifling his hair again, "as a *Dias*, a uh, a God fearing man, I will not assault you again. Nor will I flog you. I know you don't trust a word I say, and I don't blame you, but I speak the truth. You will see by my actions, or actually, my inactions."

They stood and stared at each other for a long moment. She with distrust and disbelief, he with the ruggedly hard planes of his face implacable.

"Come," he dreaded to say it. "I must return you to the dungeon." He cringed at her cringe, he felt her skin shrivel and breath quicken at the words.

His head bowed slightly to her, he said quietly, "I am sorry, Princessa, that I cannot do anything about it. At the moment. But, I will-" the rap came at the door.

McGee had arrived to take her.

Jashar opened the door and frowned at the huge friendly grin McGee gave the princess.

"Princess," McGee said cheerfully, he offered his arm.

She easily slipped her slim hand under it.

He ushered her out the door.

As they passed the threshold, Jashar said, "Princessa."

She hesitated, rotated slightly towards him, staying partially behind the protective body of the guard.

Jashar could see the wary flinching way she regarded him, as if she expected him to strike her or order her death.

"Uh," he stuffed his hands in his pockets, shook his head. "Nothing. Go on."

She turned from him without a word and smiled weakly up at McGee. Not happy to return to the dismal cell, but she seemed pleased to see McGee, and to get away from the king.

Jashar could hear them chatting comfortably as they travelled down the hall, away from him. He stood in the doorway silently watching them until they disappeared.

Then he went back inside to prepare a lock so she couldn't get the window open again.

Chapter Nine

After breakfast the next morning, Jashar skipped his normal practice and went straight to the dungeon.

As usual, McGee was present as her guard. Jashar hadn't trusted any other male to be alone with the princess.

McGee was sitting cross-legged in front of the closed cell. Maratia sat mirroring him on the other. They were playing cards.

"What is this about?" Jashar asked, his voice gruffer than he meant.

They both looked up when he came in. Maratia quickly lowered her eyes, McGee hustled to his feet.

"Sire, we are playing cards." A crease wrinkled McGee's forehead. "Is that, I mean, there is nothing wrong with it, is there?"

Waiting anxiously for Jashar's response, his gaze flipped down to Maratia who kept her head bowed then back to Jashar in time to catch the king's frown of disapproval.

Before Jashar could respond, Maratia gracefully unfurled her body and stood up. "It is not his fault, Sire. I asked him to play with me. Please," she raised her eyes carefully to Jashar, "if there is any punishment, please spare him, do it to me.

Quickly McGee turned to Jashar speaking urgently, "Nay Sire, it was me. I am in charge of her, please, if there is discipline let it be me!" He maneuvered his body to be in front of Maratia.

She stepped to the side of his blockage. "No, Sire, punish me, Robbie was only trying to comfort me, distract me."

McGee hastily moved back in front her. "Sire, she was inconsolable, she couldn't stop crying, a rat ran over her in the-"

"Robbie!" Maratia cried. "That is between you and me." Looking at Jashar, she said with bravery encased in a frightened tone, "I will accept full responsibility for-"

No!" Robbie yelled frowning at her. "It is I that-"

"Enough!" Jashar bellowed. He glared at one then the other, "*Sáith*, tis only cards, I don't care."

He let out a loud exhale. "There is no danger as long as you," he nodded to McGee, "keep out of her reach. Which," a corner of his mouth ticked up, "won't take much." He looked pointedly at her small slender arms.

McGee's eyes narrowed at the king, was that mirth coming from his liege?

Maratia, on the other hand frowned at Jashar's accusation that she would be a danger to him if she was in reach of the big strong guard.

"Have you had your breakfast?" Jashar asked Maratia throwing her off kilter.

"What?" She blinked wary, and puzzled.

"Sire, as usual I brought her oatcakes with jam and tea," McGee offered.

Pulling his hands out of his pockets, Jashar twined them behind his back and regarded McGee with a rebuke. "I did not ask you, Guard, I asked her."

His face flushed, McGee nodded mutely. The straw on the floor of the dim lime and clay room crunched under his feet as he nervously shuffled them.

One small window way up high let in faint light. The other cells were unoccupied. Crime in the village of Spiremoor was infrequent. Serious offences were usually dealt with whippings, the most serious were death.

Although Jashar insisted everyone worked for their bread and homes, he did allow for the differences in each person's ability to do work.

He demanded that the villagers live in peace, not fearful someone would steal their possessions or kill them while they slept. Everyone knew punishment was swift and could easily be lethal.

Jashar said to McGee, "You are free for a few hours. Take off."

His eyes flitting uneasily back and forth from Jashar to Maratia and back, McGee uttered an unsure, "Uh, Sire?" His lips pulled in at the sudden sign of distress that crossed Maratia's face.

Jashar inclined his head to the door and tersely ordered, "Go." A frown grew on his stern face at the guard's obvious reluctance to leave him alone with the prisoner.

But McGee knew better than to disobey an order, men had lost their heads when defying the king's commands. The guard glanced nervously at Maratia, offered her a hopeful but weak smile, saw her own anxiety blossoming, then he reluctantly left the dungeon.

Maratia slowly backed away from the front of the cell, her eyes never leaving Jashar. Her skin paled at the scowl he gave her as she kept inching back.

Jashar took the keys off the wall by the door and unlocked the door to her cell.

He took note of the meager pallet with folded blankets on it against one wall made of limestone, oil shade, volcanic ash and saltwater. The effect was a sharp, rough, uncomfortable cold hovel.

The corner of his mouth twitched, *who neatly folds their blankets in jail?*

Her eyes downcast, Maratia labored to keep her voice strong, "Am I to receive my whipping now for playing cards with Rob- uh, the guard?" She straightened her spine and bravely raised her eyes to his.

Seeing the fear lancing the huge indigo orbs, Jashar said softly, "Fear not, Princessa, I am not here to harm you. I told you I was done with that. I want to take you outside. It has been a bit since you've felt the fresh air on your face, the breeze in your hair, the warmth of the sun."

Her back was against the far wall, she could not go any further from him. Her forehead furrowed in disbelief of his words, and distrust of him.

He moved his hands to cross his arms. Even in the long-sleeved shirt the muscles in his arms bulged and flexed. He could see her looking at them with added anxiety. "Come, Princessa," he stood aside of the open cell door.

She didn't move.

"Princessa, if I wanted to harm you I could just as easily go in there and get you. Now, stop wasting our time, the morning sun will soon grow uncomfortably hot."

He waited. He wanted her to come to him of her free will, not go in and forcibly drag her out. It would defeat his purpose.

Seeing his resolve that he wasn't going away, Maratia sighed and gingerly moved across the straw covered floor to the front of the cell.

He moved further from the opening so she could exit without coming near him.

When she stepped out of the cell he let out his held breath and took a few steps towards the door then turned back to her knowing she wouldn't be following him.

"Come, Princessa," he motioned slightly with his hand. He heard her deep, anxious inhale, but she did move to where he stood by the door.

He opened the thick wooden door, pushing it aside so she could pass through.

Her head tilting away from him, she warily passed him to step outside.

As soon as she stepped from the dank dungeon, the sun shone on the golden rosewood of her hair lighting the streaks of saffron that ran through it. Her pale skin was instantly warmed. Jashar stepped out behind her.

He watched her squint up in the sky at the puffy clouds then lower to survey her surroundings. She looked everywhere but at him.

He held out an arm like he'd seen McGee do. "This way, I will show you our gardens. I am curious to see if you have any different kinds of vegetables or fruit than we grow."

She cocked her head to him as if waiting for the ax to fall on her neck, but when he dropped his arm and started moving, she fell in behind him.

"Walk beside me, Princessa. I can't talk to you if you are at my back." He held out a hand for her to take.

She glanced at it, moved up next to him but didn't take his hand. He'd hoped she would, but he hadn't expected her to.

They walked across the low grass surrounding the castle compound incurring very curious glances.

People stopped what they were doing to watch them pass by. Warriors froze in mid-strike, gardeners stopped and leaned on their hoes, shepherds stalled with their sheep.

Everyone knew she was the king's prisoner. They knew who she was purported to be. A murderer of young children.

Villagers gaped at the mighty sire with the petite killer walking unbound beside him. Astounded curious eyes followed the pair as they crossed the meadow.

When they reached the gardens, Maratia let out a happy sigh, "Oh, the flowers!" She moved closer to the blossoms that filled the area.

Stepping up to a rose, she tipped her small nose to inhale its fragrance, then with a hum of enjoyment she moved to the brilliant purple orchids. She gently rubbed the side of her cheek on a petal.

Strolling leisurely behind her, Jashar kept his hands folded behind him. Identifying the orchid in his language, "Ah, the violet *magairlíní*." He smiled, said very softly, "Stunning, but they don't hold a candle to you."

Her lips pulled into a pucker, unsure if he was teasing her, or mocking her, or worse, she didn't say anything. She let her fingertips drift over the delicate blooms.

Jashar ambled slowly trailing her as she meandered around the garden with little yelps of joy when she discovered a new flower to touch and sniff and gush over.

After an hour or so of wandering the flower gardens they moved onto the vegetables.

Jashar explained a few of the vegetables that she did not recognize, gave her a couple to taste.

He laughed when she bit into a bitter *stalet* and stuck out her tongue. His voice was lazy and gentle as he answered all of her questions.

Her face lit up animated, roses bloomed in her cheeks from the fresh air and slight excitement she exhibited at each new thing that caught her interest.

The sun grew hot, Jashar said, "We need to go in now, that fair skin of yours will fry like bacon on a griddle." He felt a tug at his heart at the disappointment that shaded her face.

"Come," he held a hand to her.

Distracted by a butterfly, she took it. Her accepting action made his lips lose their normal reticence, softening the chiseled mouth for a moment.

As they left the garden and headed across the grass, her feet started dragging, she moved slower and slower.

His voice low, slightly cajoling with a hint of mirth, he said, "If you don't make this hard on me, Princessa, tomorrow I will take you to the stables."

The big eyes swung wide at him, "Really? To see the horses?"

He almost smiled at the pleasure that bowed her lips. "Aye. But you have to stop dragging your feet now, I have matters to attend to, we need to go back, all right? *Bine*?"

Her step quickening, she smiled without humor up at him. "How, Sire, tell me how I could make anything hard on you? You merely move me about as you desire."

The easy feeling that had permeated them the entire morning dissipated as she reminded them of his cruel treatment of her.

Her mention of her making anything hard on him gave him the physical reaction he'd been fighting since he first saw her this morning in the cell. His pants grew tighter at her unaware innuendo.

His mouth firmed grimly, he didn't notice his hand clutching hers squeezed hard until she tried to pull her hand from his grip.

He immediately released her. "I am sorry, Princessa, with someone as delicate as you I fear I don't know my own strength."

Maratia kept walking; surprised that he actually had said he was sorry. The kings she had known in her lifetime never would have used that word. Ever. She glanced quickly up at him.

His broad shoulders were regally back and autocratically rigid, he'd shortened his long strides so she could keep up with him. He'd left his long hair loose, it swung against his broad shoulders.

She had been amazed earlier how the lines of his rock-hewn face had softened some of the harsh lines while they strolled the gardens. He'd seemed almost...human. Now he looked grim and stoic again. His warrior's jet black eyes inscrutable.

On the way back to the dungeon he stopped a guard telling him to retrieve McGee to come and watch over her. Maratia hid a little smile. Now that was kingly, he never asked, or requested or said please, he ordered.

She wondered how he was with his family. Was he as taciturn and cold, callous and cruel to them as he was to her?

The thought of returning to that nasty cell made her shiver. It was so ugly, and damp, cold, hard. There were rats.

Thank goodness McGee was tasked with having to stay with her at all times.

She had felt the furry rodent scurry over her leg last night and let out a peal- Robbie had woken and come immediately to her.

Of course by the time he got the main door open and hurried to her cell the creature was gone. It had upset her so much she couldn't contain the tears.

At least it was only Robbie who saw her cry like a foolish baby. He was kind and gentle and nonjudgmental. He'd told her from the beginning he didn't believe the stories about her. He had said anyone with half a mind could see what a dainty little innocent she was.

Maratia had giggled then, the first time since her capture. She had said, "So, Robbie, you're saying the king only has half a mind?"

Robbie about had a heart attack. "Hush!" He glanced all around worried someone had heard her. Seeing her hold her hands over her mouth to cover her giggles, he relaxed and grinned at her.

"Nay, King Jashar is really a brilliant man. He's brave and the fiercest warrior of them all, he is a fair man, an honorable man," he saw her lip curl. "Maratia, yes, he is extremely...tough."

She nodded.

His lip pulled in. "I will tell you about his young life and perhaps you will understand why he does, did, what he did to you."

Robbie told her about how harsh and cruel King Allon had been raising Jashar. He told her the tale of the youngster's fight with the panther.

She rolled her eyes at the part about him morphing the panther's being into himself.

Robbie smiled. "You doubt, Princess? Just look at him. There is definitely a wild savageness to him. The scar on his temple from the big cat, those obsidian eyes, they're called *daoldubh,* black as night, primal. Have you ever seen a person with such richly pure black eyes like that? They are unnatural."

Her shoulder raised, she shook her head. "I thought they were black because he's Satan."

"Princess!" he squawked. "Hush! Stop that, you will lose your head-" he had broken off at the rueful look on her face.

Chapter Ten

But that had been a day or so ago. Now, the Satan King held the door to the dungeon open for her to go back inside.

She passed through under his arm with her head down. The autumn hair covered the sides of her face, waving down the front of her.

His back rigid, Jashar caught the sad pout of her pink lips. He looked around.

The stone and lime chamber was dim and cold, the air damp and heavy. Thank *Dias* there were currently no other prisoners. He would have had to find somewhere else to hold her, and it would be worse.

Regardless of what his father had ordered, he couldn't have left such a young woman in the company of drunk, dangerous, abusive men. His shoulders twitched, hell, he was two of those himself.

Having to return to the dismal dungeon, her shoulders drooping, she trod across the straw covered floor to her cell, dust kicked up behind her.

"We'll, uh, leave the door open until McGee gets here," Jashar said quietly motioning to her cell door.

Maratia stood on the threshold of her cell. She ducked her head, peered up at him through her long curly lashes.

"Um, Sire, I want to say, it was kind of you to take me to the gardens today. I, uh, don't know why you did, but I am grateful and appreciative. I know you are a busy man, yet you took your time to take me."

She squinted at him waiting for him to reveal his ulterior motive for taking her.

He said nothing, just nodded slightly. He had moved until he was a just few feet from her.

Red color stained her cheeks. Wrapping her arms around her body, she guardedly peered up at him. Her expression turned anxious as the color infused her skin. Resigned to her fate, she asked, "Will you be having me brought to your chambers later?"

His expression impassive, his brows arched at her question. He understood now why her face had suddenly turned red. He shook his head. "Nay. I told you, I am desisting with your punishment."

Her eyes flashed with fright, the red fled from her face leaving it pale as ivory. She took a step back from him.

"You- you are going to kill me now?" Maratia tried to keep her spine straight, her voice steady, her gaze unwavering. She knew she failed at all of them.

His black brows arched higher, right up to his hairline. "Nay, *Dias* nay, Princessa, you misunderstand me." An annoyed scowl pulled the brows down, he snapped harshly, "Stop inching away from me." He regretted his sharp tone the second it was out.

She froze, strung her arms so tightly around her body he wondered how she drew a breath.

He tucked his hands behind his back to appear less threatening. "Princessa, Maratia," he cleared his throat.

"What I'm saying is, that I will not be...punishing you anymore. I found it hard from the very beginning to believe you were this- this soulless murderess. But, you know my father's orders, you heard him." He sighed heavily and advanced a spare inch closer to her.

His head slightly bowed, he looked up at her, the angles of his face were hard but his mouth had softened. "I have soldiers out now seeking the answers. They are questioning people to find the truth of the matter. If it comes out that you are in fact, the uh, Princess Butcher, then we will deal with it at that time."

She stood motionless, staring at him, obviously on edge, as if the second he made a move she would flee. Alas, she had nowhere to run to.

"Maratia."

Her head tipped at the sound of his voice, the way he said her name. It sounded quite different from the way people in her land pronounced it, he drew it out in his deep voice and rolled the r.

His sigh was audible. "I can't take back what I've done to you."

He was coolly looking at her face but she remembered how after she endured the indignation of him forcing her to disrobe, his hot gaze had seemed to sear her flesh as he had stared at her bare chest.

She recalled the pain and humiliation of the first night when he ripped off her underwear then ruthlessly penetrated her. Then...the next night, his big hard hands clutching her bare bottom...the ignoble spanking, his...manhood in his fist pressed against her mouth.

Maratia recoiled. Grief and a stinging ache struck her eyes dulling them, her face blew up red again. She wrapped her arms tighter around her body. So mortified at what he'd done to her she couldn't look at him.

Jashar was astute enough to know what she was thinking, it was written all over her devastated face. He raked a hand through his long hair then frowned when she flinched as if he was going to hit her.

"Ah, Princessa, I am sorry, for what I've done to you. I swear, if I could undo what I did, I would. I cannot. I can only promise you I will not assault you again, or," his brow cocked, "slay you. Even if you were the perpetrator of the atrocities to our children, I don't have women executed. And my father is well aware of that."

She waited, he stared at her. Curious she asked cautiously, "Why did he say I was to be beheaded then?"

Jashar shrugged his big shoulders. "It is what he wanted. If I hadn't been around he would have seen the punishment carried out exactly as he ordered."

The red poured out of her face again, she was visibly shaken. "Uh, but, I don't understand what you are saying. Your father ordered me assaulted, whipped and then beheaded, but you're saying…what?"

He took a step closer. "I am saying, Princessa, that I will not assault you again. I will not beat you or flog you or take your head."

Lips bunching, she gazed at him quizzically, then fear pulsed across her face. "Oh, then another. You will have someone…else punish me?" Her shoulders bowed inward as if they could protect her. Even as badly as the king has treated her, clearly the known Satan was better than an unknown torturer.

"Nay." His eyes narrowed in frustration at her. A frisson of possessiveness sprinted across his shoulders at the thought of another warrior doing to her what he had. And, of course, they would commit so much more merciless savagery on her than he had.

"No one will harm you now. I have told you, please accept my word that you are now safe from punitive actions."

"But your father-"

His head shook back and forth. "Nay, it doesn't matter. I agreed to what he said at the time because I really had no choice. He had ordered it in front of the entire tribunal. Tis basically our laws, and at that moment, every man there wanted your head," *and the rest of you too*, he thought to himself, drawing up a picture of her on her knees the day of her capture.

Her hair gripped in his fist, baring her neck to his knife, her half-exposed tits on display- oh aye, they all had wanted a piece of her, himself included.

Jashar explained, "If I hadn't agreed to his command I would not have been able to prevent the roomful of enraged men from taking you, gang-raping you, and killing you on the spot."

"You- you're saying you assaulted me- to save me?" Small dimples in the sides of her cheeks slivered as her lips pursed in her disbelief. Shaking her head, her teeth nipped at her bottom lip.

He dragged a hand through his hair, then seeing her stiffen again at his sudden raised arm, he clasped his hands behind his back.

"Aye. That was part of it. The other was to deny my father in front of those men would have shown the utmost disrespect, a slap to his dignity and his power. Although I am reigning king, he is my father and his words must be respected."

"Hmm," Maratia muttered with a short aggrieved glare at him. "But it was all right for him to slap me, twice, hard enough I was sent reeling." Her face fully reflected her recalling the pain and mortification she had suffered at the debasing experience, her eyes splintered in shamed misery.

Her arms had been bound behind her back leaving her woefully vulnerable, on her knees in a room filled with only males who were calling for her head, in between vulgar offers to fuck her.

Her head wrenched back by Jashar clutching her hair, her breasts about to spill out in front of all of those men. A visible shiver conveyed her dreaded feelings of fear at that time, that she was going die, and the terrible degradation of it all.

"Believe me," Jashar said, watching the play of abhorrent emotions score her face. "I had struggled to figure a way of appeasing everyone without anyone coming to harm."

Further remembering the event and his part of it, and recalling his thoughts and feelings at the time, the dark eyes crunched in despair, first of agony of the reasons why they wanted her killed, and then later shame and guilt at his actions.

Her voice filled with humiliation and loss, she whispered, "But I was hurt. You hurt me."

His full lips compressed in a severe line, he looked at her with matching pain. "Princessa, one of the children murdered, she was dear to me, Felicity. I," he winced, "saw her destroyed body, they told me what had been done to her. The unrelenting torture of men violating her young body, beating her, the unimaginable fear and agony she must have felt..."

He took a deep breath. "Every time I was to…take you," he glanced at her, her face was a mask of horror. "I pictured the child so that I could force myself to dispense…your punishment."

Maratia quietly studied the grief and guilt that marred his face, his shoulders slightly hunched with shame. "But, nothing has changed, Sire, you still are required to-"

He shook his head. "Nay. I told you. I will not hurt you again."

"But- your father, his orders, the other men-"

"Nay," he shook his head again. "I am the crowned king. I supersede everyone, including my father. I did what I did because he was right, it is my duty to mete out punishment to royals.

"Although I do not believe in flogging or executing women, or," he colored slightly, "raping them, but," he looked at the floor then back up to her, "at the time I had little choice in the matter. It was a mob scene that I could not fight alone. Now, I have the loyalty of my brothers and my closest warriors to assist me with protecting you."

Her voice tight, she murmured, "I…don't understand."

"Aye, the heat of the moment of your capture, when I brought you in front of the tribunal," they both again pictured him pushing her to her knees in front of all those men and holding his knife to her throat, they both grimaced.

"I could do naught to protect you against the enraged mass except to swear to carry out my father's order of punishment. Once I swore to it, I had to do it. And," he sighed, "as we know, I did carry out part of it."

His brain sifted through his violent rape of her virgin's body, and, he hadn't actually whipped or beaten her, but he did spank her. Color seeped up his neck at the remembrance of her naked behind and his hands and mouth on-

"Ah," he blinked the thought away. "But now I can protect you. And, I am doing what I felt was right from the beginning. I am investigating the whole *búistér-stríapach* matter."

At her confused look of the foreign words he spoke, he translated, "The butcher-whore business."

Her lips pulled in. "I don't understand your language, you have a mix of languages, from other lands, why is that? My people speak only one language."

He smiled a rare smile, this was an easy question. "We are the closest to the coast, the travelers that wash ashore usually stay here. We have not brought on the modernization like most of the rest of the world they tell us about, however, over hundreds, or more, years of mingling, our language is a blend of many."

Jashar sighed. "Unfortunately, that includes our disreputable slang and cursing. Since our land cannot be located except by those that accidentally come to our shore, we maintain our ancient ways. You understand now, *mici nua léas?*"

He smiled at her inquiring look then explained, "It loosely translates to, *mici* is little, *nua-* means fresh, and *léas-* is a ray of light."

Her eyes widened. Unsure of how to take that, she said nothing.

The door opened, McGee slowly entered leery of what he was going to find.

Seeing the two of them standing peacefully chatting, brought a look of bewilderment to his handsome face. He had expected to find her bloody and broken, maybe dead. His exhale of relief was audible.

The pair heard it but continued gazing at each other until McGee coughed.

Jashar turned slightly to him. "Ah, McGee. You're here," he said redundantly, like he hadn't remembered sending for him.

He turned back to Maratia but said to McGee, "I think it would be all right to leave the cell door open tonight. You may remain guard inside, instead of outside of the dungeon."

McGee and Maratia looked at him like he'd lost his mind.

He again turned slightly to regard McGee. "Unless there are other prisoners brought in. Then the door will be locked and you will immediately send word to me. Is that clear?"

The look on McGee's face said it was anything but clear, but he said, "Yes, Sire."

Jashar addressed Maratia who was staring at him as if she was trying to figure him out. "Princessa," he said softly, "I have a free hour in the morning. I will come and take you to the stables, if that is all right with you?"

She stared speechless, *if it was all right with her if he took her out of the frightful dungeon and into the light?* She nodded unable to speak.

His voice gruff, he said, "All right then. McGee," he said to the guard who came abruptly to attention, "keep her…safe." He bowed to Maratia then left the dungeon.

Chapter Eleven

The next morning when Jashar arrived at the dungeon, Maratia was sitting just inside her cell leaning against the wall. The despondent look on her face that shifted to uncertainty and then traced into a tiny bit of glee, told Jashar that she had not really expected him to show up.

The same look was reflected on McGee's face. They both got to their feet when the king stepped inside the door.

The two glanced at each other then at Jashar, both faces tense with question.

Jashar moved a few feet inside with his hand out to Maratia. "Come, are you ready?" He bit back a smile at her trying to stifle her eagerness to leave the frightful dungeon.

Still, she moved slowly, warily towards him.

Waiting patiently, he spared a quick glance at McGee who looked unsure, still puzzled, yet on the verge of appearing happy for the princess to have some time outside.

When Maratia reached Jashar, he took her hand and headed towards the door. He stopped briefly and said to McGee, "You are free for an hour."

"Thank you, Sire," was the guard's quick, enthusiastic response.

Outside, the sun had not fully risen; the air was transitioning from the night's coolness to a balmier dawn.

The couple stepped into the lush meadows that spread for miles cuddled in the cusp of the flourishing forests.

Dense woods bountiful with evergreens, vibrant shrubbery, and teeming with creatures encompassed most of land.

Leading her across a different field than yesterday, Jashar said, "So, you would like to see the horses?"

She nodded emphatically. "Oh yes!"

He took shorter steps so she could easily keep up with him.

Their feet shuffled over the short grass, her dress just brushing the blades that sparkled from the morning dew. Her hair was still wet and curling from her early morning bath.

As the day before, people stopped what they were doing to gawk at the couple. Some with interest, some with anger. Everyone knew about the Butcher Princess and the gossip circled with contradictions galore about Maratia.

Jashar walked quietly as Maratia plucked a few wildflowers along the way. They passed by meadows bordered by partially wooded, shrubby areas.

When they approached the stables, Maratia sniffed the air and exclaimed, "Ah, I love the smell of horses and the woody sweetness of the freshly cut hay."

Jashar smiled as she tugged her hand from his and hurried up to the first mare they reached.

Setting her bouquet on a hale bale, "Oh, she is lovely," Maratia enthused moving close to an Eriskuy Pony. She hesitated when she was within arm's reach of the grey horse with the short legs and bit of tufted hair at the fetlocks.

Jashar told her, "Go ahead, you can pet her, she has a fine temperament."

Maratia put one hand behind her back and reached out tentatively with the other to stroke the pony's nose. "She is soft, Sire, but small, what will she be used for?"

He moved up closer to her. "She has terrific stamina and can carry a light adult."

"Ha!" Maratia laughed still petting the horse. "That lets you out!"

"Aye," he agreed nodding, watching her gently stroke the horse and whisper dulcet words in the animal's ears. "She will carry mostly women and children, and do some labor. She is small but quite strong."

Noting that Maratia seemed oddly shy around the horse, he asked her, "Do you not have experience with horses?" He assumed as there was little other transportation on the land she must have been raised around equines.

The blush that crept up her face at the question drew his curiosity. "What? Tell me?" he encouraged her, watching the soft garlands of sky blue lace through the indigo in her irises.

"Um," slightly embarrassed, she turned her head from him and kept skimming her hand down the horse's nose and petting its neck. "Actually, I don't have much, uh, make that no experience, except for…" she trailed off.

"Except for?" he prodded, seeing the color intensify in her round cheeks.

"Well, I wasn't allowed near the horses much," she looked slightly forlorn. "I was pretty much made to stay inside doing domestic things, you know, sew, assist the cooks in the kitchen, and the maids with cleaning and such, and I made pottery.

"Sometimes when I could get a bit of sunshine, I snuck over to the stables and visited with the horses. I could not get close to them though." Her sigh breathily wistful, she stroked her palm down the horse's mane. "Yet, the day I escaped," she glanced sideways at him, "you will think I was so naughty,"

His mouth quirked at the childish words, but he said seriously, "Nay, I'm sure I will understand. Tell me."

Her attention back on the mare, she told him, "When I fled from my fiancé, Sammel," her lips twisted as if they tasted something bad, "his name is Sammel Valmyrjr."

Her sigh careworn, she continued, "I ran towards the stables. There was a horse there with a wagon of sorts hooked up to it." Then her lips rose in a mischievous grin.

"I scrambled into the wagon to hide from Sammel. But, I guess the darn horse got scared when I did that and it took off like it had been stung by a wasp!"

His interest showing, Jashar said, "So that's how you got out of your village and went so far from home?"

Her round cheeks turned a darker pink. "Yes. There were clothes in the wagon so I put them on so no one would be able to say they saw a female leaving. We did go for quite a ways, many days or so.

"We kept moving day and night, the horse would stop briefly to rest near streams. One time he wandered through an apple orchard so that was our food for some time. Apparently our land is near to yours because the horse went straight and smooth in that direction, but then he became less…smooth, as we both tired.

"Then we were going downhill and the wagon became detached and rolled erratically before tipping over and throwing me out." She ruefully rubbed her rump where she had obviously landed.

He couldn't quite hide his smile. "But you survived the fall."

Nodding, her gaze turned melancholy. "I did. But Sammel and his horrid men were right behind me. I was up and running, that's when you-" her eyes dropped, her face darkened with remembrance and the wretchedness that had followed. Him. Jashar the rapist king. The skin around her mouth and eyes pinched.

Jashar was not pleased when the joy left her, the light teasing atmosphere between them fell dark again. He had already talked to her about his behavior with her; it wouldn't do any good to keep rehashing it.

He saw another horse being brought out to the paddocks. "Come Princessa, that is my stallion. Let me introduce you."

Her big eyes popped wide at the enormous steed clomping towards them. She moved behind Jashar.

He laughed. "Come on, Maratia, do not be afraid. He is very well behaved. I trained him myself."

She mumbled with some sarcasm from behind him, "Huh, yeah, I bet then he's *very* well behaved."

Amused at her insinuating if he trained the animal he had probably been quite strict with it, which was true, he turned and put his arm around her shoulders drawing her out from behind him.

"There is no need for fear. I will pet him first then you can see how calm he is. *Bine*? All right?"

"Hmmm," she muttered allowing him to lead her to the giant animal.

Jashar slid his big hand under the pure black horse's chin and raised it up. Then, to Maratia's great astonishment, the aloof king kissed the animal on its nose!

The horse snorted, Maratia jumped back with a yelp, which brought another rare spout of laughter from Jashar.

"Here, I'll hold him while you pet him." Jashar gripped the harness around the steed's head and held him loosely, then reached for Maratia's hand and moved her to gently set her palm on the horse's nose.

The steed's head bobbed slightly, his tail swished and he snorted again.

Gasping, "Oh," unsure, at the great head bobbing, she leaned away. "Is he mad at me?" When she leaned back she bumped up against Jashar's chest.

"Nay, *mici léas.*" He let go of her hand and set his palm on her shoulder lightly holding her against him. "He is just saying hello. Introduce yourself to him."

Unnerved by the huge animal, Maratia was unaware she nestled closer against Jashar.

He was aware of it though, very aware. He turned his hips slightly so she wouldn't feel the bulge in his trousers growing bigger from the contact of her tantalizing behind, and lowered his nose to brush the top of her hair. She smelled fresh and softly flowery.

Her graceful back pressing against the king's powerful chest, Maratia asked, "What's his name?"

"*Daoldubh.*"

She tipped her head to look up at him. Tried to say the word and failed miserably.

Jashar chuckled and repeated it slowly for her.

Still destroying the word, over his laughter she asked, "What does that mean?"

Her face was so close to his, Jashar felt his throat tightening. The brilliant clear eyes in rapt wonderment, her plush lips curved in pleasure. He licked his own, his voice notably husky, he told her, "He is named after his coloring, it means 'pure black.' "

She smiled up at him and his heart tumbled. "I see," she said. "Like your own hair and eyes?"

His eyes were on her lips. Jashar's head lowered, the horse nickered and stomped his feet, he wanted the attention back on him. It broke the spell of whatever Jashar was about to do.

A small cough cleared Jashar's constricted throat. "Ah, perhaps I can give you some riding lessons. Would you like that?"

Her face glowed. "Really?" She clapped her hands in delight. "Oh, Sire, that would be so wonderful. I've always dreamed of riding."

Her broad smile elicited one from him.

She told him, "Sire, you should smile more. You have a beautiful smile."

His lips twitched then firmed. "Nay, Princessa, men do not have beautiful smiles." His gaze fell to her own plump mouth. "Women do."

She grinned. "Well, whatever, the cold and hard look of your face softens when you smile, and your eyes twinkle."

Now he was blushing, something he didn't ever recall doing in his life. "Ahem, let's uh," he lost his train of thought, "aye, you were going to introduce yourself to my stallion."

Seeing the tough warrior's embarrassment only made her grin wider. "All right." She moved from him and stepped closer to the steed and spoke quietly to him.

Jashar stood back. He felt funny. His chest felt oddly cold now that she'd moved her soft curvy body away, taking her warmth and sweet smelling hair with her.

They dallied for a while with the horses then Jashar took her to the castle where he led her to the kitchen.

Ignoring the stares of the help, he grabbed up a basket and a folded length of cloth, and ushered her back outside.

He brought her to a soft place where the grass was low and set out the cloth. "Have a seat, Princessa, I've gotten us something to eat."

Her forehead rolled up with surprise. She hesitated, *why would he want to sit and eat with her when he had so many things he needs to do?*

But, he set the basket down, then took her hand waiting to help her sit on the grass. Totally baffled and suspicious, she allowed him to help her sit and he joined her.

Her body stiff with uncertainty, she watched him take out a couple of wrapped pastries, some fruit, cheese, and containers of tea. He set them down and handed her a pecan and pear pastry.

When she just stared at it, he said, "Go ahead. I've told you, I am not going to hurt you again." He held it out for her to take.

Her chary eyes looked from his sincere face to the pastry. She warily accepted it. But waited for him to unwrap his own and take a bite first before she did.

They sat peacefully enjoying the day and the food. "There are egg custard tarts too," he told her, holding a plate to her and was astonished at how quickly she gobbled one up.

He teased, "Sweet tooth, eh?"

She grinned then ate another.

"Here," he handed her a plum when the tarts were gone, and then took one for himself. Biting into the crisp purple fruit, he chewed then said quietly, "Maratia, I can't let you go, not now anyway, you understand that, right?"

Nibbling at her plum, her eyes flashed up at him then away. Her nod was brief and glum.

"So, ah, but I was just curious, if you were free, what would you do? Where were you running to when I, uh, brought you here?" He edged slightly closer to her.

Pensive, she looked out over the meadow and shrugged, took a bite of her plum.

The scent spiking the air with a sweet crispness, she answered him, "I...don't know. I was just so afraid of...Sammel, I just wanted to get away from him. I guess I thought I could live happily in the forest."

His head cocked to see the naiveté scrawled all over her face. "In the woods? How would you eat? Where would you sleep?"

Damn, but she was so childlike. Yet incredibly womanly in her bravery and defiance, her strength of character, the way she carried herself with elegance, her head high even when humiliated beyond belief.

Even when scared out of her wits she struggled not to cower from him and he was twice her size and weight, and ten times her strength.

But she was still a child in her view of the world. She must have been terribly sheltered, keeping her innocence so intact. *Well, he chided himself, he certainly had taken care of that, hadn't he?*

One shoulder rose languidly, she tossed her plum pit out to the field like he had done with his. "I've heard tales of sprites and fairies that live in the forest quite happily. I thought maybe I could find some and make friends," she sighed and smiled slightly embarrassed at him.

At the amused curl to his lips, she said, "I know, I was being fanciful. I was scared and wanted to believe some kind of magic would miraculously rescue me."

Her mouth turned down. "I only made things worse for myself." She snorted somberly with self-effacement. "I ran right into what I was running from."

Knowing she meant that he was the same evil that had pursued her, he could have kicked himself. Again, he had broken their mellow, friendly mood, and reminded both of them of his brutal assault on her.

Seeking to regain the warmer mood, with a crooked grin curving up part of his harsh face, he said, "You throw like a girl."

Her autumn eyebrows flew up. "What?" Then they lowered over the narrowing indigo irises. "Is that supposed to be an insult?"

His smirk that would normally be an unnatural cleft on his hard face, was just shy of a grin. He said mocking her, "Aye, tis, so what of it?"

Her mouth dropped open. Then, seeing he was teasing her, her angst forgotten, she launched herself at him with faux anger, "How dare you! Men!"

He caught her as she hit his chest, his arms snagged around her and he fell backwards on his back bringing her down with him. "Oh yea?" he teased, "what about us men? Are you saying that we are superior to you women in every way?"

Giggling, Maratia lay on his chest and playfully punched his shoulder. He caught her hand. She braced herself over him with a palm on the ground, her body resting on his.

"Certainly not," her air haughty, nose raised. "You are wrong, it is we women who are the smarter. We just let you men think that you are!"

Her hair draped over him. Jashar combed his long fingers through the silky locks. His lids hooded over the gleaming black, he remarked, "Ah, you think that's true, aye?" He loosely grasped a handful of her hair letting the tresses sift through his fingers.

"Of course it is," she laughed impishly. "Tell me who is really in charge of your castle? Is it you? Do you run the day-to-day living? Do you clean the house, plan the menus, prepare the food, decorate, make, repair and clean the clothes, raise the babes-"

"*Bine, bine,* all right, all right, I get it," he chuckled. Still stroking her hair, his hand moved up closer to her face.

"I have to agree on that point with you. Tis true; mostly tis my mother who keeps the household running. If it were up to us men, we would likely still be naked and living in caves and eating only meat and fish."

That brought a shout of delighted laughter from Maratia. "Ha," she said pulling her hand from his grasp and slapping his shoulder in gleeful play. "I know that's true. You can thank women for your very comfort." Her pretty lips drew up in a tease.

She said smugly, "Who makes the soft linens and plush pillows for your beds? Who creates the heavy drapes that keep out the cold, hmm? Who tends to you when you are ill? I could go on and on, but I will relieve your poor ears of my prattle."

His gaze was drawn to her mouth. He knew it was wrong, but his hand was sliding around the back of her head to cradle it, to hold her while his lips-

"Jashar!"

He was torn with relief and vexation for his brother Kaer calling out to him. It stopped him from doing what he could not stop himself from what he was about to do.

"I guess our playtime is over, *mi mici nua léas.*" He put a splayed palm to her back, smoothly rolled her over, jumped to his feet and pulled her up with him.

"Whoa!" She brushed off her skirt, her admonishment teasing, "You are way too strong for your own good!"

Jashar smiled at her comment while he bent and scooped up the basket and cloth. "I can't say I've ever been told that before, but you could be right."

"I forgot what you said that meant- that 'me meechi nwa leas,' " she asked as they started walking towards Kaer.

He chuckled again at her pronunciation of the words. "I said it was something like 'my, uh, little fresh ray of light.'" His neck warmed at telling her that.

"Oh." She pondered it. "That sounds so…pretty, so…nice. Thank you." She suddenly stood on tiptoe and brushed her lips across his cheek.

His face was burning red by the time they reached his brother. Jashar could see Kaer's puzzled, yet warning look. He slightly shook his head at Kaer to tell him to wait.

Kaer fell in step with them. "Hello, Princessa, you are looking well." Kaer had never believed the terrible rumors about her. To him she was sweetly innocent and drop dead gorgeous. He held no rancor against her.

"Ah, Maratia, um, Princessa, this is *mi bráthair*, that is, my brother, Kaermon." Jashar introduced them.

Kaer bowed to her politely with a saucy wink.

Maratia hadn't spoken to another soul but Jashar, McGee and a maid since her capture; she was at a loss of what to say. She wondered if she was to fear Jashar's brother. She moved to stand slightly behind Jashar.

"Tis all right, Princessa, Kaer is one of the good guys, sometimes," he cocked a mocking brow at his brother. "You don't need to fear him, he would never hurt you. He's too softhearted, at least with women."

Kaer snorted ungainly. "Oh yea? Let's take a quick detour to the training fields and let me show you a thing or two *mi bráthair.*" His wide grin showed gleaming teeth, he raised his fists ready for sparring action.

"Uh huh." Jashar's lip quirked. "You sure you want to go there? Remember the last time we fought…"

Kaer's mouth pursed, he shot a quick grin at Maratia. "Aye, Mother about decked you for the beating you gave me." The brothers shared a sibling laugh.

Still tense, Maratia's rigid shoulders eased somewhat at the brothers' playful ribbing.

They verbally taunted each other, throwing loose punches on the way back to the dungeon. Both men observed Maratia's growing subdued face as they neared the jail. Her mouth compressed, the skin pinched around her eyes, her step slowed.

Jashar discreetly jerked his chin at his brother. "Kaer, if you would be so kind to locate Officer McGee and tell him he is needed?"

Kaer nodded. "Aye, *bine*, all right. See you around, Princessa." His smile charming and kind, he said, "Or may I call you Maratia, tis such a beautiful name."

Maratia smiled shyly through her gloom, her cheeks pinked. "Um, thank you. Of course."

Kaer bowed to her, winked at Jashar then headed to the castle leaving them alone.

Jashar held the door open for her to enter the dingy chamber. He left it open to let in more light.

Her steps heavy, she made her way to her cell.

Chapter Twelve

"Princessa," stiffness came through in his tone, this was difficult. "I will be afar out in the field for the next several days. So, uh, I won't be here to take you outside for fresh air." Jashar's stomach pitched at the desolate expression she tried to hide.

"However, when I return, I will escort you outdoors again. We have a nice lake that feeds from a river where we get our fresh fish. I can take you there. What do you think?"

She tried to strengthen her feeble smile but the words got stuck in her craw. "I...understand. You don't have to make up things. I understand that you have had your fill of my...repugnant company."

Her head slightly drooping she trudged into her cell. Standing with her back partially to him so he couldn't see her face, she waited for him to close the iron-barred door.

He strode quickly to her. "Maratia." He walked into the cell, she didn't look at him. He reached out and caught her chin, gently turned it up for her to face him. He saw the sparkle of tears in her eyes.

Brushing her cheek with his thumb, he said softly, "I do not lie. As you get to know me better, you will realize that. I do not have to lie to you. If I wasn't going to visit with you again, I would just leave without a word."

She blinked hard to keep the tears at bay, but her expression stated she still doubted him. "It's all right, Sire. I know I am nothing but a foreigner, a prisoner, your prisoner, you don't have to-"

He held her jaw and lowered his head so quickly she couldn't take a breath. His lips fell on hers in a seething ardent kiss. Sealing their mouths together, he groaned at the sweet innocence of her response.

Then she froze. He brought his other hand up to cup both sides of her face to deepen the kiss, his thumbs stroking her cheeks until her mouth responded again with soft pulses.

Nudging her lips apart, he thrust his tongue in, searching, not violent, the blood rushed to his head. She tasted so sweet, like the purest nectar from the ripest fruit. His manhood joined in the passion, springing to attention.

He needed to stop. He should never have started. He forced himself to tear from her mouth.

Wiping the back of his hand across his mouth, he struggled for something to say. She looked stunned, confused, her lips fell open.

He could see unmistakably that her eyes were cloudy with the stirrings of passion; she drew her fingertips to her mouth as if she could still feel his lips on hers.

"Uh," Jashar took a deep breath. It was going to be taxing to walk with the erection that was pounding away in his pants.

"I, uh, Princessa, ah, Maratia, I shouldn't have done that. I'm sorry. Please don't be scared, or offended. I should not have touched you against your will, again."

He watched her carefully for her to exhibit her feelings for what he'd just done. But, she held her hand over her mouth, he could read nothing of her thoughts and she didn't utter a word. Her chest rose and fell hard as she worked to catch her breath.

That was not where his eyes needed to go. Her bosom billowing, the swells of her breasts molding slightly over the bodice of her dress, he quickly pulled his gaze from them and back to her face.

"So, uh," *Dias*, he was stammering like a schoolboy. What the hell was the matter with him? "As I said...a minute ago, I will be away for a few days. McGee will stay with you day and night. When I return," he shouldn't but he did anyway, he took her hand and held it, "we will go to the lake. I promise."

Still she said nothing. He lifted her hand, kissed her knuckles, released her then left without another word.

Outside he waited for McGee, catching his breath and steadying his racing heart. He didn't dare leave her alone in the dungeon with all kinds of men roaming around.

He ran a strict kingdom with little crime, but warriors, especially those without women of their own, or the younger ones who haven't learned yet, or even the ones that have been away warring, fighting, for a long time, he couldn't leave the hen alone in the henhouse.

Fortunately McGee was hurrying towards him.

When he reached him, Jashar greeted him curtly. He advised the guard that he would be gone for a few days and to not let Maratia out of his sight, and not let anyone go near her. Then he strode off for the house.

Just inside the castle door Kaer popped out at him.

Jashar kept going.

Kaer trod alongside him. "*Bine, mi bráthair,* what the hell was that all about?"

Jashar kept walking.

"You can't say it was nothing, Jash, you had that girl lying on your…you were holding one of her hands and your other hand was in her hair, and you were laughing. *Mi Dias*, where the hell was I when you suddenly got a fucking heart?"

Not a word fell from Jashar's mouth as he strode straight to his father's office.

The elder king was sitting at a big polished oak desk. A stack of books and papers littered the desk. King Allon was always working on one project or another. He peered over the top of his glasses as his sons entered. He ignored Kaer, but scowled at Jashar.

Jashar marched up and stood in front of the desk a little to the side.

Kaer hovered near the doorway. This really wasn't any of his business, but he didn't care.

Allon pulled off his glasses and set them on the desk then steepled his fingertips. Glowering at his son, he said, "You have stopped her punishment." He sneered, "Not that you ever actually started it. "You will tell me-"

"I will tell you, Father," Jashar cut him off. "I am not going to beat her or rape her again. I have decided, as I should have in the beginning but I deferred to you out of respect and the damned tribunal, that I am not going to do anything to her until my investigation is completed."

Allon's face flushed deep red. His eyes narrowed to furious slits, he rolled his hand into a tight fist as he leaned across the desk. Then he spouted in a low shout, "How the fuck dare you defy me?"

The elder king's voice rose to a deep belligerent thunder, "You agreed to do it, you know if you hadn't at that moment the crowd would have cried for her head and likely

taken it then and there regardless of your objections. Now-"
He broke off at his son's defiant stance.

Jashar stood secure in his strength and power. He stared
evenly back at his father. Both knew Jashar was the Word of
the land.

He said calmly, "That was then, Father and this is now.
I won't say it again. There has been word brought that
infidels are trying to take over our land to the far north. I am
going into the field for a few days to defend it and run them
off. Or destroy them, whatever needs to be done."

Allon jerked his head to toss the dark hair with strips of
grey off his forehead. His sneer accusing, he said scathingly,
"I hear you take the bitch on walks, son, to the gardens, to
the stables. You had a fucking *picnic* with her which
according to my sources, you were…frolicking shall we say
with her?" Allon was contemptuous, enraged. "Laughing,
touching like lovebirds-"

Jashar glanced at Kaer but he knew his brother would
never tell tales. A number of people could have seen him
with Maratia.

He didn't care anyway what his father heard. He cut him
off like a knife, grating furiously, "Tis none of your concern
what I do with her. Do not reprimand me or question me
again."

Allon reared back in dismay.

Jashar set his knuckles on the edge of the desk and bent
slightly towards King Allon, his command solid and clear.

His voice respectful to the elder king, yet formidable,
inarguable, making it understood his indisputable directive
was to be obeyed, he said, "No one is to go near her, touch
her, speak to her, or my wrath will know no bounds." He
paused, letting his father read the unequivocal stance in his
eyes.

Father and son glared at one another for a long time in a battle of wills. Seldom did Jashar wield his power over his father. But he was patently not going to back down.

Allon leaned back in his chair. His long arms stretched across the desk, he coolly picked up his glasses, twirled one of the stems between his fingers. His bottom lip pursed before it slid into a grudging grimace. "Ah, it seems I have taught you too well, my son. Your misguided obstinacy-"

"Nay, Father," Jashar said smoothly, coolly. "I don't idly make snap decisions without great thought, for no good reason just to be annoying and stubborn, and you very well know that." His breath drawn jagged and chagrined, he uttered, "I deeply regret what I have done to that woman."

"You agreed-"

Seeing the strong features of his father's face stiffening, Jashar said brusquely, "Aye, I agreed at the time because of," his eyes clouded, "my respect for you in front of the tribunal. And, the mob was too dangerous, seething with the atrocities allegedly committed by her."

His sigh bitter, his gaze hardened. "But it, you, I, ah, it was wrong. We don't treat females that way. I am revolted and appalled with myself, and I can't forgive myself for my despicable actions."

Sucking in a hard breath, Jashar said, "You," his calm regard expressed at his father, he saw the elder man's brows rise. "That is how you lead. Tis not my way. Tis not the way of our people, tis not the **Thuas sa Spéir's way.**"

The lines around Allon's mouth deepened, the ones around his eyes sharpened. "That is the way of a strong leader, my son. You cannot give leeway. You must discipline what can be fixed, and abolish that which is pure evil." He leaned forward again. "And that woman was created by the devil himself."

His lips bunched, Jashar said wearily, "My head aches with all the debased violations I perpetrated on the defenseless princessa." He bowed his head. "May *An Tiarna,* the good Lord forgive me. I do not believe there is an evil bone in her body. It sounds to me like she's been framed."

He closed his eyes. Then he stood back, his arms at his side. "I will be gone several days. I've posted extra guards around the dungeon. Do not doubt my wrath, Sire, if a hair on her head is harmed. Are we clear on the matter?"

He waited while his father slipped his glasses back on and tugged at his mouth.

"Whatever you command, son. You are the authority. I have never, will never, defy or dishonor the Word of the Leader." His eyes narrowed. "And you know that." Offended at the insinuation, he passed a hand over the top of his head then folded his fingers together, thickly calloused and knobbed with decades of fighting and warring, on his desk.

Jashar paused for each man to gather his thoughts.

Then he glanced at Kaer who had remained silent near the doorway, and said, "Very well. Kaermon will be with me. Daron will remain here to oversee our township Spiremoor and the other villages. Defer to him for any questions."

He waited to see the gall color his father's face, but was surprised as it remained smooth, undisturbed. Instead, a small, gratified smile tipped the edges of his mouth.

"Aye, son, I did raise you right, you have a backbone of steel, and your brothers, although they were allowed to assimilate a bit of heart, are almost as brave and strong as you." He slid an arrogant glancing jab at Kaer.

Kaer scowled, that was the second implication that he was soft.

Jashar frowned. It was not a pleasing thing to be reminded he had no heart. But what was it that pained him so when he saw the female, the princessa suffer? He shook his head, these things were beyond his comprehension.

He was designed, created, for war, for protecting his people, and that was all. Pushing away the incessant evocation of the way Maratia's lips had felt on his, he bowed his head in deference to his father.

"I will take my leave now, Sire. Any problems and Daron knows to send word to me." He turned on his heel and departed.

Kaer bowed to his father then followed directly behind his brother.

Chapter Thirteen

It had been a long three days.

Jashar wiped the grime and sweat from his forehead with his filthy sleeve.

His men had finally dispersed the insurgents that had survived the fierce battle, chasing them into the mountains, where if they were lucky and did not perish in the deadly harsh conditions in the midst of the rugged treacherous hills, could make it back to their homes.

Knowing they would risk life and limb again if they ever thought to come back to any part of their region called Thuas sa Spéir and try to take it over, claim it as their own, Jashar would ensure they would all be dispatched to their God, or gods, for good.

Next time Jashar would leave no survivors. He had felt strangely more mellow, unusually merciful this fight.

A pair of indigo eyes with tinsels of blue in them wavered in front of his mind. It was the female that had softened him. He wiped his head again, lifted his shirttail to wipe his eyes and frowned.

He would be best to keep her off his mind and stay clear of her bewitching ways. Those beautiful *aingeal* eyes hypnotized him. As much as he fought it, while he had stabbed and sliced and butchered the insurgents, he had tried again and again to thrust her from his mind, but to no avail.

"Jash!" Kaer's heavy boots pounded up to him, "Woolgathering? How unlike you." A snicker in his voice he said, "I'm thinking a pair of lush tits and plush lips have put a spell on you!"

"Shut up, Kaer," Jashar growled, annoyed his brother was on the mark with his teasing. "I have nothing but war on my mind." He closed his eyes hard to extinguish the seduction of Maratia's enchanting wiles that pilfered his brain cells.

He was a warrior, a warlord king, he could not let himself be softened by a woman, he could not let thoughts of her distract him from the-

"Jash!" Kaer shouted with snickering joy. "Moon to Jashar." He laughed. "*Dias*, she's got you good, our bonnie princessa captive, eh?"

"Shut up." Jashar punched his brother in the arm, which only brought more chuckles from Kaer. "Knock it off," Jashar growled. "*Sáith mi bearránach bráthair,* we need to make sure the last of the rebels are gone. Wipe that stupid grin off your face and let's go."

"Ah, you may call me *bearránach*, obnoxious, *bráthair,* but I'm not the one being led around by the nose by a lovely pair of tits- ow!" Kaer laughed as he rubbed the spot on his arm where his brother punched him again.

He strode after Jashar who marched ahead, a grimace of fortitude making his harsh face even harder, lids lowered far over the glittering black orbs.

"Listen," Kaer said as he reached Jashar. "You don't want to claim the chit, I'll take a go at her. She'd make a fine wife. McGee says she can cook and sew with the best of them. There's a hearth in the dungeon, she's cooked him some meals and repaired his torn clothes. She's damned easy on the eyes, has the prettiest voice, sweet as hell disposition but stands up for herself as best she can in the circumstances she's in, and shit- warm my bed?

"That juicy body? I can just feel those supple tits in my hands, and those slender legs wrapped around my hips. Oh aye, those long winter nights wouldn't be- ow!" he laughed as Jashar slammed his fist into his shoulder and kept moving.

Hurrying up beside him, Kaer kept on, "Listen, Jash, you'll either send her back home, or every man with eyes in his head and a cock in his pants will be on her like ants on sugar. I just plan on taking first choice- ha!" This time he dodged his brother's swinging fist.

Jashar's fiercely dark possessive expression was hilarious to Kaer. The two men trudged back to their campsite and joined the other men who were already breaking down the makeshift camp.

Pissed off at his brother's teasing, Jashar was silent as the exhausted warriors mounted their horses and hit the long muddy trail through the smoky maple woods thick with the dawn's hovering mist.

All the way back, Jashar scolded himself for even having a thought of Maratia. Then he realized that was all he had been thinking about. Even as he slashed and pummeled the enemy, her soft sweet face was always in the back of his mind.

Even if he did want her, he sure as hell didn't deserve her, after what he'd done- he shook his head.

What the hell is he thinking? He didn't want any fucking woman. He had his pick of them, he could have a different one every night and never do every single female in their land.

And as king? He had every right to take any woman he wanted, without anyone questioning or disputing his claims. But, he'd never had to take before, sex was always freely offered. In fact, half the time he was tripping over eager females who relentlessly threw themselves at him.

The thing was, as hard as he tried to conjure up any of the women he'd been with before, those damned sultry indigo eyes floated in front of him.

Grumbling, "Fuck it," scrubbing his fingers through his matted hair, Jashar vowed to himself he was done thinking about her. Only working the investigation would he have anything more to do with the alluring vixen.

After long harsh travel, the warriors made it back home. At each village they passed, more and more men split off to go to their own towns, return to their own hearth and homes.

Watching women pouring out of their homes to embrace their returning men shot a tiny envious stab to Jashar's heart. He shoved it away. With Kaer constantly grinning at him like a buffoon he kept his mind on the business at hand. Getting everyone back home safely.

When he and Kaer and their team reached their village of Spiremoor, Jashar and his brother said goodbye to those that weren't heading back to **their castle,** *Caisleán a Chéile,* **Castle of Each Other,** with them.

It was early afternoon as they approached the castle. Jashar's thoughts were on having a hot bath, clean clothes, something rich and satisfying to eat while he lounged in his comfortable bed. A vision of Maratia languishing in the rat-infested dank cell, her eyes bright with terror, cold and-goddammit-

He dismounted and took his horse to the stables. Maybe after eating he'd dig up a woman to relieve his lusty loins on, push the princessa from his mind, and release his throbbing cock from his unrelenting thoughts of her.

Jashar took care of the cleaning, brushing, horseshoe repair and feeding of his own steed. It didn't take him long as one of the hands helped him.

He trod to the castle to see about that bath when the door opened and Thandie came hurtling out with her arms raised in welcome.

"Jashar! You are home safe and sound!" She threw herself at him, wrapping her arms around him, squeezing his strong back with her sturdy limbs.

Then she moved her hands to clutch at his lean hips, wedging her big breasts against his massive chest. "I've missed you so, it's too lonely and quiet without your mighty presence here!" She wantonly rubbed her body against his.

"Uh, Thandie," Jashar grasped her arms and carefully pushed her from him. Recalling the feeling of envy he had felt of the other men returning home and their women rushing to him, he did not feel that envy now. She was the wrong woman.

He was surprised his cock didn't react to her female curves pressing on him. She'd taken care to wear the tightest, most low-cut outfit she had ordered made for her voluptuous body. The enormous tits were falling out of it. Without the support they needed, they drooped slightly, swung loosely.

She was tall enough he didn't have to bow his head so much to look her in the eye, and her arms were thick with sinewy muscles from generations of strong breeding. Not like the petite princessa where her delicate frame tucked so comfortably in his own huge arms making him feel so manly and protective, *arggh-*

"I am filthy, you don't want to get dirt and sweat all over that pretty dress of yours." He smiled crookedly at her look of dismay when she glanced down at her now soiled garment. Dirt smeared across her half exposed melon breasts.

"Jashar, really!" She complained, "You couldn't shower, and shave," she eyed the dark scruff on his strong jaw with distaste, "before you returned?"

One brow quirked in amusement at her delicate sensibilities. "Eh, and where would I be doing that, woman? In some wintry creek along the way? Would I then be putting the same filthy clothes back on, like putting new wine in an old cask per se?" He chuckled dryly at her foolish comments.

"Of course," she conceded, pawing at him again. "You are right. I don't know what I was thinking." Her hands were all over his arms and chest. "Perhaps we could...bathe together?" she purred. "I can wash that big strong back of yours, and...other things..."

A few feet behind them Kaer smirked. "Well there ya go, Thands, thinking. What a waste of time for a female!"

Sparks of ire shot at him from her slanted golden eyes. "Do shut up and mind your own business, Kaermon." Scowling at him, she continued pawing at Jashar even though the king kept moving to the stairs.

Sniping at Kaer, she said, "You know I have told you again and again not to call me that horrible 'Thands.' I was endowed with the queen of last century's royal name," she sniffed, her straight nose high and haughty in the air, "and you will not diminish the honor of it!"

Jashar's boots hit the stairs and he took them two at a time.

"Wait! Jashar! I wanted to talk to-" she screeched after him.

Snickering, Kaer followed his brother. "I fear his thoughts are not on you, or your wants, they undoubtedly lie in a hot bath, food, and…" his brows wriggled, "the dungeon." Laughing out loud at her irritated expression he disappeared up the stairs.

"You-" Thandie dropped off with a sigh. "That stupid brother of Jashar's," she muttered, "always acting the fool." She primped her straight dark hair and sniffed again, repeated his last words, "The dungeon?"

She shook her head in disgust. Jashar had more refined breeding than to have interest in that skinny whore housed there, other than to see justice carried out with her beheading.

"Dammit," she cursed several words in a fishwife snipe. "I might as well go change into something sexier. He should be down shortly." She hurried off to change her stained outfit.

Enjoying the sting of the hot water sluicing down his back, Jashar turned and tipped his face up so the water would heat his face and chest. He combed his fingers through his hair then turned again to ensure all of the soap had rinsed clean.

Shaved and bathed, he pulled on clean breeches, buttoned his shirt and slid into his boots. Feeling fresh and clean after many days mired in mud and blood and sweat, he trod down the stairs intent on going to the kitchen to rustle up some food.

But, as he hit the last stair, his feet had a mind of their own and took him across the great hall and out the side door. He was soon on the path to the dungeon. He told himself it was just prudency on his part to check on his prisoner.

He knew nothing untoward had happened or Daron would have gotten word to him. Still…his feet kept carrying him to the stone building with the dank lime walls and floors.

A frown pulled the corners of his eyes down as he grew closer to the dungeon and saw his half-brother, Aran, standing directly outside talking with one of the extra guards Jashar had appointed before leaving on his quest to clear their land of the marauding insurgents.

Their heads together, Aran was pointing at the dungeon, the guard was nodding, neither saw Jashar coming. Both raised their heads at the clomping of the king's boots as he neared.

Aran had guilt written all over his narrow sallow face. His pale blue eyes shifted from the guard to Jashar to the dungeon. He quickly cleared his expression of anything but vague welcome and straightened his back.

He lifted his chin at Jashar in greeting. "Ah, *mi bráthair,* I hear all went well with the mission and you and the others have returned safely with few injuries."

It was on the tip of Jashar's tongue to correct Aran's misuse of the word brother, he hated that the conniving man claimed any relationship to him at all. He was a product of his father's first wife.

Aran's mother died shortly after giving birth to him. Allon had taken one look at the scrawny, pallid whiny child and knew his kingship would not fall onto blond Aran's narrow shoulders. Fortunately, Allon found Vashana and soon after they married Jashar came along.

At the birth, Allon had breathed a sigh of relief. He was satisfied with the strong, valiant sapling of his loins. If Jashar hadn't worked out, Kaermon then Daron and finally Makir had come along.

None were as perfect as Jashar with his steely determination, fighting skills, strong as a bull body, swift as the fastest racing stallion and as fearsome and fearless as they come. But the younger brothers would do if something happened to Jashar.

His only daughter, Sheera, born between Daron and Makir, of course as a female she didn't count in the mix of things.

"Aran," Jashar said, his voice brusque, manner curt, "what are you doing here?"

His pale face flushed with guilt, Aran shrugged his imperious shoulders. He had grown to be as tall as the rest of the men, and strong and warrior trained within his own right, but Jashar had never taken him with him on battles. He didn't trust him.

"Oh," Aran's blue eyes shifted again. "I was just ensuring the security of our, uh, that is your prisoner. We would not want the murdering whore to be out and about, now would we?"

Jashar's gaze tapered to slits at his stepbrother. The man lied and Jashar knew it. He also knew he wasn't likely to get the truth out of him, or the guard who was inching away from Aran.

"I will see to her. You can all be on your way. Guard," he nodded to the man, "tell the others they are dismissed as well."

Before Aran could object, Jashar strode past him, threw open the door to the dungeon, frowning because it should have been locked, and stopped with astonishment at the threshold.

His hand on the door handle, his mouth dropped open, brows slashed down over the ridge of his low brow, he barked, "What the fuck is going on here?"

Maratia was on her hands and knees outside of her cell with her arms in a hole in the side of the stone wall where the overlay of lime and hay mix had cracked. Mud mixed with straw was used to bind the mix and the dried bricks of clay. But over age, parts of it had crumbled. McGee was crouched closely behind her, making comments.

Jashar stormed in and stomped down the stone steps.

McGee's head shot up, but Maratia kept doing whatever the hell it was she was doing.

"I asked-"

McGee answered quickly, "There is a tiny puppy, Sire. Somehow it crawled into a hole from the outside and got stuck." The puppy's whimpering travelled weakly out of the hole.

His brows knit hard, Jashar moved closer, asked, "So, what the hell is she doing?" Seeing Maratia's small round behind in the air with McGee crouched almost upon her ignited his ire like crazy.

"Uh, well," McGee stammered, "she's trying to get it out."

Reaching them, Jashar ordered, "She needs to stop, it will bite her."

The guard shrugged. "Already been telling her that, Sire. She is sort of a stubborn woman."

"Why the hell didn't you just move her out of the way and do it yourself?"

McGee's eyes slanted at the king. "As I said, Sire, she's stubborn."

Jashar rolled up his sleeves and ordered, "Get out of the way." He elbowed past the guard and crouched down beside Maratia. The dog was making tiny yelps and snarls.

Jashar said to the princess, "He's scared, he's going to bite you, Maratia, take your hands out of that hole right now."

Her voice muffled, Maratia replied, "No, he can't help it, he's a frightened baby. We can't leave him in there, he'll die."

Sighing, "*Mahmen de Dias*," he ordered, "move aside, Maratia."

Ignoring him, she kept speaking soothingly to the puppy while trying to reach him. The dog snapped and yapped at her reaching hands.

Jashar grasped her around the waist and pulled her back and set her out of the way. Disregarding her squawking protests, he bent and reached in and grabbed the dog.

The puppy bit his sleeve but the cur was too little to cause much harm. He pulled him out.

"Oh!" On her knees, Maratia yelped clapping her hands. "You did it, Sire! You are so good!" Unconcerned at the scowl Jashar glared at her, she held her hands out to take the puppy.

His ears reddening at her effusive compliments, Jashar pried the dog's teeth from his sleeve. It promptly latched its baby teeth onto his big finger.

Scratching the puppy's ears, Jashar regarded Maratia's excited mien. They both got to their feet. She still held her hands out, her lit up eyes on the dog.

He gingerly handed it to her with a warning, "Careful, his tiny teeth won't damage me too much, but your hands are smaller and more delicate."

Maratia cuddled the puppy and uttered sweet nonsense to him.

Both men glanced at each other then back to her.

Wondering what it would be like to be cuddled by her, hear her soft words caressing his ears, oddly jealous of the puppy, the king felt the throbbing in his pants that being near to her normally elicited.

He remembered upon returning home he was going to seek out a woman to release his pent up lust on, but he couldn't muster the desire to even picture another woman must less lay with her.

Maratia turned her bright face up to him, eyes glowing happily. "Can I keep him, Sire? Please, he-" her face suddenly drooped crestfallen.

She looked down at the puppy and said to it, "No, little one, you can't stay with me, it's too horrible here, you'll cry every night like I-" she broke off and nuzzled her face in his fur.

Jashar and the guard shared another look.

McGee said softly, "Maybe if he stayed with you, Princess, you wouldn't be so alone and scared and crying." Since Jashar was away, he had been posted guard outside the dungeon, not inside.

Her lips pursed to keep them from trembling; she shot the light-haired guard a frown. Negating what she just about said a second ago, she sniffed, "I do not cry." Dashing at an eye, she reluctantly held the puppy up to the king. "Here, Sire, can you please keep him safe in your chambers?"

Jashar shook his head with his hand out to take the dog. "Nay, he belongs outside. I recognize his coloring, he is one of my aunt's whelps. She shuffled the lot of them out the door as soon as they were weaned. I will drop him by the pasture-"

"No!" She crushed the puppy so hard to her chest he whimpered. Jashar frowned at her.

"No," she repeated nuzzling her face in his fur again. "He is too young, too little, he wouldn't survive. Look at what he's already done, gotten stuck in the wall. He's just a baby. I'd rather keep him here in this dreadful place, at least he'd have a chance to survive."

She rubbed her face on his back. "He'll hate it, but, I will try to make him happy until he's old enough to be on his own. I will share my food with him so it won't cost you anything extra."

Holding the dog against her chest, Maratia turned from Jashar thinking he would take him from her by force.

The king stared at her, then the puppy. They both had big sad eyes, his brown, hers indigo streaked with blue tinsel. His mouth quirked at the idea that she thought she could stop him from taking the cur from her.

Shaking his head at what he was about to do, he snapped at her, "Come," and pivoted on his heel, glaring at McGee.

The guard was half anxious on Maratia's benefit, yet he also quickly hid his grin at the consternated set of Jashar's mouth as the king strutted across the room to the stairs.

Chapter Fourteen

Jashar turned back with a huff.

She was standing worriedly clutching the dog to her bosom.

His voice deepening in annoyance at the fearful look she presented to him over the dog's head, he growled, "I said come with me."

He waited, watching steeper fear creep over her heart-shaped face. His voice now rigid, chilled, he threatened, "Princessa, I swear, you try my patience. I warn you, do not do that."

Watching the exchange, McGee stood helpless, and intrigued at the war of wills. "Uh, Princess, please," he trailed off at the look the king shot at him to not get involved.

"Do as I say, now." Jashar glowered at her.

Dashing at her eyes, stroking the dog, Maratia sucked in a shaky breath and followed him.

He walked silently and slow enough for her to keep up as they made their way to the castle. Again, people stopped what they were doing to blatantly gape at them.

Keeping her eyes straight ahead, trying to ignore them, Maratia's steps faltered, she stumbled slightly.

Jashar cupped her elbow, pulling her in close to his side as they passed through small crowds of villagers.

At the castle's entrance, he opened the door and ushered her inside. Their feet clattered across the greyish-pink granite and quartz foyer through the great room passing servants who all paused to stare.

He took her up the stone stairs and down a long hall. Their footsteps now muffled from the thick loomed rugs that covered most of the granite flooring.

Stopping at a room near to his chambers, he held the door open and motioned with his head saying, "Go in."

Covering the dog's face protectively, Maratia sidled past him sideways as if expecting to be hit. This nettled his brow, bringing an annoyed scowl to his face.

The room was pretty, swathed in corals and white. Jashar towered over her, watching her trying to protect the dog from his wrath.

"Princessa," he sounded gruffer than he intended. Coughing once, he cleared his throat and said more gently, "Ah, you are right in stating the…puppy needs care, for now. I certainly do not have the time to monitor him."

He waved his hand at the room. "This accommodation is for when my aunt from Lavartave visits, which is very infrequently. She isn't expected for quite some time. Therefore," he took a deep breath, "for the time being, I will assign the dog to reside in this room, and you will need to stay here to care for him."

He watched her eyes widen in disbelief, then bounce around the room back to him. "I- I don't understand. Are you saying…that you want me to- to babysit the dog in this beautiful room?"

A pang stabbed his gut. She looked so damned frightened, unsure, always waiting for the hammer to finally slam down on her head.

From the very beginning he couldn't bear to think of her in that filthy, damp, freezing dungeon. This offered him an excuse to take her out of there.

His family will undoubtedly be shocked, accuse him of losing his mind for offering such a frivolous reason for her, an alleged criminal, to stay inside the shelter of the castle.

But, it was the best excuse he'd been able to come up with. He'd thought of little else the past days, trying to come up with a way to get her out of the dungeon without violating their laws.

But, fuck them. As far as anyone had proven other than through sheer innuendo, rumors and gossip, she has done nothing to be locked away in that hellhole.

She is a delicate princess and she deserves a comfortable dry, warm bed. And if he could use the dog as an excuse to more easily remedy the situation without appearing too soft, so be it.

He left her standing there holding the dog with bafflement on her lovely face.

Outside, he grabbed the first guard he found, gave the confused man some orders, then hurried down the hall to Kaer's room. He knocked and opened the door at the same time.

A squeal greeted him. Kaer and a blonde's heads popped up from under a jumble of sheets.

His hair mussed, Kaer's cheeky grin at his brother was lopsided. The naked girl beside him made a pretense of pulling the sheets up to cover herself, but left most of her flesh uncovered, actually smiling coyly watching the king's eyes fall to her generous bosom.

Jashar frowned and quickly looked away at Kaer with a slight reddening of his cheeks.

"Ah, Kaer, if I could have a word," Jashar said, then turned his attention to the wall.

Kaer's forehead bunched with mirth. "Really? Now?" His brows wriggled to the girl beside him.

"Ahem, ah, well, yes, if you don't mind."

That brought a chuckle to Kaer's full mouth. "Well, actually I do-"

Jashar's glinting eyes narrowed at him.

"Oh, well, then, of course I don't mind." With a smirk, Kaer threw the covers off, both of them as it happened. He swung his naked legs off the side of the bed. The girl squealed again, and then giggled.

As Kaer went to stand up, Jashar mumbled, "I will wait outside for you."

It took only a minute for Kaer to pull his trousers on before he stepped outside his room. A grin on his face he remarked, "You know I was in the middle of something, we have been gone for several days you know."

"Aye, aye, and you being the randy fool that you are you needed some sustenance," Jashar muttered. "Whatever. Listen," his hands tucked in his pockets, his boots braced on the rug, he said, "you can tumble that whore anytime you want. I just need a minute to talk to you."

Kaer shrugged, leaned a shoulder against the wall. "Sure, what's got your breeches in a bunch?"

As Jashar considered what he was going to say, his gaze swept his younger brother seeing the mussed hair, sparkle of mischief in his eyes, broad, heavily defined chest like his own, lean hips that his unbuttoned breeches hung low on.

He had always trusted Kaer with his life. He was not only his brother, he was his best friend. "I, ah, have put the

Princessa Maratia in Aunt Rochella's chambers for the…time being." He smiled briefly at Kaer's raised brows.

"She, well there was this puppy in the dungeon," he shook his head. "Anyway, I've decided she will stay in Rochella's rooms for now. Plus, I will be bringing her to lunch today."

"Whoa, what?" Kaer whistled. "Really? What about Father? Mother will absolutely kill you-"

"I don't care. I'm only telling you this because I want Maratia to have some allies. I want you to gather Daron, Sheera and Mak and meet us down in front of the salon."

Amused merriment struck Kaer's handsome face. With a devilish grin, he said, "This ought to be good."

"Hmm." Jashar nodded staring at the floor, muttered, "Aye."

"What's the change of plan? Of heart?" Kaer asked with a sly leer. "Two hours ago she was a dastardly killer about to be horribly tortured then executed. Now she's joining us for lunch? What happened?"

Moving his arms to cross them over his broad chest, his head lowered, Jashar's lips tucked in a tight grim line before he looked at his brother. "I never believed she was guilty of such dreaded sins. Not even as I brought her in front of the tribunal. However, as you are aware, due to the dire circumstances at the time, the only way I had at that moment of protecting her was to go along with Father's orders."

Kaer nodded in agreement.

"Now that I have my warriors and brothers at my back, I can treat her with the respect and dignity she deserves."

"They're gonna fight you, *mi bráthair*," Kaer warned.

Jashar straightened his body, his back lengthened into a rigid wall. He declared, "I am king. My word is law. My

137

word supersedes our statutes. If I say she is to be treated with respect and her life, skin, spared, so be it."

"Your words are true, Jash."

"I have started an investigation into the murders. I wasn't around when they were committed, but I am now. We will discover the true perpetrator and initiate the trial and execution if that's where it leads."

His grin widening, Kaer said, "I'm with you, 100%."

Jashar's jaw jerked with his sharp nod. "Good. On to lunch."

"When?"

"Right now." Jashar's lip tugged up as he looked at his brother's bare chest covered in dark hair like his own. "You probably should put a shirt on for lunch though."

The brothers grinned at each other, then Kaer went back inside his apartment to dress and Jashar returned to the coral room.

Chapter Fifteen

*J*ust as Jashar reached the coral chambers, the guard he had spoken earlier to was there. "Ah, thank you, MacNeil, come in."

He opened the door for the guard and both men entered the room.

Maratia still cuddled the dog, she had barely moved from where he'd left her. She looked at the guard who had his hands full.

Jashar told the guard, "You can put the box by the bed and the food and bowls in the pantry. Leave the straw and papers by the door."

Jashar helped MacNeil set up the makeshift bed for the puppy and layer it, and also a section near the door with the straw and papers.

When they were done, Jashar said to Maratia, "*Bine*, all right. For now, while we go to lunch, put the dog in the bathing room, cover the floor with plenty of straw and papers and," he studied her, then reached to her and removed her sashayed belt from her dress.

"Oh, but…" Her big eyes darting to the guard and back to Jashar clearly thinking he- maybe the two were going to attack her together, she moved away from him.

Damn, he could read her thoughts on her face. "Sorry, Princessa, I should have asked before just taking. Tis for the puppy. It has your scent on it, it will help calm him while he's alone."

Jashar waited, holding the sash, watching the sudden fear that had lanced her eyes diminish warily. "Go ahead, put him in the other room. It will be easier to clean if he messes it."

Maratia glanced from him to the guard who was carefully looking away from both of them. Jashar stood completely nonthreatening, waiting patiently.

"Um, all right." She carried the dog into the bathing room and set him down on the straw.

Jashar came in behind her with a pile of rags. He put them on the floor, bundling them together then set her sash in the bundle. He carefully picked up the pup, which shied from him but then licked his hand. Pursing his smile, Jashar set the dog on the rags.

He stood back, took Maratia's hand and said, "He will be fine here. We will check on him after lunch," and pulled her out the door closing it before she could blink.

"Lunch? I don't under-"

They both turned at the whimpering behind the door.

The king said quietly, "He will settle down once we leave. Aye, we're going to lunch."

The guard had already left the chambers. Jashar put a hand to her back and urged her out of the room.

"But, lunch, Sire, I don't-"

"Hush, tis no big deal. We will be eating lunch with some of the other occupants of the castle, as well as some friends and neighbors, and relatives of mine."

A daunting anxious pink stained her cheeks, she dug her heels in. "No, please, Sire. They don't want me there, you know that. They will be so angry."

He spread his big fingers across her slender back and kept her moving to the stairs. "Not to worry. I won't let anything happen to you. I promise."

Reluctantly pushed along, Maratia said with a slight whine, "But, they hate me, they think I did horrible things to their children, please, don't make me go."

Jashar encircled her shoulders with his arm. "I said tis *bine*, tis all right, I won't let anyone hurt you. I want you with me. They will get used to seeing you and eventually they will forget. People are fickle things. They rush clamoring in excitement at a scandal but it is quickly forgotten as soon as the next one arises."

Her face darkened. "But I am hardly just a passing scandal, Sire. They believe me to be a murderess, a rapist of children. I can't," she balked.

They had reached the salon, his siblings were there waiting. They all looked directly at Maratia, and smiled, even Daron who had been a believer at first of her guilt.

Maratia pulled back from Jashar, but he held her firm and kept walking until they reached them.

"Princessa Maratia Madrilena Araminte," Jashar announced. Nodding at Kaer, he said to Maratia, "You know *mi bráthair*, Kaermon."

Maratia shuffled back from them, not realizing she was pushing herself back against Jashar's chest. He kept his arm around her.

Kaer stepped forward with his hand out, a wide friendly grin, and a twinkle in his eye. "Of course we have already met, Beautiful. Welcome."

Maratia gaped at his hand like it was a snake with fangs out and burrowed closer into Jashar.

Undeterred, Kaer reached out and took her hand, gently shook it and said cheerfully, "You can call me Kaer." He released her hand, winked and stepped back letting her draw a nervous breath.

Kaer's eyes rolled up at Jashar. He pointedly looked at Maratia tucked against him then at his brother, his lip curved in a smirk.

Subtly lowering both arms around Maratia, binding her against him, Jashar ignored Kaer's knowing smirk and nodded to the stoic man standing beside Kaer. "This is my brother, Daron."

Dark-haired and dark-eyed like all the siblings, Daron was the serious one of the group. He hesitated, after all, someone, was it Aran- had declared her a killer. But, he looked deep into her soft indigo eyes and instantly disbelieved those outrageously ridiculous tales and smiled handsomely. "Welcome, Princessa."

"Aye, and," Jashar continued, gesturing to a young woman, "this is my sister, Princess Sheera. Princessa, meet the Princess." His mouth twitched with his jest.

His siblings all looked at him in surprise. Jashar being funny? Their eyes narrowed in unison. Doesn't happen.

Sheera tossed her long dark hair behind her shoulders, stepped forward and held out her hand with a big friendly smile. "Hi, so pleased to meet you, Princessa."

Seeing the nervous, wary expression Maratia tried to hide, Sheera said, "Seriously, Princessa, we don't believe the rumors. There has never been anything to substantiate the dreadful accusations, the wild stories."

Her smile turned kind. "Now that we have met you, we can see that you are way too young and sweet looking to have committed such heinous offenses. Please, welcome to our home."

Kaer had briefed the siblings on Jashar's request to have his back and to welcome Maratia.

The siblings didn't know why Jashar had incorporated Maratia into their home, or was bringing her to formal lunch, but they had always trusted him to know what he was doing.

Besides, it was fairly obvious the way Sheera's big brother looked at the princessa, and held her protectively against his chest, he was not regarding her as an assassin, or a criminal, or a prisoner, or even a slight acquaintance.

Sheera's eyes skewed at her brother. Nay, Jashar's hot gaze down at the princessa was fairly eating the girl up, he hadn't once moved his attention, or hands, from her.

Another beam curved Sheera's lips into a roguish smile. It appeared a female had finally snagged her icy brother's... interest?

Well, she could not wait until lunch, and Miss High and Mighty Thandie Mahli gets a load of the stunning Maratia, and Jashar's obvious interest in her not as a prisoner, but as a woman.

But then a frown touched Sheera's wide mouth. It was clear the vibrant beauty regarded Jashar with fear and distrust, and faint animosity. Hmm, interesting. She feared him, yet, when presented with his array of siblings, the princessa huddled up close to his massive chest, as if seeking his protection.

And when his arms enclosed her to him, she appeared more relaxed, strangely a shade less frightened of King Jashar, the ruthless brutal warlord. Hmmm.

A crafty smile pushed her lips up again, oh aye, this will be interesting to see played out.

How is Jashar going to handle a woman he's obviously very smitten with, and although she appears to feel safer wrapped in his embrace then alone meeting his siblings, she is conspicuously not only *not* into him, she is downright afraid of him, and harbors anger towards him.

This brought a frown back as she recalled Daron telling her about Jashar raping the princessa, and that she had bled like a virgin. The siblings did not keep secrets from each other.

Sheera's stomach roiled at the thought of her big powerful brother, he could be so tough and violent, hard and cold, holding this fragile petite woman down and forcing-yikes, she shook the vile picture from her head.

"Princessa," Sheera said kindly, reaching out she lifted a few locks of Maratia's hair. "You have the most glorious hair, like autumn streaked with sun."

The brothers all followed their sister's hands as they stroked Maratia's tresses down the length of her body.

"Soft," Sheera sighed, then touched her cheek. "And silky."

The two women didn't notice the men's rapt interest. It was weird to them watching their beautiful sister caressing an even more beautiful young woman.

With Maratia still in his arms and his sister close to her while stroking her, feeling his own erection growing and knowing his brothers' would be too, it was creepy being turned on watching the girls engaging. One being his sister, maybe it was just her caressing Maratia when Jashar himself

144

desired so badly to do so, that was causing the sudden lustful pangs.

"Well, so," he said abruptly and overloud.

His brothers didn't look away as he'd hoped.

"Ah, and this is our youngest brother," Jashar gestured to the teen standing there gawking at Maratia. "Makir. We call him Mak. Say hello to the princessa, Mak."

The teenager didn't hide his reaction to the beauty. "Wow," he exclaimed. Jashar frowned. "Uh," the boy said quickly, "I mean," he bowed courtly, "pleased to meet you, Princessa Maratia."

Sheera stopped petting the princessa and the men collectively sighed.

Peering out from her nest in Jashar's arms, Maratia smiled at the young man. "Hi, Mak, pleased to meet you, too. Please call me Maratia. Or Mara if that's easier."

"Uh, sure." Mak was instantly smitten with her. His attraction to her, and his adoration of his big brother the king, was blatant in his grin and his easy acceptance of the infamous butcher-whore into their realm.

"Well then," Jashar was loathe for Maratia to leave his embrace, but they needed to head to the dining-

A ruckus erupted near them.

Two teens, slightly younger than Mak were suddenly tousling. They were yelling and wrestling, about to throw punches.

Jashar released Maratia and grabbed each one by the collar and shook them. "Stop this. What is the meaning of this warring? Fighting inside the castle?"

"But Sire!" The blond yelped. "He stole my favorite marble!" The glassworks was one of the most popular places for young people to apprentice and colorful marbles were plentiful.

The other boy scowled and vehemently shook his head declaring loudly, "Did not! It wasn't me, it was Brantley, go ask him!"

"Nay! It was you!" The blond lunged for the boy with the brunet curls but Jashar held them both taut and out of reach of each other.

"I said stop this right now. Do not make the mistake of making me tell you again." The king's voice dark and dire, both boys clammed up. Their faces sullen, they glared at each other.

"Now," Jashar said, "how can we-"

"If I may, Sire." Maratia shyly stepped forward.

All eyes turned to her, including the rebellious teens.

His expression surprised, Jashar said, "What can you do, Princessa?" He didn't really want her near the fighting boys. One could lash out at the other and hit her by accident.

His jaw tight, he said, "Nay, I don't think-"

"Please," she said softly, holding out both her hands, palms up. To the boys she instructed gently, "Give me your hands, both of you."

The teens scowled at her and looked to Jashar for direction.

Jashar studied Maratia. Her face was intent and somber. "Aye. Go ahead." He wasn't sure what he was giving her permission to do. "Take her hands, boys."

They didn't move.

"Now!" his growl prompted them to both shoot their hands out.

Maratia gently took each of their hands in hers and held onto them. Her eyes closed.

Everyone, including people who had been passing by, stopped and watched, befuddled. They murmured amongst themselves, "What on earth is the prisoner up to?"

The vast room fell silent except for those that breathed heavy, all eyes on Maratia who seemed oblivious to them.

After a few moments, she opened her eyes and calmly looked at the boy with the brown curls. "You took the marble. It is in your boot."

Shocked silence as now all eyes turned to the boy with the curls. His face flushed with guilt, his eyes slashed back and forth and around the room then landed frightened on Jashar.

Jashar glanced from him to Maratia.

Her face was a veil of…what could he call it? Not an aura, or a mist, or a gossamer shimmer, but…there was something. "Give him the marble, son," he told the boy.

The teen lowered his head, his face red with embarrassment. The crowd gasped as he bent over and removed the marble from his boot and handed it to the blond who took it with smug righteousness.

Still holding their collars, "Jon," Jashar said to the blond, "how could you better handle this the next time?"

The boy hung his head. "Uh, I guess I could have asked him more nicely instead of accusing him. That just made him mad. I think he would have given it back if I'd done…uh, that."

"Hmm, good. Now, Clark, what have you to say?"

The brunet's head hung as well. He peered up at the boy who was normally his good friend. "Uh, I was, I mean, I'm sorry Jon, I did kinda get mad when you jumped all over me. I wasn't going to keep it. I just wanted to hold it for a while," his voice disappeared into embarrassed pouted lips.

Jon smiled and held the marble out to him. "It's all right. Here, I want you to hold it. Just for today, though, *bine*?"

The other boy grinned and accepted the marble.

147

Jashar released them and they both just took off down the hall like nothing had happened.

The king looked at Maratia. She had become aware of the crowd's interest in her.

"A witch!" one of them declared.

Jashar turned and glared at the audience. "Who said that?"

Dead silence.

He said, "I hear that again and the speaker will pay for their words with their hide. Understood?" He glared around the room.

A few nodded, murmured apologies.

"Now, go about your business." Jashar turned back to his siblings. "So," he said coolly, "let's go into lunch."

His siblings all shared an eerie look. Then they glanced at Maratia.

She appeared so upset at the attention she'd caused that now they breathed easily and smiled at her.

"Aye," Kaer said cheerfully, "let the games begin!"

The others laughed with him but Jashar bunched his lips and lowered his ridged brow.

He splayed his hand on Maratia's back. "Come," he muttered, "I am starving," and ushered her into the dining room.

Chapter Sixteen

$\mathcal{C}$onversation came to a screeching halt at their entrance.

 All attention was zeroed in on the prisoner princessa.

Vashana looked appalled.

Allon's lids lowered but he remained expressionless.

Everyone else just outright stared.

Jashar led Maratia to the seat beside the one he normally sat at and helped her sit.

He made sure Kaer would be on her other side so she would have both of their protection. He had instructed Kaer when they were upstairs to have the servants keep the five seats he wanted empty.

Sitting down, Jashar said in a clear commanding voice, "Everyone, please carry on, we all know tis not polite to stare."

The offending parties blushed and quickly looked away. However, throughout the entire lunch everyone's curiosity flitted back to Maratia.

The servants served the food and poured the drinks. Jashar dug into his food with gusto.

Beside him, Maratia's insides were hopping and rolling. She was keenly aware of the attention she drew. Especially from Jashar's mother after Jashar gave brief introductions.

Vashana's dark eyes raked Maratia from head to chest. Her hard stare never left the princessa even when she spoke about Maratia behind her hand to the woman beside her.

The queen was bad enough with her pinched face and insulted expression, but down the table a pair of golden cat's eyes were even more disconcerting. They glowed flagrantly at Maratia with venomous resentment steeped in blatant hostility.

Maratia peeped discreetly through her lashes at the woman who openly spewed her hatred at her.

The woman, several years older than herself, sat with her spine erect, her chin tilted up, sleek black hair hung like Cleopatra spikes down her shoulders.

Maratia tried not to stare, but the woman was dressed so- almost vulgar. Her dress hugged her body like rainwater, and was cut so low Maratia feared there would be an accidental slip any second.

Maratia observed the woman noxiously glower at her, but when the woman's attention shifted to Jashar, her lids slid sensuously down over those slanted orbs. She flipped her hair, coiling pieces around her fingers, and leaned over like she was actually hoping her breasts would spill out!

When she looked back at Maratia, the princessa felt like the woman was stabbing her long sharp nails into her skin and peeling it off in shreds. She shivered and looked away.

Thankfully, Jashar had made sure earlier that Daron, Sheera and Mak would be seated directly across from Maratia. They all kept smiling and nodding at her, letting her know they were on her side.

"You are not eating, Princessa." Jashar dipped his head slightly to whisper to her. While chewing, he cut another piece of meat and nodded at her barely touched plate. "Is the food not to your liking? I can order something else for you."

She bowed her head over her plate. "Um, no, it's just fine. I'm um, not very hungry."

"Huh." He grunted and stuffed the roasted lamb in his mouth, his lip nicked up. "I know you can eat, Princessa, you remember I saw you gobble a huge pastry, chomp up a plum and wolf down several custard tarts at our picnic."

Maratia had to clap her hand over her mouth to smother her giggles and hide her grin. She elbowed Jashar, and his crooked grin teased her. "Are you calling me a- a-"

"A little piggy?" He chuckled at her pretended outrage. "Nay, of course not, *mi mici léas.*" Pointing his knife at her plate, he said, "I'm just saying I know for such an itty bitty female you can sure pack it away."

"Oh!" Her appalled gasp and giggles drew attention. She lowered her lashes to hide her laughing eyes and covered her mouth again. "Stop it," she hissed at him with a tiny giggle.

Suddenly acutely aware of everyone goggling at her, many with scowls, her mouth turned down. She folded her hands in her lap and grew quiet.

"Maratia," Jashar's voice dropped further ensuring only she could hear him. "Pay them no mind. They will tire of their hostile curiosity eventually."

At her bowed head, he said softly, "Just pretend that it's just you and me, out in the meadows. The birds chirping, bees buzzing, soft breeze, eating our picnic lunch." He watched her, hating how his people were making her feel.

Of course, he had been just as bad, worse, he had deliberately abused her.

151

Uncaring of what anyone thought, he slipped his fingers under her chin and turned her to face him. He lifted her chin so they were almost eye-to-eye. He could see the glimmer of the tears of shame she swallowed down.

His eyes followed hers as they flit back and forth across his face. He murmured, "I'm sorry all this has happened to you, sweetheart. Forget them, concentrate on the pretty lake that I'm going to take you to after lunch. We can bring the puppy. What are you going to name him?"

Right away he saw the tears clear with his deliberate distraction. Her mouth almost turned up.

"Huh?" He teased, "What shall we call that little rascal?"

She smiled at him.

He let go of her chin.

The table had grown quiet except for his siblings who were talking rapidly and way too loud to cover for it.

Jashar's lips were almost against her cheek. "You eat up, and while you do, think about his name and how much he'll like running around the lake. *Bine*? All right?"

Her lips curved up sweetly, she nodded. Started to turn her head to look at the rest of the table but he set his hand on her arm.

"Nay, Princessa, don't look at them. Only my brothers and sister, or, even better, just look at me." The corner of his mouth tugged up. "I know I'm a big ugly brute, but-"

She swung her head at him. "No, don't say that. You are..." Her eyes travelled his face then lowered shyly. "Handsome, in a- a- kind of hard and fierce way."

When his mouth quirked, she hurried to say, "But when you relax, and you smile, you are..." Too embarrassed to continue, her eyes strayed to her plate. She grabbed up her meat knife and stabbed a small hunk of buttered boiled potato.

"*Bine*, we will talk later." Pleased with the way she was now slightly more relaxed, Jashar glanced at his siblings.

The four of them were grinning audaciously at him. If Mak wasn't with them, the boy already knew too many curse words and gestures; Jashar would have shown them all a new one.

After dessert, Jashar stood and nodded to his mother then his father.

His mother's grimace warned him he was going to have to listen to her tirade later. He didn't care. He pulled out Maratia's chair and helped her up.

Feeling dozens of eyeballs on their backs, his hand cupping her elbow, Jashar walked her out, through the great room and to the staircase.

As they trod up the steps, he said with a chuckle, "I can't wait to see what kind of mess the little guy left for us." He was rewarded with her grin and slight giggle. He cautiously opened the door.

He was surprised to see McGee there.

Chapter Seventeen

"Robbie!" Maratia rushed over to the guard and hugged him.

McGee tried not to touch her too much- Jashar's possessive glare was enough to scare a cobra.

The guard separated from her carefully and grinned. He told her, "The king asked one of the guards to scare up one of these," he held up a circle of leather.

Puzzled, "What's that?" Maratia asked.

"It's a doggie collar. We'll tie a rope to it and you can walk the puppy without fear he'll run off and get hurt." He scurried to the bathing room and brought the puppy out.

"Here," he slid the pup into her arms and put the collar around his neck and buckled it.

Jashar lumbered over, peeved at McGee for embracing the princessa. He picked up the rope that was on a table and tied it to the collar.

"Oh, this is wonderful!" Maratia gushed setting the dog on his feet. The puppy jumped and hopped and ran in circles.

"So, uh, I cleaned up the first mess, he's probably ready for another, you know." McGee coughed. "The dog eats like a damned…well, dog."

He looked so annoyed at the puppy, who cared less, that Jashar and Maratia laughed at him.

McGee regarded Jashar in surprise. The king's eyes were lit on Maratia, smiling at her glee. McGee cleared his throat again to draw his attention.

Jashar looked up remembering he was there. "Take off for a while, Guard."

He didn't have to be told twice. McGee bent and patted the dog on the head, then patted Maratia's shoulder gaining another glower from Jashar. Biting his lip, he bowed to the king and shuffled out the door.

"You ready, Princessa?" Jashar held the door open.

She wrapped the leash around her hand and walked to the door, the dog obediently followed at her heels.

The air was not as hot as usual. The lake was pure blue as the sky. The three of them strolled around it.

The pup occasionally ran after a bird or a squirrel, the very long leash gave him a lot of freedom but would keep him from running off and disappearing. He hopped around but always kept Maratia and Jashar in his sights.

"So, Princessa, um, Maratia, can you tell me what...happened, what you did to discern the truth between the fighting boys?" Jashar spoke gently, without judgment or hint of criticism. What she had done was...amazing, but, mystical?

He waited patiently as her cheeks colored and her eyes shifted to look over the crystalline lake. He said quietly, "I judge you not, Maratia. I only desire to understand."

She slanted her face to see him better. His expression was candid, interest shone from his night eyes.

"It's hard to...explain. It is, called vérité, truth. If I hold both of a person's hands, I can...tell, feel, I don't know exactly what it is. I can tell who possesses the truth. Because

I linked with both of the boys, the vérité flowed, channeled from them through me. My grandmother had it too, she could suss out the truth, détenir la vérité."

He strolled contemplating her words. "What about your *mahmen*, the other women, people in your village, does anyone else possess this- gift?"

A tiny snort came from her curled lip. "Gift? I think not. I reacted today without thinking. It was a mistake. People, as you saw today, fear me. They called me a witch. At least in my village, after my youth, my growing up there, they got used to it. Sort of.

"When a terrible dispute could not be resolved, they would come to me and have me...discern. It's one reason I was kept strictly sheltered. My parents feared someone would go crazy and, well, burn me like they would a sorceress. They were thrilled with the engagement, it meant someone else could take over their burden." Her loveliness became marred with bitterness.

"No," she shook her head, "it is most certainly not a gift."

He glanced from the ground, the soft grass that they walked on to her bent head. "I'm sorry, Maratia for all the pain you have suffered."

They walked without speaking for a few paces then Jashar said, "I know I've made you suffer too, and continue to by keeping you prisoner."

Jashar stopped and touched her arm to stop her too. She stiffened, drew back, eyes blanched.

Their conversation forgotten, he said, "Ah, Maratia, please, I've told you, do not fear me. I swore to you I would not hurt you again. I've apologized, I've said I wished I could take my actions back, but," his voice desolate, "I cannot."

Her lashes fluttered, her hand went to her neck. Her pretty features turned fallow, suddenly cheerless. The rawness of what he'd brutally done to her still haunted and humiliated, sapping the joy and roses from her face.

Jashar covered his eyes with his hand to dispel the images of him violently thrusting into her, tearing her tender body. Then later, forcing her to her knees and trying to shove his cock down her throat, making her bare her beautiful breasts to his greedy gaze.

Bile rose in his throat. Even thinking at the time she was a whore, it had still killed him that he was doing such despicable things to her.

The last obscene deed he'd done to her, when he had forced her to disrobe and expose herself, he shuddered, how arrogantly sick of him, what a despot.

Remembering though, how perfect, soft, how unbelievably pretty her tits were, his shaft stirred. *Dias* he'd die to see them again. Hold them, clutch them in his hands, put his mouth to them.

He dragged his hand down his face. He opened his eyes to see her studying him.

Her anguish had turned to…compassion? Huh, that sentiment would instantly flee if she knew what he was thinking now. Jashar trailed his fingertips down her arm, barely touching her.

He dropped to one knee, bowed his head. Then he raised it, clasped one of her hands. With all earnestness, he said softly, "Maratia, forgive me. Can you forgive me for what I did to you?" He could feel her slightly withdraw, imperceptibly tug from his grasp.

As he was about to let her go, he felt her ease.

"Maratia?"

Sadly, she said, "I can forgive you, Sire, because you seem to genuinely regret what you've done. But, I don't know if I can forget. You savagely took away something from me that can never be replaced." Her gaze followed the torment marking his face.

She continued, "And, worse of all, I don't think that I will ever forget your...the way you treated me with...such rage and hatred, and," she looked away, "the worst was your cold, complete disdain, callous indifference. Like I was a- a- nonhuman with no rights that you would destroy and throw away, without a shred of pity-"

A sob choked in her throat, she jerked her hand from his and covered her face with it.

He stood up and grasped her upper arms. "Ah, Maratia, never, I never felt any of that for you. It was so hard for me to do what I did to you. I had to," he thought about it. "I had to block your feelings from my mind. I couldn't look at you, your eyes tore me in pieces. But we were told you were, well you know.

"I had to keep dredging up the horrors that befell our young women, to- to- force myself to assault you. Maratia, it was my fucking *duty*- I thought you were a whore." Now his voice was fraught with despair.

Her voice small, she said, "But, your...body was, uh, you were," she was too shy to say out loud about the way his manhood was erect and pounding whenever he was near her, in her.

His mouth crinkled up the side acknowledging the truth of her words, "Aye," he rubbed the bare skin on her arms with his thumbs.

"I admit, *mi mici léas*, there is no doubt I am heavily attracted to you. That was part of the...issue. As horrible as it sounds, it was because of that I was able to follow through with, well at least that first night." He quailed at her cringe.

His thumbs brushed her skin softly as he finished, "I was able to, assault you because you excited me so."

Confusion at his words clear on her face, she cocked her head, scanning his face trying to comprehend what he was saying. She didn't pull from his hands stroking her arms.

His skin darkened with his shame. "Maratia, I am not proud of any of this, please believe me. But if you hadn't been so beautiful, so alluring, the sight of you stirred my body the split second I saw you, the day I...took you. If you'd been fat or old or ugly," his shoulder lifted in a shrug.

"I don't know what I would have done. It certainly would have been better for you. Being homely would have saved you, at least temporarily. I wouldn't have been able to fuck- uh, assault you, and I can't beat a woman, so," he shrugged again.

"I don't know what I would have done to comply with my father's directive. I might have had to turn you over to another man to do it. That would have been devastating in ways I won't begin to explain, to not fulfill my duty."

She looked down. The bulge in his pants was quite visible.

He blushed slightly. "Aye, my sweet, even now. You have that effect on me. Always."

When she drew back from him he said quickly, "Nay, Maratia. I will never, I swear, I will never assault you again. Unless," his voice silky and low, he trailed a finger back up her arm and slid his hand lightly around the back of her neck.

She didn't move from him, her head tilted to the side, she whispered, "Unless?"

His eyes on her lips, he whispered back, "Unless you are willing." Bending his elbows more, he moved closer to her.

She stared at him, her eyes wide, then they dropped to the ground as pink stained her cheeks. But she didn't back away from him. They were so close that when she took a deep breath her breasts brushed his chest.

That was like throwing a bucket of fire on him. His shaft surged in his pants to get at her.

Jashar swallowed and dropped his hands. Last thing he wanted to do was negate everything he just said to her.

The puppy was yapping and running circles around them. Neither had even noticed him.

"Um, let's," the dog jumped up on his leg yelping sharply to get their attention. Jashar smiled at the pup. "Carry on with our walk, *bine*?" His mouth went dry when he looked back up at her.

Her neck was slightly arched, lids low and heavy over her eyes, so sultry Jashar's legs melted.

"Maratia," his hand went to her face, he cupped it and leaned carefully to her, brushed her lips lightly.

The dog jumped and hopped and yelped. Jashar glanced down at him with a short smile.

"*Bine, bine*, we get it, come on, we're almost back to the castle." He swept up Maratia's hand and held it as they walked.

She did not demure, just trod peacefully beside him holding the leash in her other hand.

Jashar let out a heavy sigh. He felt like they had cleared the air between them, maybe they could start anew. For now, he'd keep things light, let her get used to him as a person, a man, not the monster that had attacked her.

Jashar asked mildly, "Well? Have you thought of a name for him?" He smiled when she scratched her chin and her brow furrowed so adorably.

"I just haven't settled on something that suits him," Maratia murmured watching the puppy dash after a butterfly, tripping over his feet as the butterfly stayed just out of his reach.

She slowed while thinking. "Tell me, Sire, what is a word for tawny, he has tawny fur."

"Aye, and big feet," Jashar said, coming to a stop.

"Hey," she pretended pique at his comment. "He is a puppy, he will grow into those feet."

"Aye, and what about those long floppy ears?"

She batted him lightly on the arm. "He will grow into those too!" Giggling, she looked up at Jashar and scolded, "Stop making fun of our dog!"

His heart warmed, *our* dog? He gazed down at her.

The sun lit the side of her fair face and brought out the flaxen streaks in her amber hair. Before he thought, he reached out and sifted his fingers through her tresses. "Ah, my sister was right," he said softly.

"Mmm?" She smiled up at him. Her gaze scrolled from his dark eyes that were heating up again, to his full, masculine carved lips. "About what?"

He tracked her gaze tracing his face. He could feel his manhood harden, more. "She said it was like silk, she was right. But, the dog," his eyes were drawn to her lips again. He remembered their taste when he had kissed her, in violence, his mouth twisted sadly.

Then when he kissed her that day he took her to the stables, her lips had tasted like honey and were as soft as glossy confection. He had hungered to taste them again; he had ached to kiss her again since that day, not with brutish force, but with both of them willing.

"The dog?" She imitated him, her eyelids limp as well. She licked her lips, her body ever so slightly leaned into his.

"What about him?" Jashar drawled absently, his head moving closer to hers.

"Who?" Her lids were almost closed, only slits of indigo radiating ingénue desire were barely visible.

"*Tenné,*" he whispered so husky his voice was a mere scratch, pupils enlarged and pulsating, burned at her.

Her lids almost completely closed, her neck arced, tilting her head up to him, a breathy murmur, "What?"

"The dog." Lowering his mouth to hers he murmured against her lips, "Yellow-brown, is *tenné.*" His fingers webbed the back of her head, cradling it, holding it as he faintly touched their lips together.

"Tenny?" She distorted the pronunciation in a hush lilt.

He smiled. Pressing his mouth to hers he said against her lips, "Close enough." When her lips pulsed against his, his shaft moved with them. She wasn't rigid and scared, and she wasn't pulling away.

"Sire," she whispered at his mouth, letting her lips part. He circled them with his tongue.

"Jashar, Maratia, call me Jashar, please," he murmured, moving to seal their mouths when they heard someone calling his name.

Jashar cursed in several languages, fortunately none she knew or her ears would have burned. "Not again, dammit." Regardless, he cupped her face, his thumb on her cheek, tilted his head and pressed their mouths-

"Jashar, come on, for crying out loud!" Kaer was shouting across the pasture.

Jashar moved slightly to look over her head, he moaned, Kaer wasn't grinning. Something was wrong.

"Come on, sweet." Jashar rolled his arm around her shoulder to steady her while she pushed out of the fuzzy net of desire that had overtaken them both.

He was used to being glazed with lust around her. Still, it was a struggle to shake off the filaments of rapture that had tied up his brain and his balls in sensuous knots.

These feelings were new for her. Jashar regretted they were interrupted at that pivotal, wonderful moment. Now, she would be left with confusion and uncertainty, and have the opportunity to remember he was the beast who had viciously taken her virginity.

He feared she would put her walls back up and he would not be able to get her back to where they had been. In his arms, trusting him, willing to accept his kiss- *damn*.

He gave her a butterfly kiss, soft and fleeting, to remind her, then took her hand and started walking towards his brother.

"What is it?" Jashar asked as they reached him.

His hands on his hips, Kaer glanced at Maratia, nodded to her. "Princessa." He said to Jashar, "We need to talk." He glanced at the princessa again with meaning. "Tis not an emergency. Just important."

"I see." Jashar said to Maratia, "I will take you to your room."

They all headed to the castle, the puppy bounced beside them, but did so less and less as he grew tired.

Jashar picked him up and carried him in one arm balled in his big hand against his chest.

"Who have we here?" Kaer asked, scratching the puppy's ears. The dog licked him a couple of times before he succumbed to sleep.

"His name is Tenny," Maratia told him, smiling at the dog curled in Jashar's arm.

"He's cute, your puppy is darn cute." Kaer grinned.

"He's *our*, puppy," Jashar said watching Maratia adoring the dog.

Kaer's brow arched like a boomerang. Jashar's meaning wasn't lost on him. "Oh yea?"

"Aye," Jashar grumbled holding the door for Maratia. "I'll be right back, Kaer. I will meet you in your chambers. Can you find McGee for me?"

"Sure." Kaer strode off towards the guards' quarters.

Upstairs, Jashar settled the pup in the makeshift bed next to the one Maratia would be sleeping in.

He stood up and faced her. He couldn't resist touching a part of her. He picked up a lock of hair, let wind it around the ends of his fingers.

"Tomorrow," he sighed, "I have work to do in the far eastern field. I won't be back until the next day. You can walk the dog, but only if you are with McGee, and you aren't to go any further than five feet from the castle. Anna will see to your meals here in your room."

He could see the ambiguity rifle across her face, the surprise at her sudden freedom, but with strict limitations.

He tucked his hands in his pockets. "I uh, I want you safe. That's why I don't want you to wander too afar of the walls."

Her small smile wistful, she set a hand on his chest. They both stared at it.

Jashar could feel the warmth of her palm through his shirt, through the matting of hair on his chest, his loins stirred.

"You mean you want to keep me from…escaping."

He had meant to wait until he had time to soften her up again, but he couldn't help it. Her freely touching him made it seem she would be all right with it.

His hand cupped the side of her face, he gently kissed her. This time he could feel her slight resistance, she lightly pushed her hand against his chest.

"That is true in a way, *mi léas.*" The pads of his fingers stroking her cheek, he touched her lips again softly, a brief buss. His mind begged for more, he steeled his control.

"But tis for your safety. You cannot go home right now, it isn't safe. There is nowhere safe for you right now, Maratia, except for here. I fear you will think tis all right to leave Thuas sa Spéir. I cannot let you." He also wasn't ready to give her up yet.

"Sire," she protested, faintly pulling away. "I can take care of my-"

He put a finger to her lips. "Nay, please. I know tis hard, but please trust me. Don't try to leave. There is nowhere for you to go except your home, and that isn't safe for you. Wait until we can talk, *bine?*"

Maratia studied his granite face, his enigmatic eyes. She looked at his mouth, then nodded.

His hand wound behind her head. "Promise me, Maratia, promise you won't try to leave," *me*. He kissed her, whispering at her lips.

Urging, "Promise me," his other hand stroked down her hair, down her back. McGee would be ensuring she didn't leave, but he wanted her to feel she was making her own choices.

Leaning back, he scanned her lovely face for sincerity. He checked her high, round rosy cheeks, her small nose, tiny full lips, then her eyes. Pure as crystals, the indigo shined at him.

"I promise, Sire."

"Jashar, call me Jashar, Maratia." He kissed her slightly harder, then he let her go. "I have to leave, I will be back as soon as I can. *Bine?*"

She nodded again then turned her head smiling to the other room as tiny yelps could be heard.

"Aye, take care of our Tenny, my sweet." Jashar kissed her briefly and went to meet his brother.

Chapter Eighteen

When Jashar went to Kaer's room, his other brother Daron and his sister were there too. He closed the door behind him and took a chair, sinking comfortably onto the thick cushions.

Kaer liked his comfort. His room, like Jashar's was filled with strong heavy furniture that had thick stuffed cushions. It was sparsely decorated although he had some paintings on the walls and a few family portraits on the mantle of his fireplace that more than likely Sheera had put there.

The furniture was mostly cedar, the material made up of woven browns and dark blues.

Sheera sat on one end of the sofa with her legs curled up beside her, her shoes were on the floor in front of her.

Daron sprawled at the other end, his legs spread comfortably.

Kaer took up another big cushy chair. Leaning back, he crossed an ankle over a knee.

"Well? What is it?" Jashar settled back, laid his arms along the chair arms. His gaze flit around the room at his siblings.

167

"Aye," Kaer said, "we've gotten word from some of our recon far afield, a few miles outside the boundaries of Thuas sa Spéir." He glanced at Sheera and Daron. "That Sammel Valmyrjr, uh, the princessa's fiancé, is searching for her. He has gone to two other regions with his inquiries."

"Her ex-fiancé," Jashar muttered.

The siblings shared a look. Gossipy Kaer had already told Daron and Sheera that he'd interrupted the couple kissing.

"Aye, well," Daron glanced at Kaer then said to Jashar, "whatever. The man will eventually find his way here."

The king stood up. He trod over to the window, stuffed his hands in his pockets and stared out. The sun had set, lanterns glowed in the dark throughout Spiremoor.

"Jash," Kaer said quietly, "what are you going to do?"

Jashar stood immobile at the window, not responding.

Kaer looked at Daron and Sheera, then he got to his feet.

"Jash, we need to know what your plans are, to know how to proceed when he arrives here. Will you hand her over?"

Daron said from his chair, "What about the charges against her? If we keep her in custody does Valmyrjr have the right to take her? Maybe they will prosecute her themselves?"

"Nay," Sheera interjected thoughtfully. "He wouldn't come for her to do that. The claim is that she hurt our women, there's no indication anything happened to theirs."

"Aye, he is looking for her, to take her back home with him, to be his wife," Kaer said.

Still Jashar remained at the window, silent.

"Jash, what are we to do when he comes here-"

Jashar swung around cutting Daron off, his face dark and hard, his hands clenched in furious fists. "Nothing." He let out a harsh breath. "We will do nothing." He crossed his arms over his muscled chest, his long black hair settled around his shoulders.

The siblings looked at each other.

Kaer spoke, "Nothing? We can't just do nothing. He will ask for her. We will have to hand her over to him-"

"Nay we will the fuck not!" Jashar roared uncrossing his arms and taking an angry step towards his brother.

Kaer's mouth nipped up in amusement at his brother. Now Kaer had finally found a button to push on his mighty granite brother. "Jash, he will ask for her. He has rights to her, he's her fiancé."

"Ex-fucking-fiancé," Jashar snarled. He growled, "After the way he abused her, he has no rights to her."

Daron sneered, "And you do?"

His face darkened with shame. Jashar replied harshly, "If he comes around, she will stay ensconced in her room, with guards. He will not be allowed to enter the castle, and he will not see her."

Sheera's gaze slipped to Daron, then Kaer. There was already gossip about Jashar bringing the princessa into the castle.

Exasperated at his older brother, Daron said, "Jash, he will ask around, he will learn that she's here. He will demand we give her to him."

"We have security, guards," Jashar informed him. "We have warriors continually patrolling our perimeters. No one gets onto our land without our knowledge, and we certainly have the ability to stop them if they do.

"Her people, the Saorghlanadhs, while they have a military it is meager and a mile less than par. They are inferior to most of the other factions in the land. No one attacks them because they have nothing anyone would want."

Daron said drily, "Apparently there is a princessa that normally resides there that someone wants."

The siblings watched in amusement as Jashar glowered at his brother.

"Whatever," Jashar said firmly. "We will instruct the field warriors to say no one of the princessa's description has been seen here. Aye they will-" he spoke over Kaer's objection, "they will do as they are told under penalty of death. Every soldier knows that. Valmyrjr will be turned away, and that will be that. *Bine*?"

The devil's advocate, Daron asked, "What if her father is with them?"

His smoldering glare and set mouth was the king's answer.

"Are you going to tell her?" Sheera asked evenly.

They looked at Jashar. His eyes glazed like onyx.

"Nay. And neither are you. None of you. No one is to tell her he is looking for her. Or that he is near here. I don't want her running from the castle afraid that he will get her, or fear that her presence here will put us in danger."

Uncoiling her legs, Sheera stretched her arms over her head with lackadaisical indolence. Her head inclined to her brother in feminine forewarning. "She finds out and learns you told us not to tell her, she is going to be-"

"Pee-issed," Daron filled in.

"Oh, aye," Sheera agreed. "She will be furious with you. You can't treat a grown woman as a child, Jash. You can't keep information that is all about her, from her."

The king rolled his muscled blocks of shoulders. "I will deal with it then, if it happens."

"Oh," Sheera gave him a sly grin, "these things always come out. When they do-" she grinned harder. "You will be dead meat."

He glared at her but said nothing.

"Humph." Kaer crossed his arms and said to Jashar, "Jash, what are you planning to do with Maratia? What if we never find the truth of her charges? Or even better, clear her name? What will you do with her then?"

Jashar's face scrunched into a darker scowl, he didn't answer the question. He stalked to the door, yanked it open,

"You have my instructions. I will see you, Kaer and Daron in the morning before I leave. Good night." He let the door slam shut behind him.

The siblings stared at the door.

"Aye, that went well," Daron muttered with a loud exhale.

Kaer shrugged. "He is right. If we run the guy and his men off before they can get inside our land, if they believe us and there's no reason why they wouldn't or shouldn't, he will go away and search somewhere else for her."

"And if he can't find her anywhere?" Daron asked.

"He will assume she was taken by animals and exists no more. Eventually he will be forced to let it go and return home," Kaer told him.

"What about Jashar?" Sheera's provocative voice slipped in between her brothers' deeper voices.

"What about him?" Daron asked.

"Come on, Daron, even if Kaer hadn't told us what he saw, the two of them together acting more than captive and king, twice now. And he took her to lunch with our people," she smiled, a mischievous curve to her wide lips. "It's written all over his tough glacial face, he's got it bad for her."

Her brothers nodded in agreement. "It gets more interesting every day," Kaer chortled with mocking glee.

"Aye," Sheera laughed. "Big bad brother has finally fallen. And what a fall, eh?"

Daron scowled at them. "I don't see how any of this can end well. She's a prisoner. She has horrendous charges against her and she's a foreigner with a fiancé hunting for her. And, she has family she will eventually want to see again. " He shook his head grimly. "Nay, I'm not seeing a happy ending here."

Kaer grinned at his pessimistic brother. "Daron, have you no faith in our king? He is brilliant, he fights to the death, he never gives up, and Maratia is his prisoner, *his*. You can see how possessive he is of her. Nay," he shook his head, "he won't be giving her up."

"What if she doesn't want him?" Daron inquired.

Kaer's grin deepened. "Huh, you didn't see her in his arms, her pretty face sloped up to his. She was not fighting him, she wanted him."

"As much as he wants her?" Daron said, "What if she's playing him, lowering his defenses so she can make a run for it?"

The siblings looked at each other. They would have to wait to see how it all played out.

Chapter Nineteen

Jashar had gone out with a squad of men.

He spoke with every single warrior patrolling the land and told them if anyone, no matter whom, comes asking about the princessa, they are to say they have never seen such a woman but will gladly spread the word and let them know if they hear anything. They are to be polite and appear fully cooperative.

It had taken longer than he had thought, even on horseback, and he had told each man he came across to tell the others to come to him to make the linkage quicker.

He wanted to get back to Maratia. He had not liked leaving her again without his protection. At least his brothers were there with her, and McGee.

Jashar touched his lips with the pads of his fingertips recalling them on hers. He remembered the feel of their soft sweetness as she responded to his kisses. He had only once been able to push them open and explore her mouth with his tongue.

Her body had been melting into his when his brother had interrupted them. Again. His manhood was throbbing; his bollocks were so tight it sucked riding.

Ahh, he crossed into Spiremoor, then soon the castle was finally in sight. Exhausted beyond belief, he quickly took care of his steed then hurried inside to bathe.

As his boots clunked across the great-room floor, his mother swept from a hallway to stop in front of him.

She kissed his cheek. "My son, I am always relieved when I see you have returned safely from yet another mission." She never asked what he was doing when away, it was male warrior business and she had no interest in. She only cared that he was uninjured.

"Darling," she started.

Jashar's eyes rolled, *here it comes*. He tried to keep moving for the stairs but she hustled in front of him.

"You have put that- prisoner- in Rochella's rooms. What on earth are you thinking? She could murder us all in our sleep for heaven's sake!" She pushed at loose hairs that swung from the chignon and wafted in her face.

Jashar held his temper in. "Her door is locked and Officer McGee is with her at all times. She is a titled princess from an honorable land." He tried to move around her but she blocked him.

He sighed heavily trying to conceal his irritation and his desire to see Maratia.

Vashana smoothed her long skirt then fussed with the cuffs on her sleeves. "I hear that when the guard is not with her that…" she regally crossed her arms and pursed her lips, "you are…entertaining her. Is that true?"

Jashar took a deep breath to calm his anger. "I am not sleeping with her." He held a hand up at her shaking head. "You are well aware that I do not lie. However, I'm not saying that I don't want to sleep with her."

His eyes narrowed with his edict, "Let me be clear. What I do with her is none your business, and I will not hear you bring it up again. To me, or anyone. And, I will not have her treated with anything but the utmost respect."

She opened her mouth to speak, he cut her off with a snap of anger, "She is a princess, and she will be treated as such. I do not believe she is guilty of the foul accusations against her and I will not allow her to maligned or mistreated." Rolling his anger in, he worked to keep his fists unclenched.

Exhaling in irritation, "Anything else?" he asked with unconcealed impatient sarcasm.

Affronted at his tone, her mouth pushed out. "Really, Jashar, this is ridiculous, ludicrous. You brought that- that-butcher-whore to our table! Your younger brother, so impressionable and vulnerable was there, what if she-"

"What, Mother? What if she leapt on the table swinging her soupspoon threatening to kill us all?" His smile was twisted and dry. But a dark warning flushed his skin.

"Now, I won't say this again. There will be no disrespect to her. That is final. She will stay here as my honored guest."

Streaks of red striped Vashana's sharp cheeks, her mouth dropped with dismay. "You cannot have an infamous murderess as your guest. You cannot-"

The corners of his lips edged in, crinkles around his eyes should have warned her his temper was fueling. "I can. I've had feelers out questioning, our people, her people. There is absolutely nothing to substantiate the accusations against her. There is zero evidence. We can't event trace how the fucking, sorry Mother, rumors started."

His mouth tightened in aggravation, he continued, "Where the goddamned, sorry Mother, the name Princess Butcher came from, or who even started it." He inhaled with an obvious struggle trying to hold onto his temper. "Tis all unknown conjecture."

"Jashar-"

"Nay. I won't have more slander said against her. She is my guest and she will be treated as such. That tis it. You have my orders." He gently elbowed past her.

"Aye," Vashana called out, "and when you tire of- of-shafting her, then what? You send her back to her people and they come after us for keeping her here against her will and you raping her? You can't tell me that you aren't-"

He swung on her. "*Sáith!*" he shouted so harshly she jumped back with her hand at her throat.

She knew he would never harm her, but his eyes were spitting black fire, his fists clenched, and his ruthless, legendary vicious fighting methods came to her mind. She wisely backed away.

Jashar was known for his cool control, he looked anything but calm right now.

He glared at her for a heartbeat, then turned and marched up the stairs.

Vashana let out a shaky breath.

"Tis her," a voice came out of the hallway. Aran had unapologetically been eavesdropping.

"Aye, tis that bitch that is making him behave irrationally," a lofty voice with pretentious undertones joined him. Thandie came to stand beside Jashar's half-brother.

Vashana folded her arms over her chest covering the top of the tiny flower print. She watched the pair approach. "I agree," she said.

Her eyes flashed back and forth in growing pique. "She has shown her colors as a true witch and she has bewitched my son. A spell," her brows rippled down, she nodded vigorously. "Yes, that's it, she's put some kind of spell on him."

"The question is," Aran said, smoothing his light hair back with both hands, then straightened his jacket by tugging at the hem. "What are we going to do about it?"

Vashana lifted her shoulders. "What can we do? You heard him. He refuses to hear a bad word against that-mesmerizing murderess."

"Let's put our heads together, we should be able to come up with a plan." Thandie set her long-nailed fingers on her hips that were surprisingly angular for the huge bosom that she had.

The other two turned to her with peaked intrigue.

Chapter Twenty

Jashar cleaned up and changed his clothes. He sat on the edge of the bed to untie his boots. The bed felt so soft and welcoming, he would just take a short nap and then be fresh to see Maratia.

As soon as his head hit the pillow he was asleep.

Hours later, the brilliant rays of the setting sun pierced a crack in the curtain and pushed his lids up. Rubbing his eyes, Jashar yawned and stretched. He peered at the window and saw the sun was going down.

"Shit- I must have been asleep for hours." He sat up. He hadn't meant to nod off for so long. The eagerness to see Maratia struck him, already his body hardened with thoughts of the fey beauty.

After tying his boots and binding his hair back, he strode quickly out the door and down the hall.

Just as he reached her door, he heard her scream.

Jashar yanked at the door handle, it was locked. He lifted his boot and kicked the door open then stormed in behind it.

Maratia was on her back on the floor, a guard was on top of her. He had wrenched her dress up and was yanking at his belt.

Maratia was screaming, "No!" Her thin bare legs kicked as she bucked and squirmed punching at him, struggling to beat him away from her.

The guard leaned back slightly and slapped her. "Shut up, quit screaming," he snarled. "I was told you like it rough, honey, so rough you're going to get!"

He spread his hand, large and calloused on her chest and harshly slammed her back on the floor. Kneeling over her with his legs between hers shoving them apart, he tore at the clasp on his trousers.

Jashar roared as he ran from the doorway and sprung in the air. Colliding with the guard, he knocked him off Maratia but he didn't stop moving.

Jumping to his feet, Jashar bent and grabbed the guard's collar jerking him up- then he picked him up by the collar and his belt, lifted him and hurled him at the window.

The guard crashed through the glass and disappeared with flying shards of glass and a scream. The scream was sharply cut off.

The king stood with his arms bowed, shoulders bunched and fists clenched. His skin mottled with rage and blackness, panting, he glowered at the window as if expecting the guard to reappear.

Hearing a choked gasp behind him, Jashar turned around.

Maratia sat with her bare legs curled beside her, her hand covering her mouth. The puppy's frantic yelps barraged from the bathing room.

"Maratia, I-" Jashar dashed his hand, running it over the top of his head, pushing loosened hair back, what could he say? He'd deliberately thrown a man out a second story window.

He couldn't tell if the terror afflicting her face, etching egregious circles around her eyes was for the guard's actions, or his. She now had both hands clamped over her mouth.

He took a step towards her. She didn't shrink from him, but her shocked expression seemed carved in solid marble on her frozen face.

Jashar said softly, "Maratia, I won't hurt you, I swear." He crept closer then sank slowly to his knees. Her dress was torn, the top wasn't covering much, the guard had also ripped the skirt in his violent attack.

"Sweetheart, are you all right?" Jashar was surprised to hear his voice shaking. His arms ached to hold her safe.

She just stared at him. A cut bled slightly from where the guard had struck her.

The king moved to sit beside her on the floor. He dabbed at the cut with his fingertips. "Maratia, please, tell me if you are all right. I am dying to hold you but-"

She flung herself into his arms weeping.

"Oh *Dias*, baby," he groaned. Holding her tightly against his chest he stroked her hair. "I'm so sorry. I don't understand how this happened. No one would dare to come here," he could hear his voice dark radiating with fury.

Struggling to keep his voice calm and even, he gripped her shoulders and held her back. "Ah, *mi a stór aingeal,* my precious angel, your pretty eyes are like misty jewels. Hush now, you are safe. He will never harm you again."

Jashar plucked at wisps of hair with his thick fingers that stuck to her damp face and lifted them back.

"Is- he dead?" Her chest shuddered, she wiped at her tears with the heels of her palms.

Jashar glanced at the window and shrugged. "Likely." He rolled his arms around her and pulled her into his embrace. She felt so good in his arms, cuddled against him, her face resting on his shoulder. He curled a finger under her chin to pull her head up.

"My sweet, I hate like hell that since you've been...ah brought here, that you continue to suffer violence at our hands. Tis so damned wrong, you are a woman, we men should be protecting you, not constantly attacking you."

Her smile watery, she replied, "You did protect me today." Her brows drew down. "But, Sire, you shouldn't have thrown him to his death!"

He didn't make a comment to her statement. The guard had been trained and sworn to protect the people of Thuas sa Spéir, yet he had broken into her chambers and had struck her, for that alone he would have died. Attacking her? He shook his head, the man was lucky he died quickly and painlessly.

Jashar asked, "What happened, how did he get in?"

Her pupils dilated with the remembrance of her terror of only moments ago. Her voice hitching, she told him, "He...uh, someone had slipped a note under the door that Robbie was needed, that you were looking for him. So he left to find you.

"The door wasn't locked. We thought he would be right back, he told me to lock it from inside. Just as I reached for the handle the door burst open. That- man came barging in. I told him you weren't here, he-" the words clogged in her throat, she gulped, wiped at her tears.

"I didn't send for McGee," Jashar said gently, caressing her face.

181

The dog must have heard Maratia no longer screaming and Jashar's deep calming voice, the frantic yelping diminished.

She nodded. "I know. He- closed the door behind him and looked at me with a- menacing smile as he locked it. He said he wasn't here for you, he was here for- me. Then he suddenly leaped at me. He grabbed me around the neck and held me, crushing the breath out of my windpipe."

Her hands went to her throat as she spoke. She looked away from Jashar in shame. "When I weakened from the lack of air, he tore my dress, trying to rip it off me. I fought him, he pushed me to the floor."

"Sweetheart, this is not your fault. You have nothing to be ashamed of. Tis the wildness of our times. People do things to women that they don't think twice about. They think tis all right if tis what *they* want. Women don't have the same...rights."

His mouth straightened in a hard line. "I will work to change that, I swear. But for now," his tender voice soothing, he said quietly, "I'm only concerned about you."

Her face crumpled in baffled misery. "Sire, I don't get it, what did I do? Why do people want to hurt me?"

Cupping her face like she was treasured china, she looked so woebegone Jashar felt like a fist was squeezing his heart, he drew in a long slow breath.

"I don't know, Maratia. I guess because you are so sweet, so innocent that we people with darkness in our souls want to destroy that goodness in you. I guess it scares us, we feel our lack in the comparison, it brings into the glaring light our own evil."

She thought about his words, they were disturbing. Her big eyes rolled up at him. "But you, do you still want to destroy me?"

"*Dias*, Maratia, I never wanted to destroy you. I-" his breath caught at how much she'd been hurt since he brought her to the castle, much of it at his hands. How truly angelic she was, it killed him how hurt she's been.

"I want to take care of you, protect you, hold you," his voice dropped to a bare whisper, "kiss you." He tipped her head up, his thumb stroked her lips before he replaced it with his mouth. The kiss was sweet, and gentle. He felt his cock harden like an iron rod. *Fujon*, he could kiss her like this forever-

"Damn, Jash, what the hell?" Daron exclaimed.

Pulling from her with a sigh, Jashar looked up to see his brothers coming through the broken doorway.

They tromped right in, stopped a few feet inside the room and stared at the pair sitting huddled on the floor, with a speck of shock inside their amused surprise.

Behind them was a series of concerned, and nosey, faces. McGee burst in right behind the brothers.

"Jash, *bráthair*," Kaer huffed with a grin. "There's a damned guard lying on the ground right below," he gestured with his head, "that broken window."

"Aye, I know." Jashar kept Maratia wrapped against him. She was sequestered in the corner of his arm and shoulder. He strapped his arms over her as if he thought someone was going to take her from him.

"So, ah," his grin deepening, Kaer asked, "what happened? How the hell did a guard fall from this window?" He crossed his arms, a grin lingering around his questioning face.

Beside him, Daron copied him like a twin, but without the grin.

McGee stood still, his face red with guilt and alarm.

"He didn't fall, he was thrown," Jashar replied matter-of-factly, turning his face back to Maratia. He cradled her jaw, his eyes went from hers to her lips looking like he wanted to eat them.

"Huh," Kaer snorted. "Well, someone has some cleaning up to do. I'd suggest you get something rolling before Father arrives. Did we mention he's on his way here now?"

Jashar dropped his head back and stared at the ceiling. He wanted to shout out a slew of curses, but now, there was a growing crowd trying to peer inside the room. He needed to get the door and window fixed so Maratia could have privacy.

Groaning, he stood up and helped Maratia up. He saw both his brothers' eyes widen. He looked at Maratia. "Ah shit, here sweetheart," he moved facing her to block his brothers' view of her.

He put a hand on her waist, just below her breast, the other he put across the side of her neck. "Your ah, dress," he nodded looking down.

She followed his gaze and gasped. "Oh, my goodness," her breasts were more exposed than not.

Jashar growled at his brothers over his shoulder, "Get the hell out you perverts and close, uh, lean the door against the opening. Keep the gawkers out and give us a minute."

Kaer and Daron snickered their way out the door pulling McGee with them. Kaer said, "I can now see how the door was kicked in and the guard got flung out the window."

Jashar heard them arranging the door so it covered the doorway.

He'd called his brothers perverts, but it was his own eyes that were devouring Maratia's plush mounds. His hand, toughened from years of killing men, at her neck slid to her breastbone, the other spread on her waist with his thumb slightly between her breasts.

"Um," Maratia put her hands on his arms to hold him back. "I, uh, need to change my clothes." Hearing the pair sound calm, the puppy who had started barking at Jashar's brothers' loud voices stopped yelping.

"Hmm, aye," he mumbled, lowering his mouth to her neck. He licked her skin, smiling at the goose-bumps rising where his lips were. He was surprised when with a small moan she rolled her head to the side so he could have easier access.

"Maratia," he whispered, moving his hips to press his erection against her belly.

He slid his hand to cradle the back of her neck, the other skimmed slowly up the front of her to spread over the top swell of one breast. He licked his way back up to her mouth and covered it with his.

He felt her hesitate at his kiss, then she melted against him and responded to his tongue's demands. His big fingers stretched over the curve of her breast that mounded over the bindings.

Sliding his fingers under the fragments of her torn bodice, Jashar carefully pushed it so it slipped down one of her shoulders, exposing more of her luscious skin.

Murmuring, "Ah, Maratia, I want you so badly," he left her mouth and sank his face against her plump globes. He moved his hand to cup her breast, shreds of her dress still clung to it, he sucked her plump flesh until it was red and she whimpered.

His brain flooded with searing sparks as his swollen erection grew to bursting. He released her head and slid his hand down the curve of her back to grasp a rounded cheek.

Squeezing it, he pulled her hips hard against his. The friction of their bodies rubbing together filled his head and cock with breathtaking rousing heat.

Maratia stood on her toes and shifted her pelvis to accept the thick hard ridge of his penis, letting it fill and stroke the throbbing folds of her womanhood through the thin dress and swath of underwear.

Her fingers spiked through his scalp, she grabbed tufts of his long hair.

He needed to have her now- Jashar slid both hands under what was left of the shoulders of her dress and pushed it down until it bunched around her waist leaving her breasts mounding well over the light bindings that held them.

His eyes glazing at their curvaceous beauty, he palmed them, crooked the tips of his fingers under the top of the binding to pull it down and fully free her breasts for his raging, unleashing consumption.

But she panicked. "Please," she blinked to clear the erotic cotton from her eyes. Repeating, "Please," she arched from him, her hands clutching his arms.

Jashar pulled back, pushed away the lock of black hair that had fallen over his eye with a trembling hand. Sucked in a taut breath. "*Bine,* sweetheart, tis *bine,* uh, tis all right, I'm sorry, I," he tugged the fragments of her dress back up to partially cover her.

She pressed her hands against them to hold her modesty.

"I'm sorry, Maratia, I pushed you, and on top of what happened earlier," he raked his fingers through his hair and scrubbed them down his face.

"Again, I act the rapacious beast. Forgive me." He had forgotten he wanted to make amends to her first before trying to move forward with her physically.

The crowd outside the door was growing rambunctious. Through the haze still firing inside his skull Jashar could hear his father's booming voice.

He took Maratia's hand and brought her into the other room so she wouldn't have to deal with King Allon's questions.

Chapter Twenty-One

*O*ver the next several days Jashar and a team of warriors were miles across the land squashing another insurgent skirmish. Daron was with him. This time Jashar ensured Kaer stayed back to watch over the castle.

He breathed easier and could put his full concentration on the battle knowing one of his brothers was keeping an eye on the people, and Maratia.

As soon as he returned and took care of his horse, taking the stone stairs two at a time, Jashar hurried to his room.

After a quick bath and change of clothes, he brushed his hair, tossed the brush on the dresser and was out the door and down the hall.

He knocked, waited. Frowned. There was no answer.

Grasping the handle, he was surprised, and not happy, that it turned easily and the door opened.

Furrows digging into his forehead, he needed to have a word with McGee. His rule was that her door would remain locked from the inside and out when both McGee and Jashar weren't present.

Stepping inside, he called out, "Maratia?"

Nothing but silence.

Where was the puppy? he wondered. The dog should have been barking like crazy at his intrusion.

Jashar strode through the chambers calling Maratia's name. The rooms were empty. His heart started racing, where could she be?

Panic rising up his chest, he strode out of the room and hurried down the stairs.

After a cursory check of the gathering rooms in the castle, he left the building and checked the guards' quarters.

The dorms were mostly empty except for a few guards that were sleeping off night duty. He didn't wake them, but he had thought to perhaps find someone who knew where McGee and Maratia were.

Where they hell were they?

He dashed outside and scanned the surrounding grounds. The panic was gripping his heart when he heard a bark. Not just a bark, but a tiny squeaky yelp.

Jashar followed the sound of the dog.

Around the east side of the castle, out in the meadow, he could see Maratia's golden rosewood hair fluttering in the breeze, the dog was bouncing around her on his leash. Maratia was laughing, and touching, Jashar's brother.

And, Kaermon was touching her back.

Jashar's shoulders bunched, his arms bowed, steam poured out of his ears as he stomped across the grass ignoring the greetings of villagers as he passed them.

They didn't see him until he was almost upon them. They were laughing, pointing at the dog. Kaer kept touching her shoulder, her arm, her hand, her hair- then Kaer spotted Jashar.

He slid his arm around Maratia's shoulders and hugged her to him, with a shit-eating grin directed at his brother. The darker Jashar's expression got, the tighter Kaer hugged her and the bigger his grin.

Clipping sharply, "Kaer. Maratia." Jashar clomped up to them, his boots smashing the grass.

Maratia turned around. Her hair swung, the indigo eyes shone brilliant, and her plush lips rose in a big smile when she saw him.

"Sire!" She broke from Kaer's embrace and strode quickly to him. As she neared him, she shyly slowed with her hands behind her back.

Jashar's heart leapt at her genuine pleasure at seeing him. The dog bounded between them yapping and jumping on her and then on him.

"He missed you," Maratia said with her shy lilting voice.

"Did he then?" Jashar stooped and scooped up the little dog.

Tenny slathered his tongue all over Jashar's face. Jashar scratched the puppy's ears for a minute.

Ignoring his brother's deliberately obnoxious grin, the king said to Maratia, "What about you, Maratia, did you miss me too?" He smiled at her blush. She didn't reply.

Jashar turned to his brother and said in a growly terse, "What the hell," he glanced at her, then glowered at Kaer, "are you doing out here? I left explicit instructions that she was not to leave the castle without McGee."

He turned and frowned at Maratia, berated roughly, "And you were not to be more than five feet from the castle walls."

He regretted his harsh tone and words the instant her lips fell and the sparkle in her eyes dimmed.

"I," she glanced at Kaer whose grin finally stalled at the anger in his brother.

"Get a grip, *mi bráthair,*" Kaer's voice was chilled. "McGee needed a few moments to himself, the dog needed a walk, she," he smiled at Maratia who looked crestfallen at Jashar's tantrum, "she needed sun. I took it upon myself to take her and the pup out for some fresh air." His eyes told his older brother to back off.

"I did not want her far from the protection of the castle, Kaer, I made that clear." Jashar got in his face.

Kaer leaned his nose close to him. "Am I not about equal with my older brother's warrior skills? She was safe with me, Jash, ease off, *bine*?"

Maratia stepped between them. "I can choose for myself if I want to walk my dog and with whom." Her small chin in the air she sniffed with irritation.

Both men turned to her.

Jashar glanced at his brother and muttered, "They need help at the carpenters' stalls."

Kaer got the hint. "Aye, sure." He grinned and bowed to Maratia. "I can leave you in my brother's safe hands," he winked at her. "Don't let the big angry oaf boss you around, honey."

He snatched the dog from his brother, gave him a few scratches on his ears then set him on the grass. Winking again, he turned and whistled while he strolled away.

"Maratia," Jashar said quietly waiting for her to look at him.

The welcoming smile had turned into wariness in her eyes and pique in her pursed lips.

His heart sank. "I, ah," he rubbed his chest with his palm. "I only have concern for your safety. I," he paused, searching for the right words, "am not used to…dealing with women. I mean on a personal level. How to talk kindly to them. I speak mostly with men. The females I converse with, well, I don't actually converse with them, I'm used to just-" this wasn't working, he was making things worse.

"Hmm," she hummed, crossing her arms. The dimples in her cheeks puckered as her peeved lips pushed out. "You're saying you don't speak to women like they are regular people, like men. You only sleep with them, take from them, and don't give back."

Jashar spoke quickly, "Aye, I mean nay, I mean, I give back-" ah, that was surely the wrong thing to say. Last thing he wanted was to put pictures of him with other women in her mind.

He stuck a finger under his shirt collar and tugged at it. The back of his neck heated. All he could think about was how cute she was when she was mad. Her little show of temper only made her appear all that much more captivating to him. At least he was smart enough to keep that to himself.

Her cheeks colored with pique and embarrassment, her foot started tapping on the grass. "Oh? You are kind enough to reciprocate to the women what you take from them?"

Her pretty eyes narrowed at him. She remarked, "I seem to recall you only taking from me." Then she turned from him about to stalk away.

He reached out and grasped her shoulders, turned her back to face him, holding her still.

She put both palms against his chest and pushed at him. It did about as good as a mouse against a bull.

Jashar pulled her closer so her elbows bent, her forearms pressed against his shirt giving her no leverage to push at or hit at him. "Maratia," he said softly, but she looked away from him. His hands moved down to squeeze her upper arms.

"Let me go, Sire. Go *give* to one of your women. It will be easier for you to take from them then have to fight with me."

"Stop it, Maratia," he said, shaking her gently. He brought her closer, so close her forearms were the only things between them.

"Don't throw other women in my face. Since you …came into my life, I have not desired," a half-smile perked his harsh face. "I have not looked at or even thought about another woman." He moved his hands up to caress her shoulders.

Keeping her head averted, she said, "Sire, you don't have to say anything to me."

He sighed her name, "*Maratia*. I do have to tell you what I feel. When I said I didn't really talk to women, well, that was a lousy egotistical male thing to say. Implying women only have one use. Unfortunately, I have to admit that," he ran his fingers through his hair then put his hand back on her shoulder, "that was how I felt."

With a snort, she tried to shrug from his grasp. "Fine, then, Sire. Please, take me back to your chambers where you won't have to talk to me. Just do- what you were commanded to do, get it over with. I can't stop you, you easily overpower me." Her last words were said with a teary sniff.

He dropped his head back and rolled his eyes. Squeezing her shoulders in frustration, he said, "Stop this, Maratia. I have told you over and over, I will not force you again. I want you to freely come to me."

Taking a quick breath, he went on, "I enjoy talking to you, being with you. Sure, I want to have sex with you, that is not in doubt," his cutting laugh short, even now his erection was straining against his breeches.

"So then, just do it, just get it over with." She squinted bitterly at him and said, "But I will fight you to the death." She wrenched at him, trying to free herself from his grip.

Groaning, "Ah, Maratia, please," he released a shoulder to cup her jaw and raise her head. Her hands dropped to set on his hips.

He pulled her closer to him until their bodies were touching. "I will never rape you, force you to do anything again, I've told you that. What I want is, what I just said. I want you in my arms, willing, and wanting me as much as I want you."

He tipped her chin up, waited for her to look at him.

When she did, he could see the hurt and bitterness, and anger in her eyes, but he could also see her lids lower over the heat that was starting to cloud them.

Her breasts were nestled on his chest, they molded over the low blouse from the pressure. His eyes dropped to drink them in, and he moved his hips so their lower torsos were touching.

"Maratia, I don't just want to have sex with you. I want you to be with me, make love together. Freely. I also want to wake up every morning with you curled happily beside me. That's not something I have ever desired before with a woman. I," he sucked in a breath.

Gripping her shoulders, lowering his mouth, he said quietly, "I care about you, Maratia. A lot. Not as my prisoner, or just any woman, but as a...mate. Please believe me."

"Sire," her breath hitched. She studied his face for any hint of mean trickery or guile. But his mouth was soft, the black discs warm for once, exuding interest in her, genuine caring. "I'm not sure…"

"Baby," he hummed against her mouth. "I won't pressure you, just," he licked the seam between her lips, then kissed her cheek, peppered kisses along her jaw. "Give me a chance." He bent to kiss her neck.

When she tilted her head to the side, he pressed his lips against her skin and sucked. Caressing her back, his big hands curving over the blouse, stroking down her spine, encircling and squeezing her waist until she moaned and shivered against his mouth.

Jashar moved a hand to cradle her head, the other spread across her back to hold her tighter against his chest.

Her hands slid from his hips to circle his own lean waist.

His erection jumped when her breasts pressed harder against his chest. Jashar moved slightly so she could feel the hard length of his erection straining at her abdomen, letting her feel his desire for her. His lips moved down to her collarbone.

Nipping her skin, his hand lowered down her back to spread over her bottom, he pulled her in tight and another soft moan slid from her parted lips.

He moved back up to capture her mouth. His loins burned as she responded by opening her mouth letting him explore the threshold of her lips. His tongue sliding under the inside rim of her mouth, relishing the taste of her, he searched for her tongue.

At first she shied from him, then, as their mouths sealed and he slanted his head to fit them together more tightly, her tongue pirouetted with curiosity tasting him.

Their breathing rushed, chests heaved with the heat that poured around them. Their lips pitched at and over, licked and sucked with crazed heat until he groaned her name, "Maratia…"

She nibbled his bottom lip and said with a soft questioning breath, "Sire?"

He moved his hand to net the side of her neck just under her jaw, his thumb stroking the side of her chin. He tipped her head, her lips parted, eyes drifted dreamily up to his.

He said gently, "Jashar, Maratia, please." He couldn't have her lying under him at some point if he's lucky, and hear her breathlessly moan, "Sire."

He wanted his name on her lips. He wanted her to scream his name when he finally had her willingly while he brought her to sweet explosive release. He needed her to be fully aware that it was her man, not her king that was ravishing her.

His shaft ached and strained against his pants to get at her. But slow, he needed to move slowly, carefully, woo her; he didn't want to scare her off. Everything was so fragile right now. The wrong move, the wrong word, could send her fighting, and running from him again. He needed to earn her.

Whispering, "*Jashar*," her eyes closed, her mouth opened for his kisses.

He about came in his pants at the way her accent curled around his name. Her parted lips beguiling him to plunder it, and her, all of her.

Murmuring, "Ah, thank you, my sweet," and he invaded her mouth. His brain soared with the thrill of her, the desire, the…love.

Gathering his breath, Jashar webbed her jaw with his fingers and said, "Maratia." He waited while she blinked away the cloud of scorching passion that was burning between and around them.

"Maratia, if I, cleanse myself of the evil I did to you, can you, would you, accept me?"

Her brows knit. "I don't understand, Jashar, accept you?" she said his name shyly, sweetly.

It sounded so bloody different on her lips, the intoxicating sound went right to his already burgeoning cock, and his toughened heart, and damn it felt so good!

His adoring gaze drifted down the soft contours of her face, soaking up her innocent beauty.

"Aye, I need to excise, from myself, the unforgivable violations I inflicted on you, body and soul. I cannot claim you until I suffer recompense for my abominations, my terrible actions, and am made clean, deserving of you. Worthy of you."

His breath warm, his masculine scent enveloped her. Whirling hot spindles and oozing ribbons of excitement surged up and down her body saturating the core between her legs.

Maratia scanned his tough face made up of flint and scars and brawn, his mouth hard with his serious rectitude. In his enigmatic eyes she could see the pain he'd caused her, his guilt and shame, and pleading for her forgiveness all clashing in a turbulent nebulous of remorse.

She laid her palm against the side of his face, he leaned into it. "Jashar, I have already forgiven you. We've talked about this. What do you mean by accepting you?"

He took the hand that warmed his face and kissed it. A hitch in his confident deep voice betrayed his apprehension over what he wanted to say to her. "Ah," his gaze stroked her, settling on those indigo orbs that radiated passion and forgiveness.

"I, want you," he paused, *how was he to say this?* "I want you to stay with me, Maratia, for good. For forever. I want you to be my wife. My queen." He waited, but could read nothing of her thoughts.

Her lips pressed together, the long lashes lowered shadowing the blue eyes.

"Maratia," his voice rasped deeper, he kissed her hand again and held it aside his face. "I don't want to take your...body...again...without an agreement between us, that, you will marry me. I don't want to lie with you without making you mine in promise, promise of my name, my allegiance, my commitment.

"You deserve the honor of being engaged, to me," he frowned remembering the fool she had run from, "before we, consummate…uh, our relationship."

He cocked his head at her silence. "Unless, I mean, I feel the energy, the magnetism between us. The passion is like none I've ever felt before. I feel like my heart, and my…uh, manhood will explode with every kiss, and," he smiled in question, "you don't seem immune to me?"

His mouth quirked. "And if I am judging the feelings between us correctly, we aren't going to be able to wait until the time we can properly wed. Between the banns and the other stuff, it would be too long…" His lips curved wryly.

"I know I can't wait. By our laws, people marrying have to be housed apart for 120 days. I cannot bear to have you out of my sight, out of my reach until we can make it legal. Maratia," he held her hand, "I don't want to be without you."

Still, her eyes just kept flitting around his face, setting on each feature as if studying it before moving to the next and the next and back again, she said nothing.

"Sweetheart," he regarded her carefully, his stomach plummeting with pending despair, *she doesn't want me.* "Talk to me. Tell me what you feel. I promise, whatever you want, I will do."

Her head moved to a slight cant watching every emotion that flickered over his normally implacable face. With a small smile, she asked, "And what if what I want is to go home? To **Ailanthus?**" The indigo orbs trailed all over his face, landing once again on his own suddenly panicked ebony eyes.

He stiffened like a knife had plunged into his gut. The sting at the back of his eyes was unfamiliar, but he knew what it was. He had to struggle not to squeeze her hand, crush her to him, get on his knees and beg her-

"Jashar? What is your answer?" Her voice such a soft lilt, Jashar had hoped to hear it every night as he fell asleep, and every morning as he rose to a new and wonderful day, with her beside him.

Now, his ribs compressed, all the air in his lungs squeezed out and he seemed to be unable to draw more in. His throat strangled with the fear of losing her.

His head lowered, loose threads of long black hair swept over the sides. It took a minute for him to get a grip. He dragged in a hard breath, exhaled harder, looked up at her.

Now she was the one who wore the stoic expression, and he knew fear and dread crisscrossed his own scarred face.

"Ah, Maratia, you own my heart. You took possession of it that day in the field that I held you thinking you were a boy."

A short snort of disbelief that he could have thought that, he grunted, "My sex was hard just looking at your ass as you fled. But when those eyes, those beautiful pools of blended blue moons wide in fright lit on me," he shook his head. "I was gone that split second."

"You had a funny way of showing it," she said with dry reminder.

"Aye." His shoulders slumped slightly. "It took everything I had, to bury my feelings for you, to be able to, perversely, harm you. You don't know how I agonized over my behavior," his voice strained. "I suffered, I know, no where's near the pain and humiliation you did, my sweet, but I suffered to see you hurt and to know I was the cause of it."

His fingers slid under her chin, he kissed her with hungry gentleness as if it was for the last time. "I love you, Maratia, I want only what will make you happy. If that means you leave me to return home, then I will let you go. It will destroy my heart, but I will do as you ask."

"Jashar-"

He put two fingers over her lips to stop her words. "Let me state, though," he said with his usual commanding voice, "you will not travel to Ailanthus without me and a cortège of men."

Her brows shot up, he moved his fingers, her lips parted, "But you just said-"

"Aye, my sweet, I will set you free as you ask. But hear me, tis too dangerous for you to cross the land alone, or with only a retinue. I don't trust anyone but myself to see you home safely. I will escort you there. On that there will be no discussion."

His fingers wrapped around her upper arms, he craved to pull her to him and devour her mouth again. But he resisted, she was declining him to be her husband.

"Additionally, I will speak with your parents. That ass, Valmyrjr," his mouth twisted, "will not be allowed near you again, ever. I will see to that. Your parents will be made aware of his…danger."

"Jashar," she tried to speak, he cut her off.

"I will also be…*speaking*…with him." Jashar used the term 'speaking' loosely, very loosely, figurative actually. "He will never lay a hand on you again, Maratia. Never." His fingers tightened around her arms.

"You must be given the adult choice to choose the mate that your heart desires. When you find him." His head drooped. "Even though it would not be me."

"Jashar," her voice hushed she asked, "and, what if I ask you to tell, my parents, what you did to me?" He still held her arms as if afraid to let her go, but she clasped her hands in front of her.

His face hardened at her words. His head lowered in his shame. He raised his dauntless gaze to her, straightened his shoulders and spine like the king that he was, and nodded stiffly.

"Of course. I mistreated you and I will inform your parents of my actions and about your incarceration." Immense regret and ignominy rippled over his face and glittered in his black eyes.

She stared mutely at him, scrutinizing the sincerity of his brave words.

He kept his head raised but lowered his eyes to her. His chest tightened like there were chains wrapped around it and squeezing the breath out of him. He looked her sadly, but directly in the eyes.

"We're all right with all of this, then?" Creases deepened across his forehead, lines pinched around his mouth and eyes at the thought that he would have to free her…from him. Ah well, he knew he didn't deserve her, she was too-

Maratia pushed free of his hold and slid her hands up his chest. Her fingers slowly skimmed over the slated bricks of muscles, feeling them bulge through his shirt, then flex with his shudder as she grazed his nipples. She smiled at the way they hardened from her touch.

His hips convulsed.

She moved hers to just barely chafe his pelvis and he about jumped out of his skin.

"*Mahmen a Dias*! Maratia, stop, you don't know what you are unleashing!" He caught her wrists, pulled them from his body. "Sweetheart, I want you too badly. I can't bear, I mean, you need to not touch me. It's too hard already to let you go as it tis-"

"Ah, again, Jashar," she purred, "you are always talking about this hardness of yours," she glanced down with deliberate coy.

His shaft reacted at her attention. It was already a thick ridge in his breeches. It swelled even more.

When she moved to press her body against his, her breasts wedged on his chest, her hips brushing his, her hands slipped from his shaking grasp and slid up over his shoulders to caress his neck. His breathing heaved so hard his growls seared her ears.

"Maratia, what are you doing? You've denied me your life to bind with mine, I don't-"

Her fingers strolled over his collarbone, her thumbs slid just inside his shirt to brush the top swells of his pectorals. She smiled as his flesh quivered under her touch. He kept his arms at his side.

She drew the backs of her fingers up his neck to stroke the underside of his jaw and around and behind his ears, then she drove them up into his hair.

"*Dias*, Maratia," he breathed fire, desperately trying not to touch her. "Baby, don't do this, I will not be able to stop myself from," a deep inhalation dragged up his lungs as her lips met his neck.

"From what, Jashar?" she whispered. Her lips parted on his neck, she kissed then sucked his flesh like he had done to her, and received the same reaction.

Shudders surging up his body, he instinctually pressed his loins against hers. His big hands moved to cup her bottom to heighten the contact, but he let go instantly. Dredging up his diminishing control, he dropped his hands back to his side.

Her soft lips minced little puckers all over his skin, kissing and stopping here and there to suck across his neck and down his collarbone. Her small hands were back on his chest stroking, clutching, kneading his hard body.

Jashar stood as a statue, not moving, hardly breathing, more like completely holding his breath. His eyes closed at the sweet torture she was inflicting on him.

When she moved her mouth to kiss around his ear, her tongue slipped behind it, so inexperienced she didn't realize how sensitive the area could be until he groaned and pushed her from him.

"Maratia," he panted holding his palms up to ward her off. "What the hell are you doing? Don't you realize what you are doing to me?" His agonized eyes ate her up, he craved to hold her, be inside her, so badly his gut hurt.

He begged, "Don't do this to me just to push me away and walk out of my life."

She crossed her arms and with a coquettish smile, narrowed her eyes at him. "I never said I was leaving, Jashar. I asked what if that was what I wanted. I needed to know how much you really cared. If you cared enough for me to set me free."

Confused, he shook his head as if to clear it. "What? I don't understand. What exactly are you saying, Maratia? Do you want me, or not?" His mouth clenched prepared to hear her turn him away again.

Her endearing smile held him aloft as she replied, "You said I should have the right to choose my own mate. I choose you." Her eyes lowered shyly, she cupped his face, then moved her hands around his neck, then she slid them over his shoulders and down his chest before dropping them to her side.

Her gaze rolled now uncertain up to his. "If, um, you want me. If what you said was true, oof-"

He grabbed her, slamming her against his chest, his arms crushing her to him. His mouth fell on hers, so aggressive, taking, feeding the grinding hunger he felt for her since the day they met.

Fearing he would frighten her with his fierce intensity, Jashar withdrew, holding her from him, even though he ached to take her right then, right there. "Maratia," he panted, watching her for any clues of distress.

Instead of distress, her bosom pumped with quick shallow breaths. Her pupils flared covering most of the indigo irises that glowed with vestal passion. Her lids hooded sultry over them, her tongue slipped around her lips as if asking for more.

He held her in his arms loathe to not be touching her with his hands and mouth.

She held her palms flush against his chest, peered up at him under quickly closing lids, her head tipped up, lips parted for his.

Jashar stroked a hand around the back of her neck, kissed her, then pulled back gently. "You need to answer me, I need to know if you will give me everything. Will you be my wife, Maratia? Will you marry me?"

Her eyes opened partially, her smile sweet, she replied, "Yes, Jashar, I want to be your wife."

He gathered her up in his arms swinging her off her feet, and whooped, "Thank the great *Dias*, I am blessed this day!"

Something was hitting his leg. He looked down and smiled. "Well, you have been quite patient, little Tenny, eh?"

He lowered Maratia to her feet, enjoying her body sliding down the length of his, the hard rod of his shaft stroking her female parts on the way down.

Jashar smiled at the sudden blush that burned her cheeks. He kissed her then bent and scooped up the puppy.

Holding the dog against his chest and laughing as the tongue swept his neck and chin and everywhere he could reach, Jashar kept an arm around Maratia, cradling her against him.

His cheeks ached from the enormous grin that had taken over his face.

Chapter Twenty-Two

"But I don't understand, Jashar," Maratia wrung her hands as she followed him down the stairs all the way to the front of the castle. "I thought we worked everything out, we can marry and-"

"Aye, we will, sweet," Jashar said, hooking a wineskin of water over his belt. The only weapon he carried was the rapier in the sheath at his thigh.

"Then why are you leaving? You don't have anything to prove to me, I have told you I forgive you."

They both looked up as the guard tasked with carrying out the whipping sentences came in through a side door.

He was big, a shade bigger than Jashar, and he was thick, colossal with cords of muscle strung across his back and over huge shoulders and down arms that looked like they were made out of iron.

It was his face that frightened Maratia the most.

Gouges from past duels covered most of Hagan Codkill's body. A strong nose yet crooked from decades of warring anchored his unpleasant face. His head was as big as a wheel but rough with hard angles.

His hooded eyes were unreadable, only dark flashes of dispassion seared from under his slit lids. He stood just inside the door, his arms crossed, his frosty gaze on Jashar.

Jashar nodded to Hagan, then, caressed Maratia's face with a thick finger. "Tis not about you forgiving me. I must do penance to cleanse the obscenity from my body. I can't come to you with the same body, the same ugly soul that did what I did to you."

Protesting, "But scourging? Please, no Jashar," she clung to his arm.

"Tis what I have to do to feel right to take you. Now," he kissed her cheek and hugged her, "don't make this hard on both of us. Kaer and Daron are unfortunately across the land on a mission. McGee while stick to you like glue.

"When he can't, then Officer Vachkianna will see to your safety. I am not pleased leaving you without my brothers to watch over you, but they might be gone for months and I," his kiss voracious in his need in taking her mouth, he didn't let up until both their legs were unsteady.

He sighed, drew a finger down the side of her face admitting, "I am too greedy for you to wait, Maratia. I want you now. So-"

"Jashar, this is ridiculous for you to go- go- beat yourself." Maratia twined her hands around his neck as if she could keep him there. His strong arm curled around her holding her close.

His face rigid in his seriousness, he ordered, "Stay inside, Maratia, do not leave the castle, even with McGee. Let him walk the dog. Promise me you won't leave these walls?"

"Of course. I will stay in until you return, but Jashar, please-"

"Thank you, baby. I will be back in," he glanced quickly at Hagan who stood completely immobile waiting. "A week or so. I love you." He bent and kissed her protesting lips one more time before releasing her.

He nodded sharply to Hagan and the two men left.

"Maratia, where is my brother going?" Sheera came out just as Jashar was leaving.

Seeing Maratia's bleak look on her bone white face, Sheera felt instant alarm. Touching the princessa's arm she asked anxiously, "What is it? Is everything all right?"

For once Maratia did not struggle to stop her tears. They rolled out one after the other. "He…is going to the forest…to purge the uncleanliness from his body so we can be, so he can, oh," the tears cascaded, her chest hitched with her sobs.

For a second Sheera stood stock still. Then she said, "Are you saying he's going to commit the," her voice dropped to a whisper, "ar'dhéana?"

Maratia nodded unable to stop the flow of tears. "Yes," she took a deep breath. "He's going into the forest where he's going to have Hagan flog him with first the whip and then the cane."

Her voice rough where it raked over the knot in her throat, the words came out in a tremble, "Then he will seek the bear, not the panther from his youth. He said he will look for the snow white bear that according to the stupid axioms of the decree, he must take down, kill, to purify his- soul, so he can be worthy of…me."

Her hands crossed over her heart, Sheera stood rigid with terror for her brother for the first time in her life igniting inside her heart. He was always so strong and confident she had never doubted him before, but this-

Nodding her head and pressing her hands on her eyes to stop the damned tears, Maratia sobbed, "Yes, after he's beaten horrifically, Hagan will leave him. He'll leave him alone, weak and bleeding, hurt. Jashar has gone out there with no food and little water, and only a knife to protect himself. Oh Sheera," she sobbed, the girls clung to one another.

"Huh. At least we will know if that ridiculous episode everyone claims he did as a child was real." Aran's snide voice drew near the girls. "Fighting a damned panther for fuck's sake, who believed that tall tale?"

Sheera lifted her tear-stained face from Maratia's shoulder and scowled fiercely at her half-brother. "You've always hated him, Fang, always were jealous of him. First, although you were Father's eldest, Jashar surpassed you as next in line as king, and then as a great warrior."

Aran glared at her. "I have never been jealous of that big bruiser. He is all muscle and no class."

"Shut up you horrible man," Maratia cried at him.

"Hush, Princessa," Sheera said. "He isn't worth wasting a thought much less a breath on. Come let's go to-"

The front castle door swung open. A guard was in the doorway, three women flanked him.

"Ah," Aran's wide mouth scooped up in a big pointed smile, "you made it. You came." He turned to Maratia and announced, "I have a lovely surprise for you my dear princessa." He motioned to the guard. "Come, come in."

Maratia and Sheera dabbed at their tears and watched with trepidation as the trio of women approached, the guard stayed by the door.

Aran scurried forward to greet them. He brought the women to where Maratia and Sheera waited in a perplexed huddle, holding onto each other's arms.

Aran nudged one of the women. As a tall, athletic woman with short dark hair and a plain face, moved a step forward, he said, "This is Miss Shalonda Calixte."

He drew one of the other women to stand next to her. This lady had auburn hair that curled down her waist with a curvy figure, blue eyes and pretty face.

Aran introduced her, "This is Janine Leudo." He smiled broadly at Maratia. "And this is Hollyanna McDonald," he gave Hollyanna a little push forward.

This young lady had dark wavy hair that swirled around her shoulders, a slight frame and big brown eyes like a doe.

Maratia stared blankly back at him and at the three women. "I'm not sure I understand what, um," her confused eyes hopped from one person to the next.

Nodding briskly, Aran said, "Of course, of course you don't. I shall explain."

His narrow face brightened as he said, "Well, Miss Shalonda and Miss Janine were, shall we say, in a relationship. But," he shook his head side-to-side with fake sadness. "Recently," he nodded at the third woman with the doe-eyes, "Miss Hollyanna came and gave Miss Shalonda a little visit the other day."

"Really, Aran," Sheera snapped, "what on earth is this all about?"

Aran shot her an irritated frown. "Don't interrupt, little sister, I'm getting to it." He swung his phony smile to Maratia. "As I was saying, Hollyanna came to see Shalonda and she told her she has been having an affair with Janine."

The tall, plain Shalonda immediately burst into tears.

Pretty, red-haired Janine looked wildly from Shalonda to doe-eyed Hollyanna then she grimaced. "It's a lie! I've told you, Shal, she's just trying to make trouble between us!"

Hollyanna moved close to Janine and said, "Oh no it's not. You and I have been having relations for weeks now and it's only right that your lover knows all about it!"

Shalonda jumped at the smaller dark-haired Hollyanna with her hands like claws, and shrieked, "I'll kill you!"

Aran grabbed her around the waist to hold her back.

Shalonda screamed again, "I will kill you!" Then she looked at Janine who stood with horror etched on her pretty face. Shalonda's plain face fell. "I loved you, Jan, I really did. I thought you loved me too." She broke down in sobs.

"I do, Shal, please," Janine begged her, "believe me, she lies!"

Her hands slammed on her hips, Sheera demanded, "What is this all about, Aran? Why have you brought these women here? What foolish-"

"Hush up, Sheera." Aran glowered at her, then smiled at Maratia. "I brought them to you. You can tell who is telling the truth, can you not?"

A pin could be heard dropped, all eyes were on Maratia.

Her face blooming with red, she tried to shrink within herself. Shaking her head, she opened her mouth to deny but no words came out.

"Aye, you can, I saw it myself. Those boys with the marble. I was in the great-room that day. There is no way anyone could have guessed what was the truth. But you could and did. You need to do that now. Give one of these three women the peace of truth that she needs."

His voice silky soft, he said, "Let Shalonda know if she is in a true relationship with Janine." He glared at the auburn-haired Janine who cringed at his angry look. "Or if she needs to kick Janine to the street for cheating. Relieve her mind, Princessa, help her with the truth."

He didn't mention the gold lining his pockets that Shalonda had paid him to come in front of Maratia. She desperately needed to know if her and Janine's love was true.

"I-I-" her palms out and up, Maratia stammered.

Sheera swung her arm around her shoulders. "You don't have to do anything you don't want to, Maratia. In fact, I'm pretty sure Jashar would be highly annoyed at this-intrusion." She leaned and whispered in Maratia's ear, "You know he doesn't want anyone near you, he doesn't trust anyone with your safety."

Even now, to keep him away, Aran had sent McGee on a wild goose chase to go to Maratia's rooms to get her while he'd snuck her down a different staircase.

Shalonda threw herself on her knees in front of Maratia. Clutching her fingers together in prayer, she begged "Please, Princessa, please help me. I love Janine with all my heart, but," her wet eyes flit to her mate.

Janine stood with her arms wrapped around herself.

Her homely face pale, Shalonda whispered through her tears, "I have to know the truth. Please."

Maratia wiped at her eyes and pushed her heavy length of hair off her shoulders and sighed. "All right. Please, get up."

Having the woman on her knees at her feet greatly disturbed the princessa.

She waited while Shalonda climbed to her feet and lifted the hem of her skirt to wipe her face. Then Maratia said quietly to Janine, "Give me your hand."

Janine hesitated, her blue eyes flicked from Maratia to Shalonda. When her gaze landed on Hollyanna, her eyes hardened then lowered. "*Bine*," she agreed and slipped her cold hand into Maratia's.

Maratia nodded to Hollyanna. Saying, "Now you," she held out her hand.

Hollyanna looked like she wanted to flee. Her doe-eyes darted to the door.

"Miss Hollyanna, you agreed," Aran reminded her with a nasty chill in his voice.

Her attention aimed at the floor, Hollyanna moved to Maratia and slowly slid her hand into hers.

Maratia took a deep breath.

Sheera and Aran and Shalonda stood as if on nails, afraid to move or speak. Holding their breaths, their wide eyes intent on Maratia.

Shalonda's hands covered her mouth to keep from sobbing. Janine refused to look at her.

Both Janine and Hollyanna's heads were lowered, their gazes arrows to the granite floor.

Holding their hands, Maratia said nothing, just closed her eyes.

The room was dead silent, fortunately the time of day there were few people out and about. No one moved, no one made a sound for what seemed like hours but was only a few minutes.

Maratia opened her eyes and released the women's hands. She looked straight at Hollyanna.

Hollyanna blanched.

"What?" Shalonda fairly shrieked. "What is it? Does she speak the truth?"

"No," Maratia stated flatly. "She does not. She wants Janine for herself. She thought to drive a wedge between you, turn Janine against you."

The hall rang with first silence and then gasps.

Shalonda turned to Janine. "You spoke the truth. Oh my darling, I am so sorry I doubted you. You know how much I love you-" she paused not sure what to do next.

Janine raised her arms with globby tears blurring her blue eyes. "I know. I love you too, Shal."

The girls ran into each other's arms crying.

"So," Aran rubbed his hands together and watched as Hollyanna, her face as red as a beet streaked to the door and slipped out while the two lovers hugged.

He grinned hugely at Maratia, mouthing, *goldmine*.

Chapter Twenty-Three

*H*agan hadn't hesitated to whip his king. As a warrior, he understood what Jashar was doing, and he admired him even more than he already had for years. Hagan would follow Jashar off a cliff if the king told him to.

What he didn't like was leaving his liege alone, lying face down in a blanket of grass with his back ripped open. He couldn't believe the king hadn't passed out from the flails. He'd seen other big, strong warriors break down long before Jashar had finally buckled to his knees.

But still, he kept hold of a thread of consciousness even as Hagan slathered ointment on his wounds to prevent infection from settling in, and the warrior knew that had to be as painful as the whippings themselves.

"Sire," Hagan said quietly.

His face in his arms, Jashar mumbled, "Leave me."

It was an order, but, Hagan crouched beside his king. "Sire, let me at least get you food, you will be too weak to hunt-"

"*Leave,*" it came out in a groan.

Hagan reluctantly got to his feet. He stood hovering over the badly wounded man. *Maybe he could-*

"Warrior," Jashar coughed, wheezed through his tight lungs, "leave."

"Aye, Sire." Hagan sighed unhappy to leave him like he was, severely injured and unprotected. He wouldn't be able to move for a while, maybe days. The warrior turned on his heel and marched out of the forest to where they'd left the horses and returned to the castle.

Jashar drifted in and out of consciousness. His temperature rose desperately high, nightmares plagued him.

He woke one night burning up. Knowing the issues he would face, he had planned his scourging near a creek.

It was agonizing, but he crawled to the edge of the creek and slapped water on his face and chest and arms. He avoided getting his back wet and taking the chance of getting his wounds infected. It mustn't have been long before he passed out again.

He was trying to fight back to lucidity when he heard it. A growl.

Ah, he had hoped to get to the winter bear before having to dispatch any other threats. He had no idea how long he had lain there. It had been a danger itself just for him to lie near the water as the animals of the forest could be drawn to it.

His mouth was dreadfully dry. He painfully raised a hand to touch his jaw. A layer of scruff covered his lower face. He had to have been lying there for days. First thing he needed was liquid.

He wasn't worried yet, about the growl, he knew what it was, he'd spent enough time in the forest. A wolf. He hoped there was only one.

The wolf would carefully stalk him for a bit to see if he was dead or alive before attacking him.

When he reached for his skin of water the movement would relay to the wolf that he was alive, and within seconds, hopefully more like minutes, the canine would jump him.

As slowly and quietly as possible, Jashar rolled to his side and carefully reached for the liquid container Hagan had made sure was near him. He needed to drink or he wouldn't have the strength necessary to protect himself and fight.

What he really wasn't looking forward to was rolling onto his back. But he would have to. He would not be able to get to his feet to fight the animal, he was too weak.

As he silently sipped, he could hear the tall grass further away by the dense trees ruffle. The wolf was still in stalking mode, he wasn't yet ready to pounce.

Inch by agonizing inch, Jashar rolled onto his back and pulled out his rapier. It was enough movement- he heard the wolf's paws striking the ground as he raced through the grass, then just as he reached Jashar he lunged-

Jashar jerked to the side as the wolf was airborne and jabbed his knife into the wolf's gullet. The wolf howled and fell kicking next to Jashar.

Still alive, it twisted, his incisors gleaming as he thrust out to bite him. Jashar needed his knife back, he twisted and jerked avoiding the wolf's snapping serrated jaws and curled spiked claw.

He got a good punch in the animal's nose and when the wolf fell back, Jashar snatched his knife from his belly and plunged it into the wolf until it stopped howling and moving.

Sweat dripped in his eyes, he slung his hair back with a toss of his head. He knew his back had started healing and he had ripped parts open from his scuffle. He struggled to sit up.

The animal lay beside him. Jashar stared at the dead wolf. Damn, he hated to kill unless it was to feed. Panting, he needed to rest a few minutes before he started carving, he would not be letting the meat go to waste.

A week passed, he was feeling closer to normal, but Jashar hadn't yet come across the white bear. He knew the vague location where they traveled as they were periodically spotted throughout the temperate year.

Unusual for bears, these particular mammals stayed in packs. While keeping his eyes moving, aimed straight ahead then flashing back and forth, and down scanning the ground for tracks, he listened, and inhaled deeply through his nose for the scent.

More days passed before he saw them. The tracks. Unmistakable. They were different from the colored bears, the winter bears' paws turned out slightly.

The tracks were fresh. Jashar followed them cautiously, listening, keeping an eye behind him and up in the trees. The forest was filled with hungry animals.

He caught up with the beast pretty quickly.

Damn it was big. On its hind legs it stood close to seven feet high, had to weigh a ton. It was beautiful, fur as downy and white as snow, hence the sometimes name of Winter Bear.

It had black shiny eyes that were leveled straight at Jashar.

Jashar stopped moving, it would be hard for the bear to detect him if he was immobile, and he had been careful to keep downwind.

Meanwhile, he studied the enormous creature. Jashar put a hand on his knife still in the sheath. It was different when he was three, he'd been sent out then to kill, he was little, and he didn't have a choice.

Now, he had the choice to destroy a beautiful animal for no reason other than he had to follow the dictates of the hallowed ar'dhéana to complete the purge. He had to take down the bear.

He looked around his area. The slight movement instantly drew the bear's attention back to him.

A low growl traveled across the thin bush of the woods.

Twin trees in a V shape caught Jashar's eye. He moved towards them, the bear stood up on its hind legs and roared.

It dropped onto all fours and raced at Jashar.

Chapter Twenty-Four

$\mathcal{I}$t was a long hike through the forest to where Jashar had left his horse. His ride home when he was done had not needed to be secured. Jashar wouldn't have wanted to tie the horse up, he wouldn't be able to flee if danger came after him and he would require food and water.

Jashar had left him near a stream. He whistled.

Instantly he heard hooves pounding through the scrubby edge of the forest.

The horse trotted right to his open palm and put his nose in it. "Ah, good boy, *Daoldubh,*" he patted the horse's flanks then brushed his hand down his mane. "You ready to go home? Because I sure the hell am."

He swung up easily on the steed's bare back, made a tsk sound and the horse started a quick but not racing trot heading towards the castle.

In the time Jashar had traveled the forest, he had occasionally bathed in clear streams, and had easily caught small game to eat. But he missed his warm bath and bed, food prepared by someone else, a shave, his family. And most of all he missed Maratia.

Finally, though, he felt cleansed inside his skin, purged of his shameful acts. He had suffered his penance so he could have her with a pure mind. *Dias*, he couldn't wait to get to her, wrap her in his arms and take her straight to his bed, and make her his.

His hard-on pressed him to urge the stallion to move more swiftly.

As he neared the castle, he slowed taking in the odd occurrence of a crowd of people lined up at the castle door. *What the hell?*

The horse deserved food and a brush, and his hooves checked, Jashar took care of him first.

That done, the king strode to a side entrance to the castle. All of the entrances were guarded.

The guard at the side bowed and quickly opened the door for his king.

Jashar stepped inside and saw the line of people went across the great-room and all the way to the other side. His curiosity, and rising trepidation caused him to pause.

"Guard, what the hell is going on?"

The guard bowed again then answered, "Sire, it's…" he glanced at Jashar then quickly away.

The king was in grungy breeches, his boots muddy and shirt was so torn that it barely covered his broad chest. His skin was dark from long hours in the sun, his jaw covered with a black beard, and his hair was as wild as his eyes.

They looked like he had the entire savage jungle churning in the depths of them. Jagged cuts curved under the scar from the panther of his youth. He did not look like a patient man, or a man to be reckoned with.

"Tis what, Guard? Speak up," he commanded, trying to peer through the crowd to see what they were lining up for.

His eyes straight ahead, the guard gulped nervously. The word was the king was smitten with the lovely princess from the foreign land. Who knows what his reaction would be? "Ah," he cleared his throat, "the ah, Princess Araminte, she uh-"

"What? What about her, tell me now before I rip your tongue out!" Jashar grabbed the guard's collar, clutched it in his fist.

"Sire, sir, tis your half-brother, Prince Aran. He's got her, uh, I don't know how to say it, she can tell if people are lying. He's charging people to see her to resolve their conflicts with-"

Thrusting the guard away, Jashar was already striding across the floor.

The crowd quickly parted as he muscled through, and grew silent as he passed to the front of where the line seemed to begin.

When he reached the front, his face already dark and weathered, his shirt torn revealing dark hair that covered the thick slabs of his muscled chest, and his face, now with the marks of a bear claw, he looked like a savage native about to go in for the kill.

Near a wall, Aran was beside Maratia holding a basket.

McGee stood on the other side of her looking fit to be tied.

Jashar's sister Sheera, along with some of the guards were trying to keep the crowd contained, organized and patient.

Against the pale ivory and pink wall, Maratia was holding onto two different people's hands, a man and a woman. Her eyes were closed, her head lowered.

Jashar latched onto her face. Even with her head lowered he could see purple shadows under her eyes.

Already quite slim she looked like she'd lost weight and her shoulders slumped. Maratia somehow looked more worse for wear than Jashar did!

She was clearly so exhausted she looked about to fall off her feet. Jashar could feel the rage roiling in his chest, his ears grew hot. How had she gotten into such a sickly condition?

He stomped over to Maratia and stopped in front of her.

"Maratia," he said in a low, quiet voice, struggling to suppress his growing anger.

Between her exhaustion and the trance she was in, it appeared it was a struggle for her to lift her lids.

Now that he was closer, he could see the shadows were even darker, her skin translucently pale.

She looked at him as if trying to clear her vision. The long autumn lashes swept up and down as she blinked eyes so weary Jashar's heart hurt.

Then she focused on him and her face brightened with a big smile. "Sire, you're home safe, thank our Blessed Lord!" she cried with happiness in her voice, her face wreathed in relief.

He said not a word, just bent, slid his hands under her and swooped her up in his arms so fast the people who clasped her hands jerked forward with the motion.

Ignoring the stunned gasps of the crowd, like a fierce warlord carrying off the fair princess, holding her high and tightly against his chest, his boots clunked across the floor leaving a trail of mud as he strode aggressively to the staircase.

Her arms wound around his neck. Maratia laid her head against his shoulder and sighed, "I am so glad you are safe, Sire, I've been worried to death." She sighed again, the weariness in her bones hushed her words, "And I've missed you so."

Her hair was up in a bun, the loose tendrils swirled around his face and neck as he made his way from the now loud crowd.

His voice harshly gruff, he muttered, "*Jashar*, Maratia."

She snuggled in his arms, this time her sigh slipped out with a smile. "Yes, Jashar. I called you Sire to be respectful in front of the villagers."

"I don't give a fuck about them right now, only you. Respect my wishes and don't call me sire again." He sounded angry, but he nuzzled his chin against the top of her head.

"Hey! Jashar! She's working! What the fuck are you doing?" Aran yelled across the great-room.

The crowd started fussing, growing louder with boisterous annoyance.

Sheera called the guards over and told them to disburse the people, have them leave the castle and go home.

"Hey," the male part of the couple Maratia had been working with complained. "What about us? We weren't done, I need to know-"

"Oh yea," Sheera swung on him. "You want to take that up with the king? Wait just a second and I'll call him back."

"Uh, well, never uh mind. Come on Bess, let's go." Scowling, the man grabbed his wife's arm and pushed her towards the door. No way did he want any contact with the king. He had looked livid, like an enraged battling warrior about to take heads.

The women in the room were swooning. The king had swept the princess up in his arms and strode up the stairs with her, just like in a fairy tale, so romantic!

Aran decided it would be prudent to make himself scarce.

When Sheera looked over, he was scuttling down a hall.

Upstairs, Jashar fumbled the door to his chambers open, stepped inside and kicked the door closed. He strode to his sleeping chamber and to the bed.

Looking down at the tired beauty in his arms, he whispered, "Maratia," and waited for her to push her heavy lids up and dazzle him with those indigo orbs.

She did, slips of blue peered up at him. Smiling shyly, her plush lips curved up in such a lovely bow, Jashar could not resist kissing them. He lowered his mouth.

Meshing their lips he held back the bone-wracking hunger he had for her that he'd carried with him the entire time he was gone. His kiss was deep, he couldn't help it, he needed to taste every inch of her, but he was gentle. She looked so damned weak and direly fragile.

He laid her on the bed. Pushing up some pillows he moved her to prop against them. She started to push herself up, "Sire- Jashar, what are you doing? You are the one that needs the care."

Her hand went to the already scarring gash of the bear's claw. She touched it gingerly, delicately. "You are injured, you need aid, medicine, let me-" she tried to move off the bed but he sat on the mattress and put his hands to her shoulders holding her back.

"Nay, my sweet. You are the only medicine I need." He leaned into her, his hands still on her shoulders and kissed her.

Her hands fell to his chest. The torn shirt hid little of his strong chest. She nestled her palms against the mat of black hair and caressed his flexing muscles.

He grasped her wrists and held them from him. He voice soft, he said, "Nay. Not now." His tone turned rugged with anger, "You will tell me what the hell was going on downstairs and why you look so," his gaze stroked her face, "tired, weak, thin." His palm brushed her face, his fingertips smoothed over her pale skin.

When she hesitated, his black brows descended, eyes flashed with ire. "No hesitation, Maratia, I haven't the patience or energy for it. Just tell me."

"I will, but please," she pulled her wrists from his grasp and set them back on his chest, "I have hungered as well, Jashar, for a mere touch of you. It's been weeks, indulge me."

He looked down at the graceful hands cherishing his chest. His shaft hardened at her touch, but he smiled. "*Bine. But fair turnabout later, promise?*"

Her sinfully wicked smile turned up, an eager avarice lit the indigos brightening some of the weariness amassed there. "I can't wait, my liege," the smile broadened at his swift irritation at her formality.

"I tease you, Jashar." Her facile palms plied over every hard angle and curved muscled depression on his slated chest.

The corners of his mouth turned up in a rapacious grin. "Aye, well, I will punish you later for that," he lowered a rough hand to encompass a breast. His grin now gleamed with wolfish avidity at her sudden flush and swift intake of breath.

Her nipple pebbled against his calloused palm. "I promise a punishment we both will enjoy." He watched her face change from teasing to soft wanton desire. But, her cheeks pinked with still virginal shyness at his bold touch.

Seeing her discomfiture, he knew he had to move slow and gentle with her, he skimmed his hand from her breast to slip around her neck.

"All right my shy innocent sweetheart, later." His brows darted down. "But right now, back to the matter at hand. Tell me what was going on, and why you are so weary, and thin, and don't hem and haw, spit it out. We both need food and rest."

The weariness overtook the desire on Maratia's anemic face. "All right. Aran," seeing Jashar's scowl she took a breath and paused, but he just stared at her, waiting.

"He happened to be there that day I…helped those boys regarding the marble. He came to me and told me I must earn my keep." She paused again at the thunderous cloud that descended over Jashar's face.

He nodded sharply. "Go on."

"Um, so he said he came up with this scheme for us, that is for the castle, to earn a lot of money. He sent word out to all of Spiremoor and the surrounding villages that I…you know…can tell who is telling the truth in a situation."

Her mouth turned down ruefully. "He called me 'Princess Solomia,' you know, a female Solomon."

"Continue," his voice so tight the word barely scraped out. The hand around her neck tightened as well. Aran had certainly changed his song quickly from butcher-whore to Solomon when money became involved.

She twisted slightly. "Jashar, you're hurting me."

Grimacing, he lowered his hand to set it loosely on her shoulder. "I am sorry, Maratia. I find this abhorrent and unsettling. I ache to touch you. I certainly do not wish to hurt you. I will be gentle. Please, always tell me when I am too rough with you."

Her tender smile made his heart flip flop. It wasn't she who deserved, and would suffer, his ire.

He said more calmly, "*Bine*, I get the gist. Tell me why you are so weary, and thin." He stroked her face feeling the hollows under her cheeks that weren't there before he left.

"Um, I am all right, just a little tired," her eyelids drooped, the purple shadows under them darkened.

"Maratia," he warned.

She sighed. "He, Aran, uh, made me work as long as there were people lined up."

Jashar held his breath. "What are you saying? How often were they there?"

She looked away from him as she answered, "Pretty much all day…and into most of the nights."

His words choked out. "When did you sleep? I've been gone weeks- answer me quickly before I lunge the fuck out of here and go after him."

"I- I- took naps when there were lulls. Unfortunately, that wasn't too…often."

He couldn't believe what she was telling him. His eyes wide and aghast studied her wan face. "Food? Why are you so thin, didn't you eat?"

She nodded. "Yes, but it was in between people and it was awkward and difficult. I couldn't hold hands and eat and talk at the same time. But I'm fine, Jashar, really." She put her hand over the one he still stroked on her face.

"You are the one who has been terribly injured. Please let me-" When she tried to move he pulled his hand from under hers and set it on her shoulder holding her still.

He suddenly stood up in one fluid motion, dragging his hands through his dirty hair.

"Tell me," he ground out the words, "why did McGee and my sister allow this to go on?" His lids narrowed at her so hard his eyes were indiscernible.

"It- wasn't their fault, Jashar, they both tried to stop him. But he threatened McGee with…beheading if he interfered, and he was obviously too strong for Sheera to control. But she did try."

"My mother? Father?"

"Uh, I believe your half-brother told them all was well and I was totally agreeable to it all. After the first few days they left the castle, they traveled to…" she thought to remember. "Um, Forálacha. It is a nearby village-"

"I know where the fuck it is," he snapped. Then seeing her wilt against the pillows he sat back down, his weight sinking the mattress, and took her hand.

"I'm sorry, Maratia." He ran a furious hand over his head. "I'm just so- mad." He leaned in and lightly kissed her. "I need to go see Aran." He went to get up but she held onto his hand.

"Please, Jashar. You've been gone so long, please don't leave me," Maratia wheedled. She was afraid he would critically harm his brother in the rage he was in. He already looked so- savage. "Tell me, about the bear."

She petted his face avoiding the fresh cuts. "You have new scars," she nibbled at her lip, "did he hurt you anywhere else?"

His hand went to the marks the bear left on his face. "Aye, more scars." He smiled at her. "I'm sorry I can't be handsome like my brothers. They have been lucky so far, their ugly scars can't be seen."

Her brows dropped at him. "Don't say that. You just look more," she put a finger to her chin while she studied his added afflictions. "Well, you look even more the legendary warlord, the Warrior King of Thuas sa Spéir. You are very handsome, Jashar, in a...tough way. You know women throw themselves at your feet. To me, you are manly rugged, harshly beautiful."

The smile went from ear to ear, he leaned in and kissed her. "I care not about any other women but you. You are the best thing that ever happened to me, Maratia."

Enjoying his kisses, she murmured, "The bear, Jashar, I'm dying to hear how you bested it. I was so scared for you." Her shoulders quivered with the fear she'd lived with for weeks not knowing if he was dead or alive, or injured and unable to return home.

His orders had been if he didn't come back, no one was to look for him until his brothers returned.

His mouth quirked. "In truth, it was nothing. I stalked the poor bear until he saw me. When he rushed at me," he kept talking over her sudden frightened gasp, "I was standing in front of a pair of stalwart trees that were in a V shape.

"Just as the bear reached me I jumped aside and the bear ran into the V. It slightly stunned him and briefly held him immobile. I picked up a rock I'd prepared and," he shrugged a shoulder.

Enthralled with his escapade, that he survived a bear attack, she prompted, "You what?"

A grin ticked up the corner of his mouth. "Well, honestly, I was feeling guilty that I had hunted the bear for no reason other than to kill him to honor the warrior dictate to purify myself of my ill deeds. So, I just clobbered him a few times with the rock until he was knocked out."

He stroked the new scar near his temple and said ruefully, "He did manage to get in a few claw swipes, but thankfully I worked on him so swiftly he couldn't get in more than a couple of wicked slashes. Then I started for home."

"You didn't kill him?"

He grinned fully. "The dictate said I only had to take him down and 'out'. He was definitely conked out. I heard his roar roll over the hills echoing off the trees far behind me when he woke as I raced away. The deed was successfully completed without his cruel and unnecessary death at my hands."

She stared at him like she couldn't believe his courage and his compassion for an animal that he had provoked into attacking him. "I- Jashar, I am so proud of you!" She hugged him.

He wasn't used to praise like that, for doing a deed that was considered normal for a warrior of his league. He was slightly embarrassed, but it felt great. He reveled in her embrace.

Leaning back, she said with concern, "But your wounds from the- the flogging. You must see the physician-"

"I am good, sweet. The ointment Hagan spread over the slashes healed them quickly, they are already barely visible scars. Now," when his hands started wandering over her body she pushed him back with a giggle.

"You need a bath," she stroked his scruffy jaw, "and a shave, some food, rest." She eyed his torn shirt. "And clean clothes. Although, I have to say," her cheeks blushed, "seeing this glimpse of your, um, chest, I," she lowered her eyes to his torn shirt.

His voice warm with desire, he cooed, "You what, baby?"

The indigo blended with light bands of blue turned sultry again, but her weariness drooped her lids over them. "I would like to see, feel, more," her lids drifted closed.

Jashar leaned over her and pulled out the pins that held up her hair. He set them on the nightstand and drew his long fingers through the burnished locks spreading them around her.

Seeing the blood from an animal still on his hands, he sighed. He needed to get that shower, and some rest. He would deal with Aran later. No doubt the coward would already be in hiding knowing Jashar would be coming for him.

Aran likely assumed and hoped the bear would best Jashar and he would never return to the castle and Aran could carry on using Maratia.

Feeling sick, he combed his fingers through her hair smoothing it off her face. That fucker had treated her like a circus act. Animals are treated better than what his half-brother had made her endure. At least they are fed and allowed rest.

His hands tightened into fists, when he got his hands on him- Maratia stirred slightly, turning her head towards him. He touched the purple shadows gently, leaned over and kissed her softly.

Then he got up and trod to his door. He found a guard and told him to bring food and drink to his chambers.

He bathed, ate, left food on the table for when she woke, then Jashar lay down in the bed in his clean breeches and shirt and pulled Maratia's back against his chest, his legs curved behind hers.

Curling a possessive arm over her, he drew her close. Sighing deeply in abundant contentment, he was asleep in moments.

Chapter Twenty-Five

Other than a few dozy moments when he woke her to have her eat, it was hours before they stirred again.

Jashar was on his back, Maratia lay with her head and a hand on his chest, the rest of her luscious body was snuggled against him. When he opened his eyes, she moved.

Her lids cracked open slightly, she started to shift away from him but he caught her, holding her where she was.

"Nay, sweet, I've dreamed it seems forever about you in my arms like this," he sighed, "let me enjoy it for a moment."

Her body relaxed back against him. Her palm on his chest, she slipped her fingers through the buttons stretching her fingertips to feel his hairy steel.

"Ahh, Maratia," he moaned, feeling his body grow harder than it already was. He cupped her chin raising her head to kiss her parted lips.

When the kiss grew heated, he pushed her to lie on her back and lay partially over her with a leg between hers, his erection pressed on her thigh.

She set her palms on his chest holding him back and turned from his mouth. "Jashar, I have not bathed for," her

233

forehead wrinkled. "I don't remember. I would dearly love to be clean…for you."

His lips recaptured hers in an increasingly wild kiss, his hand at her waist moved up to the side of her breast. Against her lips he murmured, "You smell as sweet as always, baby. I want you now."

She kept both hands flat on his chest to hold him back. "Please, I am not comfortable."

His exhale blew pained but indulgent. "*Bine*, I want whatever makes you happy. But," he wriggled his brows at her until she giggled.

"But what?"

"I want to bathe with you." He slid a finger down her face and kissed her. "Is that all right with you?"

"But- you took a bath, you won't-"

"Then I will bathe you. I cannot wait!"

The color bled into her cheeks making them shine, her eyes sparkled. "Um, I'm not sure…I've never been, you know…" She asked as deeply shy as ever, the color spreading to her chin and across her nose, "Would we be-naked?"

His grin was wide and greedy. "Aye. A person cannot bathe with his clothes on. Come, let's go." He rolled off the bed. Bending to her he grasped her hands, pulled her to her feet and into his arms.

He couldn't resist kissing her again. His hand at her back, he tucked the other in her hair, grasped a handful and gently tugged her head back so he could look at her. Jashar wanted to make sure she was ready and agreeable to what he had in mind.

His heart warmed and his loins burned at the sight of the passion brewing in her darkening eyes, her lids were half-mast over them now with desire instead of weariness. Her lips were still parted from being pulled from his kiss.

Murmuring, "Sweetheart," he slid both big hands on her back holding the lower half of her against him, the rest of her still arched back.

His eyes dipped down to the front of her then back up to those steaming eyes of dark indigo, the lighter blue lacing through them like melting oceans of azure gossamer.

"Let's go before I throw you on the bed and ignore your wishes for that bath." He smiled at her hazy look, like she didn't remember she wanted to bathe.

"Here, let me pin your hair up." He grasped the pins he'd set on the table and fumbled trying to put her hair up. He was not successful with his attempts. The heavy locks kept tumbling down.

"Let me," she laughed at his ineffective efforts. Twisting her hair on top of her head, she took the pins from his palm and tacked the tresses up.

He shrugged. "Sorry, I've never really had my hands in a woman's hair before." He let a loose tendril twine around his finger. "Your tresses are the only ones I've ever desired to touch. They are exquisite beauty."

The lock twirled around his thick finger. "Like satin, just like the rest of you." He let go of her hair and stroked his hand down her arm.

He took her hand and brought her to his bathing chambers. The room was mined marble polished until it was smooth and glossy, the tile floor warm to their bare feet.

Releasing her hand, he moved to the round tub, huge enough to hold eight people comfortably, and turned the levers connected to aqueducts made of clay pipes that brought the water over heated coals.

While the tub filled, he grabbed thick towels and laid them beside the smooth marble tub. The rimmed ledge circling the tub was rounded with wide tiles, containers of soap and colorful bath salts were placed neatly along one side.

Jashar dug into the bowls scooping handfuls of the scented salt and dropped them into the water. The water bubbled right away showering the air with pleasant flowery aromas. Then he turned to her.

She stood with her arms wrapped around her body, suddenly unsure.

He took each of her hands and held them. "Sweetheart, we won't do anything you do not want to. You say stop, and we will. *Bine*?"

She nodded slowly.

His expression serious, he said, "Tell me, though, so I know how far to…" his lips pulled in at her lashes sweeping down over her eyes, hiding them.

He forged ahead. "Maratia," he angled her chin up, waited until she looked at him. "I want to make love to you. Right now. Do you want that too?"

Jashar hadn't realized he was holding his breath until she nodded.

Very quietly she answered, "Yes." Her soft smile shy, but her direct gaze told him all he needed to know.

Looking her straight in the eyes, he said gruffly, "I love you, Maratia." His fingers wound around her neck and into her hair. He pulled her head up and kissed her.

She was slightly stiff, still bashful, hesitant.

He nibbled at her lips. Licking the inside of them, he grazed his tongue along her teeth then finding her tongue he sucked on it until she felt like a ribbon of hot chiffon in his hands.

His mouth on hers, Jashar reached between them and unbuttoned her blouse. Her hands went to his upper arms, she clutched handfuls of his shirt to hold steady. Her blouse undone, he stepped a bare inch from her.

With his eyes on her face, he grasped her blouse and drew it off, letting it fall to the floor. His gaze dipped to the tie of her bindings under her chest. He untied it, then unwound the soft cloth from around her body and dropped it.

His pupils grew so large, like passionate black spheres they took over his dark irises and smoldered at her naked skin.

"Ah, you are so damned beautiful, Maratia," Jashar groaned. Having not been able to clear the sight of her bare breasts from his mind when he had forced her to expose herself, he had craved to see them again with so much need, his stomach had wept with the agony of his want.

Now, with relief and the purity of his lust, he raised his hands drawing them over her breasts, cupping them, another heavier groan drew out. "Watch me caress you, my sweetheart."

Her eyes lowered to see his big hands covering her breasts. His darker fingers gripping her ivory flesh, her own pupils expanded turning her eyes into liquid storms.

He kneaded her plump globes until he heard her sighing with kittenish moans, his own rougher growls echoing in his ears mingled with her soft sounds. He lowered his head to kiss one breast, then the other.

She watched him, saw his dark head at her bosom. His long black hair sweeping against her fair skin as he took one of her mounds in his mouth while continuing to caress the other one.

He cupped both breasts, squeezed them to swell in his hands then he kissed them, nipped both nipples between his teeth, suckled and flicked his tongue over them until she cried out with hot pleasure.

Sucking a breast, his lips on her damp skin he murmured, "You taste wonderful, my sweet, I can't wait to taste the rest of you."

Jashar dropped to his knees. Releasing her breasts, he reached around her for the clasp to her skirt. Looking up at Maratia, he saw her gaze mesmerized still on her woman's flesh wet and reddened from his mouth.

He smiled, thinking, *she liked that, wait until I taste the rest of her.*

Unhooking the skirt, Jashar looped his fingers in the waist and drew it down her hips then down her legs until it pooled on the floor. She stood in only a swath of the under garment.

When he sat back on his heels to look at her, she had one hand over her breasts and one over her sex. He smiled. She wasn't covering anything too well with those small hands.

"Sweetheart, don't be shy with me. Show me your beauty. I've waited so long for it." Her eyes glowed wide at him with embarrassed uncertainty, she didn't move. He pushed at her hand over her sex and grasped her underwear pulling it down.

"Jashar," her voice timid, shaky.

"Hush baby, look how soft and lovely you are." He removed the swath of silk and set his palm on the inside of her thigh. She made a small sound. He looked up at her.

Even with her eyes almost closed, the heat building in them was unmistakable. She watched him slide his hand up until it was touching her naked sex. Her body swayed, her breath hitched.

Another small sound escaped her. He looked at her while brushing his thumb ever so lightly over her woman's bud. Her face was pink with shyness, and desire broiling in the depths.

He brushed his fingers around the outside of her feminine folds then at her moan he stroked his fingers down her slit, her sex quivered in his hand. His fingers were glistening with her silk.

"Come," he said to her. Standing up he took her hand. She blinked away part of the haze to awkwardly follow him. He brought her close to the tub.

When Jashar started unbuttoning his shirt, she slowly moved close to him and slipped her hands in to tentatively touch his bare chest. He shrugged his shirt off while looking down at her small hands exploring him.

"*Dias*, baby," he shuddered. How could it get any better? She was buck naked, like he'd always dreamed of, and her virgin's hands were all over his chest like she enjoyed touching him, learning the feel of his body.

His hands hesitated on his belt buckle, he needed to take a moment and gather his control. His chest expanded with a deep calming breath, but then quivered as her fingertips scraped lightly over his nipples.

She seemed so intent on what she was doing, his voice husky, on the edge of shaky, he asked, "What are you thinking, my love?"

He watched her soft smile as her palms skimmed over his muscles, her fingers sifting through the dark hair that covered them.

Her big eyes followed her ministrations with wonder. "Jashar, you have the body of one of those gods that tumbled from heaven." A hand slid up his shoulder, then the other, she drew her palms over the cordons of muscles across his shoulders and then down to his biceps.

"So big, so strong, your shoulders are so huge, you feel like steel under my hands." She couldn't get her small hands wrapped around his biceps; she tried to squeeze them and giggled.

"Your arms are like rocks, and here too," she slid her hands back to his chest. When she rubbed and stared so hard at him, his nipples puckered. She moved her hands down slowly to his abdomen.

"Even here, Jashar, you are like solid chips of granite, what are you like-" a moan growled from deep in his chest as she moved her fingers down his abdomen and to his belt.

He grasped her delicate wrists, kissed one hand then the other. "I fear, sweetheart, if you keep that up our real first time will be too short. You can touch me all you want, later. *Bine?*"

Her autumn brows drew down, her cheeks flushed. "But I am…nude, and you are…not." Her eyes were intent on his breeches, on the erection that looked about to tear his pants open.

"I would like to see, you know, what you look like, too." She reached for him but he caught her hand again, with a hoarse chuckle.

"Wait," he undid his belt and his pants, then shoved them and his undergarment down and shucked them off. His eyes were on her as she watched his iron hard manhood spring up, he was so ready for her he fair burst with it.

Unfortunately, she had seen his manhood the time he tried to force it in her mouth, but she'd had her eyes crushed closed too scared at the time to look at it.

Jashar prayed she wasn't thinking about that horrible night now. His own face stiffened with the memory.

"Uh," she backed away slightly, her mouth dropped. The pink in her cheeks paled. The indigo eyes swept from his man's shaft to his face. Something in the dark harsh planes of his hard face frightened her.

The ebony in his eyes glittered, the claw of the bear under that of the panther, his jaw like stone, he looked every bit the menacing warrior that he was.

"Nay, sweet, don't be afraid of me. I am just so," he held his hand out lightly to her. "I want you so badly tis a strain to not-" his black orbs pulsed with need, he wanted to always be honest with her.

"I want to lay you down and- shove right into you." He saw the panic flash across her face.

He lowered down onto one knee to appear less threatening. "I won't, baby, you mean too much to me. I won't hurt you, I promise. I want this to be perfect for us. Please, trust me to take care of you."

He didn't move. Neither did she. Then he saw the warmth pass over her eyes, pushing the fear aside.

"I trust you, Jashar."

Rising to his feet he held his hand out.

Her gaze was on his face, studying the honesty in his eyes, it fell to the burgeoning manhood. Her cheeks bloomed full pink again. She blinked wide-eyed at his heavy erection, then looked to his hand. She set her small hand in his big palm. He closed his hand over hers.

He led her to the tub, helped her walk down the steps to sit inside the roiling warm water. He sat on a step and pulled her into his arms with her back against his chest.

"How does this feel?" he asked, his voice tight with his own need.

"Mmm, s'nice," she murmured. Her head lolled back against his shoulder.

He smiled into her hair. Reaching for the soap, he lathered it in his hands and drew his palms down one arm then the other. "Lift your leg for me, baby." He waited until she lifted her leg then soaped one then soaped the other slender limb.

Jashar ordered, "Stand up," and he helped her to get to her feet. The water was to her waist. "Ah," his throat tightened, his gaze strolled from her breasts down to her flat belly.

"Up on this step," he told her. Helping her to turn around so he could soap her nape, her shoulders, down her back and to her bottom.

He lathered his hands over her behind. Rubbing and squeezing, drawing the side of his hand up her crease and squeezing some more until she finally said with a little giggle, "I think I'm pretty clean there, now, Jashar."

Wrapping his fingers around each cheek he gripped and squeezed, said reluctantly, "Hmm, if you're sure. You said you wanted to be clean, I'm just doing as you ask, sweet."

She turned around to face him.

His face reflected the strain of looking at her nudity and holding back. He stroked his soapy hand between her legs and caressed her until her shy writhing and moans drove him crazy.

Then Jashar sat down on a step. He pulled her down to sit between his legs with her back against his chest again and soaped up his hands.

"Your breasts look like they need some cleaning, Maratia." His deep chuckle fanned in her ear while fondling her breasts pretending to wash them. He lowered his head to place his lips against the side of her neck and held her globes in his soapy hands.

He tugged at her nipples, crushed the weight of her flesh in his hands, kneading her fullness in his long fingers until she squirmed against him, arching her back, pressing her breasts into his gluttonous palms.

Sliding his lathered hands down her chest over her belly, he moved them until he cupped her sex.

She started slightly, her legs closed. Carefully nudging them apart, he gently touched her sex. He smiled when after stroking his fingers over her little bud a few times her legs widened.

When he circled her bundle of tender nerves with his fingers then pinched it, she squirmed hard against his chest. Her hips bucked at his hand, her moans came raspy and rushing.

"*Bine*," he murmured in her ear. "I think you're pretty clean." Wrapping his arms around her, he half-picked her up and moved her to where he laid out a thick towel on the wide rim of the tub. Her limbs were so loose she could hardly stand.

"Jashar," she moaned. "I feel so…"

"So what, my sweet?" he asked softly, guiding her to the side of the tub.

"Oh," she wriggled, her body shivered with heat. "I- I don't know. I feel burning between my…you know, legs."

"Does it feel good?" His eyes on her breasts that jiggled with her shivers, he leaned her against the side.

"Mmmm," she nodded. "I feel, like, there's a flush or- or something building, a strumming pressure. I don't know," she sighed as he put his hands on her waist and lifted her to sit on the towel on the rim of the tub.

"Ah, it gets better, sweet, trust me. I'm just getting you warmed up, used to the feelings." He put his hand on her chest and gently pushed her to lie back with her lower legs dangling over the edge inside the tub.

"Jashar?" she sounded confused.

"Tis all right, baby, trust me. Open your legs for me."

When she didn't, he nudged her thighs apart. He felt her legs rigid with unease.

She was lying on her back with her legs spread and hanging over the edge of the tub with Jashar in the water standing between them.

"Jashar, I feel so…exposed." Her voice tiny yet flushed with the heat from his fingers from a minute ago.

He leaned over her and set his palms on either side of her. "*Dias*, you look like heaven, baby, all pink and ivory." His eyes devoured her tender femininity.

Her hands were up near her head, her legs open. The heavy lidded eyes gazing up at him were anxious, but emanated heating desire, and trust.

As he leaned further to kiss her, his shaft brushed her core. He smiled at her twitch, and unsteady sigh.

He grasped his manhood to lightly stroke it over her sex to get them both wet, then rubbed up and down her plump femininity.

Watching her lids lower further over her burning eyes, he slid up her slit slowly, listening to her rippling excited breaths. Her body undulated with his movements, trying to push harder against him. He dragged his shaft down, then back up until he needed to stop. He bent and kissed her.

Jashar stood back. "Ah," his voice tangled in his throat. He put his hands on her thighs and stared at her womanhood. "Every part of you is beautiful, baby, soft and tender, fresh."

Gripping her thighs to hold still her but loose enough she didn't feel forced, he said, "I'm going to taste you, sweet, just lay there and feel me, trust me. *Bine*?"

She shuddered with the feeling of his big hands holding her open for his full perusal. He was looking at her most intimate female parts. The room filled with his shallow fervent breathing as it grew heavier. Then, he put his mouth on her-

"Jashar!" she started to sit up, close her legs. But she couldn't close them because he was between them. His hair brushed against her thighs as he kissed her most private parts.

"Lie back, Maratia, relax, just feel me loving you." His voice soft and deep, thick with his desire coaxed her to lie back down. He kissed her again, touched her with his thumbs, gently opened the tight folds of her tender skin and licked her slit up to her throbbing bud-

She gasped loud, her body bucked, but she stayed on her back.

"Ah, good girl," he praised, squeezed both of her thighs and licked her again. He stroked his fingertips up her slit, pressed her folds and sucked and licked her until she was writhing, frantically clutching handfuls of the towel.

He could hear her breaths, fast and heavy. Her bottom squirming, he held her thighs more tightly to keep her in place.

She was so wet; he circled her woman's nub with his tongue then nipped it with his mouth while he carefully put a finger to her opening. "Relax, sweet," he crooned, bit her bud and pushed his thick finger gently just inside her.

She immediately stiffened. He said softly, "Just feel me, baby, relax, trust me."

It took a minute, he didn't move until he felt her thighs loosen slightly. He kept his mouth on her sex and moved his big finger inside her small sheath slowly. His thumb and mouth brushing her swollen bundle while he kept pushing until he felt her hips moving back at his hand, with urgency, not fear.

"That's it, sweetheart," he said, "let it build, feel the heat, let it build." He moved his finger a bit deeper, then started moving it in and out faster, while kissing and stroking her clit until he heard her whimper, then cry out- her hips bucking and twisting at his hands and mouth.

"Let it go Maratia, come for me," his voice thick and rasping, he drove faster, biting her nub until she yelled his name in a gush of a scream, her back arched.

He felt her sheath clutching his finger. While she cried out her release, Jashar stood up and pushed another finger in to stretch her.

She folded up forward with a cry, he kept moving, keeping her orgasm going, until she lay on his shoulders, her lungs weeping and hitching.

When the tremors calmed, he grasped Maratia and laid her back down, leaned over her with his hands braced beside her shoulders. He smiled down at her.

Her mouth was still puffing, her head rolled and she peered at him through a blur. He bent and kissed her. Long, hard, until she was breathless again.

Moving to the side of her, he put his palms on the edge of the tub and pushed himself out of it to sit next to her.

Her lashes fluttered, she looked dazed, and puzzled. "Jashar, are we not…going to…"

"Aye, right now, sweet." He wanted to take her to the bed but knew he couldn't wait that long, and he didn't want her to lose her fluidity of her orgasm. Rolling a thick towel down he shifted her on it then knelt between her legs.

"Right now," he repeated. He nudged her legs apart, braced over her on one elbow and kissed her.

Her arms rolled up to wrap around his neck. As the kiss deepened, he gripped his shaft and placed it at her opening.

Without breaking their lips apart, Jashar slowly pushed the mushroom head of his manhood just inside of her.

Feeling her stiffen, he waited until she relaxed around him then pushed some more.

He worked himself inside her, deeper, moving slowly so her body could adapt to him. Feeling her tender walls pressing hard against his throbbing shaft, he felt her chest hitch with uncomfortable breaths as her hips twisted trying to get away from the extreme tightness.

Jashar paused and laid a palm on the side of her face. He said, "You're so small, Maratia, are you all right? Do you wish for me to stop?"

Her face pained, she asked, "Will it get better?"

His heart clutched at her pain, but he smiled. "Aye. Your body will accept me, give it a minute."

She smiled up at him, he kissed her.

Feeling her body relax around him, her silk making them both more slippery he moved again, pushing slowly until he finally was buried deep inside her.

They both sighed.

He waited, then pulled out carefully, almost completely out, then pushed back in, so slowly it was agonizing for him.

The strain of holding back from pounding into her was killing him. But it was an exquisite death. She was tight and wet, the more he moved in then back out the easier it got. He began a rocking a rhythm and her hips started arching up to meet his.

"Better baby?" he whispered, kissing her cheek.

She smiled, her face now showing more pleasure than pain.

"Yes, Jashar. I can feel you, instead of a tight, too fullness, you feel, ahh," she moaned as he shoved deeper. "I can feel you," her blush came on, "like throbbing against my insides. It's, uh," she gushed, her head fell back.

"It's what?" He kissed her chin, her jaw, moved down to suck on her neck. Knowing he was going to mark her, he wished he could make it permanent. Brand her as his own. He would do that as soon as he could with a ring.

Now he began the deeper plunges, rolling his hips with rapid pistoling, driving his hard thick member deep inside Maratia with each thrust.

Her body shivered, face and neck flushed. She couldn't talk, her head rolled side-to-side with rasping breaths, her chest heaving. Soon whimpers issued loudly from her rosy lips, her hips jerked up to meet his harder faster thrusts.

Jashar could feel her rushing to her peak, rising to the edge. He slid a hand under her to raise her hips and told her, "Wrap your legs around me, baby."

When she did as he said, he moved his hand between them and stroked her nub. Her fast breaths, mewling moans and writhing hips made him start to lose his control.

His own deep breathing roaring in his ears, the blood rushed from his head to his nether parts. Her cries and gasps grew louder, Jashar plunged in and out now so hard so deep he had to let go of her hips to hold her shoulder so he wouldn't push her away from him.

"Jashar," she cried, her spine arched, her head dipped back.

"Go baby, let go. I love you. Look at me, look at me Maratia." His voice harsh with his need, he watched her until her bleary indigos peeped at him, she smiled, then her face scrunched.

"Look at me, Maratia," he almost shouted. He wanted to watch her come.

She pushed her eyes wide. Tumultuous and misty, they wobbled around his face, then with her gasps scraping from her depths, she cried out, "Jashar!" Her pupils zoomed huge then her eyes rolled back.

He felt her spasm around his shaft. Suddenly milking, squeezing him, her body convulsed in his arms, under him, around him. He clutched her shoulders and finally let himself go.

He thundered her name, drove in and out of her so fast the friction was on the precipice of pain and pleasure.

Maratia screamed as another orgasm struck her. It undid him. He pushed his girth as deep in her as he could, then cried out as his seed burst into her tender sweet channel with his undulating body.

His breathing so hard and heavy he was squashing her with his chest. His hips still rocked into hers as his shuddering tremors diminished, until finally, crazed with the intensity of his orgasm he collapsed.

Jashar felt blind and deaf with the feeling of his wracking body. In the back of his disjointed mind was a thread that told him not to fall on her and he was able to angle off just before crushing her completely.

He lay half on her, her arms wrapped around him, their hearts crashing against each other's.

It was a while before either of them calmed, their heart rates slowed. A vein at his temple lessened its thrumming pulse.

They rested. He rolled on his back and pulled her to lie on his chest. His fingers stroked through her hair that had fallen out of the pins.

"Jashar?"

"Mmm?" He had no intentions of moving. He had prayed for this day, these moments, and he was not giving them up. His arm tightened around her.

Her voice faint, still thick with their passion, she murmured, "You, you released your seed, in…me."

"Aye. It was wonderful," he uttered slightly sleepy. "What do you think?"

"Hmm." Her smile apparent in her sigh and her wriggle against his big body. "I want to do it again. But…"

He cupped her chin, lifting her so he could kiss her. It was warm and sweet, and he was already stirring, hardening. She tasted insane, yet he knew he had to wait and let her body rest.

"But what, baby?" Their lips pressed lightly together not in a full kiss, just touching.

"Your, seed, won't…I can get pregnant? Aren't you, you know, concerned about that?" A tiny worry threaded through her drowsy tone.

"Nay. We are to be married. I want nothing more in this life than to have you, and our children dancing around us like colorful butterflies."

He smiled against her lips. "What about you? Are you afraid?" He stroked under her chin with his fingertips, felt her shake her head, then relax back against him.

"No. I just wanted to make sure that everything was all right with you."

Hearing the slight doubt in her reply, he lifted her head again, looked her in those indigo eyes. "You are thinking now that I've had you, I've gotten what I wanted, your willing surrender, I will move on, eh?"

Seeing the apprehension in her slight nod, he wrapped both arms around her, compressing her into his possessive embrace.

"Maratia, since the moment I saw you I've died for this day to come. Now that my dreams have come true, I will never tire of having you. I will never tire of you. For the love of *Dias*, I only crave you more!

"I will never want another woman. I've told you that. I want us to marry, to call you my wife. To hear you say to me, 'Jashar my husband.' Are you trying to tell me maybe you have doubts? Second thoughts, about us?"

Her head shook against his shoulder. "Never. I love you, Jashar. I will always love you." She snuggled against him.

His heart tripped. It was the first time she'd said she loved him. He grinned, tucking the moment away in his heart.

Sighing, he held her tighter, the world was perfect.

Chapter Twenty-Six

*T*hey spent days in bed.

Took a few short strolls outside with the puppy, then grabbed food to eat while laughing and talking and making love.

Jashar knew the entire castle and surrounding villages were rife with gossip, he'd seen Kaer a few times. Enduring his brother's teasing, Jashar just ran him off and hurried back to be alone with his fiancée.

Jashar made his intentions clear to his family. His mother about fainted on the spot. His father remained stoic, his brothers and Sheera were thrilled for the couple.

Life was bliss, until, Kaer came to their bedroom door. Hating to knock, he could hear their giggles and moans through the door. But he had to.

It took Jashar a long time to answer the door. When he did, his undone pants were barely hanging off his trim hips, he wore no shirt or shoes, his hair was haphazardly finger-combed. The look on his face could burn tar.

Kaer only a caught glimpse of an equally mussed Maratia sitting in bed with the sheet pulled up to her bare shoulders. Her eyes were dreamy, mouth thoroughly red and plumped, well kissed. She smiled bashfully.

Jashar moved to stand in the doorway blocking his view inside and growled, "What brings you here, *bráthair*? Make it quick."

His grin deliberately riling, Kaer tried to peer around his brother. "Jash, we need to talk."

Jashar leaned over with his forearm along the doorway to stop him from seeing Maratia. "*Bráthair,* spit it the fuck out, we're busy."

Kaer crossed his arms, his legs braced. "Geez, Jash, save a little for the honeymoon, eh?" He chuckled at his brother's scowl.

As Jashar went to close the door, Kaer said, "It's," he dropped to a whisper. "Valmyrjr, her-"

Jashar stepped outside the door closing it behind him. He growled like an animal warning as its food was getting snatched.

"What the fuck, Kaer, if this is your idea of a joke-"

Kaer's countenance turned grim. "Nay, tis true. We have word he never left. A few men came in from the exterior and said they heard he had feelers out, has snuck into Spiremoor to find word of her.

"It seems someone let them know she was here. The men say he's coming in ready to fight to take her." Kaer stood watching his brother's face grow dark, his brows slashed over eyes that were growing cold and fierce.

"Jashar?"

Both men turned guilty at the sound of Maratia's lilting voice.

Jashar went to put a hand to her shoulder to hustle her back inside but she planted her feet. She had the sheet wrapped around her.

Kaer's eyes dropped to the full cleavage that was half exposed and stared until Jashar jabbed him hard in the side with his elbow.

"It's Sammel? He's been looking for me? He's here?" The words trailed out of her closing throat. The round cheeks rosy with the glow of a satiated woman bled white. She saw the guilty looks on both brothers' faces.

Her brow drew down. "What, Jashar?" Her eyes flit from one to the other. "You knew? You knew he was already here to get me?"

"Sweetheart," Jashar glowered at his brother, reached for Maratia. "Tis ah…he, I mean tis been awhile since he came…looking…for you," he fell off at the look on her face. First terror that Sammel had been so close trying to find her, then anger at Jashar for not telling her.

Indigo eyes flashing in pique, she declared, "You didn't tell me? I had the right to know!"

"But baby, there was nothing you could do. I just wanted you to stay safe, here in the castle."

Kaer stifled a grin at his big warlord brother shaking in his boots at the fiery little maiden's ire.

"Safe?" she squawked. "No, don't touch me!" She slapped at his hands as he tried to catch her hands. "I am not a child, how dare you?"

Then she pointed at Kaer with her face crunched up. "You knew too and you didn't see fit to tell me either?"

Now that her heat was on him, Kaer's lips pulled in. His hands came up, he stammered, "Uh, well, he-" he motioned to Jashar. "He told us not to tell you, he-"

"Oh!" Maratia snorted. "Don't you have a mind of your own?" She turned and started down the hall to her own chambers.

"Baby, where are you going?" Jashar called out. "Maratia, wait, we need to talk-"

She snapped over her shoulder, "I need to think, alone. Don't follow me," and swished down the hall. They heard her door slam shut.

Jashar turned to glare at his brother. "Goddammit, Kaer, what the fuck were you thinking bringing this to my door like this?"

Kaer's shoulders shrugged, his palms up. "Hey, sorry, really. I can't imagine how you feel with that curvy ball of honey leaving your bed- ow, hey- " he rubbed his arm where his brother punched him.

"Where you going?" he shouted as Jashar went back into his room.

He followed him in. He watched as Jashar gathered a shirt, boots, socks, then unlocked a large container and started taking out a trove of weapons and started fastening them around his body.

When he was done, the king started for the door. "I am going to go get the fucker before he gets near here. Let's go."

"There are a good deal of our men already across to Graerdom to quell the disturbance there. We don't have enough men to go with us." Kaer watched the play of feelings cross Jashar's face as he thought. "Jash, she will be safe here inside the walls."

Jashar turned with a fierce growl. "Oh aye? Like the last time when Aran hired her out while I was gone and practically worked her to death?"

Kaer nodded. "I know, I know, but you have little choice. We need all hands with us. The information is that he will take her even if she has become betrothed to another. He has announced that she is his. Forever."

He waited for the fury to clear from his brother's face. "There will be McGee and a group of other guards to watch over the castle. If an army comes, the villagers will fight. You know that." He waited until he saw the resignation sink Jashar's shoulders and pull his face down.

Jashar said in a hard voice, "Get the men ready. I will meet you." He strode off down the hall hearing Kaer's footsteps heading down the stairs. He went to Maratia's chambers. He knocked.

She didn't respond.

He said, "Maratia, I must come in. I have little time, open the door, I don't want to kick it in." That reminded him of the guard who had attacked her. His stomach turned. But he needed to go after the threat to her head on.

The door opened a crack.

He pushed his way in making sure he didn't crush her against the wall.

She stepped back, surprise, wariness, and anger colored her face. She had pulled on a dress and shoes. "Jashar, I don't want to talk to you now, leave me-"

He gripped her arms to halt her words. Her eyes popped at his aggressiveness. "I don't have time to fight about this now," he barked.

"I need to go after him, Valmyrjr. He has made it clear he is coming for you and is prepared to fight. I must stop him before he gets close. Understand me," he gave her arms a squeeze. "I will remove this threat to you. If I have to kill-"

She put her fingers to his lips with a gasp. "No, please, Jashar. Let him come. I will tell him I'm happy and he will go away. He will-"

Jashar shook his head. Took her hand and kissed her fingers. "Nay. My men tell that he says he will take you by force regardless of the situation. Even if we had married, he vowed to take you."

He lowered his head so their foreheads met. "You will see, Maratia, I will protect you. He will not take you."

Shaking her head she said with determination, "No, I will go with him."

Moving from his clutch she cried, "I won't have him hurt you or anyone here. It isn't right for anyone to suffer for my foolishness." She turned to reach for her jacket.

Jashar jerked her back to him. He lifted her almost to her toes and ground out, "Nay. You will not leave this castle. You are not going to that bastard. I mean it. Do not make me lock you in again, because I will to keep you safe."

"No, Jashar, I don't want you hurt-"

"Tell me, Maratia," his voice dropped cool. "Do you love him? Do you want me to release you to him?" He could see her eyes shift around; she was going to say yes, just to protect him.

He shook her. "Stop it. You are mine. I am yours. The end. Right? Look me in the eye and tell me you don't love me."

"I," she couldn't look at him and tell him that. A hard breath exhaled. She loved him too much to say she didn't. Her voice threaded with despair, she begged, "Please, Jashar, please don't go after him. I would die if anything happened to you, especially because of me."

She clung to his sleeves. "Don't go, please, let me go. I'd rather go with him then let him harm you."

He gripped her chin holding her head taut. Pure unyielding steel in his voice, he told her, "Listen to me. I am going after him. You cannot stop me. You can only help me by not making me have to worry about you. Just promise me you will not leave the castle walls. For any reason."

He waited, holding her with his grip and his eyes. "I am going. Promise me, Maratia. Please."

The fight went out of her, but fear crowded into her eyes. "I…promise, Jashar."

He hugged her to him. "I love you, Maratia. I will return to show you how much." Then he kissed her and was gone.

Chapter Twenty-Seven

Jashar and his men traveled for days seeking out the danger to Maratia, with no luck. There was not a sign of him.

Yet word kept filtering to them from the villages they passed that Valmyrjr was there.

Kaer rode up beside Jashar. He could feel his brother's frustration. He was on edge, had been since they heard Maratia's ex-fiancé was on the hunt for her. Jashar was not going to rest until the threat to her was gone.

"Jash," Kaer moved closer.

"Aye?" Jashar not once stopped scanning the area.

"He's not out here. We would have found him. The only other un-scouted area is the far side, opposite from where he would have come."

"Then there is where we'll go." Jashar hooked the reins turning the horse. "Spread it through the men."

"Aye," Kaer nodded. Kicking his steed with his heels he turned back to advise the league where they were going.

They travelled back to the far side of their lands.

The wind was brisk, it was growing late, the night clouds were gathering overhead. The horses were twitchy; they thought they were heading back home.

Jashar had a strange feeling in the pit of his gut. It grew increasingly uneasy by the minute.

He stopped his horse and dismounted. Then he crouched to the ground.

Daron and Kaer came right up, the other men grouped in a semi-circle behind them. They had all been experiencing an odd floating feeling of agitation.

"What is it?" Daron leaned over with his forearm resting across his saddle, the thick worn leather of his jacket creaked on the leather saddle.

Restless, the horse stomped, tail swished. Daron grasped the reins in his gloved fist and made a quieting noise. The horse immediately settled.

"Tracks. Many. A team." Still crouching, Jashar peered into the surrounding woods. He stood up and trod over to nearby scrub. His arm reached out, he touched some leaves.

His brothers followed him.

His hand on his hips, Jashar, looked around the area.

"Broken branches, lots of horses. They aren't ours, none of our teams are out in this section." He scrubbed his hands through his hair and stared up at the night sky.

Everyone waited silently watching him. He turned slowly towards his horse, then glanced up at his brothers.

"What?" Kaer asked.

The other horses were getting restless, jumpy. They started lifting their legs to stomp on the dirt trail, and snorting their unease.

Mounting his stallion, Jashar dragged a sleeve over his eyes. Dawning crept with tiny footsteps across his face. "Fuck, Kaer."

He jerked his reins announcing, "They came in opposite from their land knowing we would have gone in their land's direction to begin looking for them. They must have gone straight to the castle as soon as we left!" He kicked his horse.

The horse's hooves pawed up in the air before he jumped and took off to the castle.

Kaer and Daron shared a quick worried glance before galloping behind him. The steeds pounded the ground, sounding like thunder rumbling in the sky.

It took so long to get there Jashar could hardly think. His head pounded with the horses hooves, he had a bad feeling.

When he reached the castle his heart plummeted. It was too quiet, no one was around. He hopped off the horse, for once not seeing to the steed's immediate care, and raced to the main doors.

He grasped the big iron handle and thrust the door open.

"*Shit-*" Daron barked, his brothers almost ran straight into Jashar.

The three men stood stunned.

There were guards lying around the great room. Blood was everywhere. At least some were still alive, they could hear moans.

Jashar saw McGee lying by the staircase. He ran to him, dropped to his knees beside the fallen guard.

He shoved his hand under McGee's head and gently lifted it. The guard's eyes were closed, he was bruised, beaten, and was covered with blood.

"McGee, McGee," he called. Jashar could hear the guard breathing, he was alive, he gently patted his face. "McGee, tell me what the hell happened."

McGee's eyes stayed closed.

Jashar yelled, "Guard! Robert McGee!"

McGee's eyes cracked, they rolled under bruised swollen lids, then flickered with recognition. "King, Sire," he let out a pained breath.

"McGee, talk to me, what happened, answer me."

"Aye, Sire." He put a hand to his stomach and winced. "It was her, the princessa's people, her fiancé. They...came through the back woods, someone let them into the rear of the castle. They were-" he tried to sit up. Jashar put an arm around his back and helped him.

Grunting, McGee sucked in a wounded inhale. "They, came upon us secretly, Sire, they were inside and scattering like rats. There were too many of them, an ambush." His head drooped, he shook it. Sweat and blood sprayed.

His heart beating hard, voice tight with fear, Jashar ground out, "The princessa, Maratia, is she-" he broke off at the pained, shamed expression on the guard's dirty face. He gripped the guard's shoulders and shook him. "Tell me, McGee, tell me!"

McGee put a hand to the floor, his arm rigid to hold his torso up. He glanced fuzzy-eyed at the king.

About to blow up with aggrieved impatience, Jashar was watching him, waiting, but McGee's eyes were hard to see under the black and blue swollen lids.

The guard looked away quickly in guilt. "I tried, Sire. I ran to barricade her in her rooms but I was waylaid by men hiding on the second floor landing." His head shook miserably. With terrible remorse, he told the king, "He," he lifted his head to look Jashar in the eye, "took her."

"How long?"

McGee squinted to the open doorway to judge the time. The sun indicated the morning had moved well on. He blanched when he realized how long he'd been out cold. "Four, five hours." McGee spat out blood and a tooth.

"My sister? My parents, my little brother Makir? Tell me they're all right?" Jashar's fingers dug into McGee's arms like steel pegs.

McGee struggled to stay sitting up, he nodded, blood dripped to the floor from his mouth and nose. "Aye, Sire. I believe they are safe, locked in the back rooms of your father's chambers. They only wanted Maratia. They only hurt whoever tried to stop them or get in their way."

The guard nodded at the men sprawled around the room. "They are all valiant, Sire, they fought to protect her. After they beat me they threw me down the staircase." He slumped.

Jashar called over one of his men. "See to this guard, soldier, get him care. Have people check the injured, bring in the physicians." Then he jumped up and headed for the door.

Kaer and Daron were already outside preparing the horses.

Kaer looked up at his brother's approach. "He has her?" He could already tell by the mutinous rise of Jashar's jaw, he could see his face was implacable, clear of emotion.

But Kaer knows Jashar too well. The tenseness of his broad shoulders, the unblinking of his eyes, the grit of his teeth.

Jashar was scared to death for his princessa.

Chapter Twenty-Eight

She had fought like a tigress, but Sammel Valmyrjr had bound her arms behind her and put her on his horse.

He held the reins as the horse danced, kicked up dirt, neighing his urge to gallop across the meadows.

Then Valmyrjr stuck his boot in the stirrup and climbed up to sit down heavily behind Maratia.

The horse again danced sideways at the sudden weight.

Maratia breathed in leather from the saddle and Sammel's clothing. Her nose wrinkled at the odor of sweat on his skin, dust from the shuffling horses prickled in her eyes.

Sitting behind her, Sammel had given the signal to head out. No longer worried about stealth, they kicked their horses, whipped the reins and pounded out of Spiremoor.

Now they had ridden for hours, and Sammel's arm was like a steel belt around her middle holding her tight against him. He hadn't said a word. His men had brought her kicking and screaming down the stairs.

Maratia had cried out when she saw McGee lying in a bloody pool on the floor. She didn't know if he was dead or alive. They dragged her past the other men lying injured on the granite tiles.

When they went outside, the men had thrust her at Sammel.

He had gripped her jaw, jerking her face up so he could look at her. He clenched her face with his fingers so hard it brought tears to her eyes. He had only stared at her. Then abruptly released her.

When they slowed the pace, Maratia was so tired, she tried not to lean against Sammel, she shuddered to think of touching him. But he still had his arm wound tightly around her.

She finally lolled back against his chest almost asleep. His hand moved up to clutch her breast. She tensed then struggled to get away from him.

He only chuckled in her ear, nipped the tip of it and laughed when she shrugged away from him. She squirmed against his leather vest feeling his weapons, various knives and throwing stars digging into her back.

"Ah, my sweet fiancée, you were just getting cozy with me. Relax back against my chest. I have waited months to hold you again." He pressed his lips against the side of her face, brutally crushing her breast in his hand when she kept struggling.

Growling in her ear, he said, "Damn, Maratia," roughly groping her now with both hands. "I can hardly feel you beneath that heavy dress and tight bindings."

With her hands bound behind her she was defenseless, she could only try to twist from his grasp. Her wrists were tied so tightly she couldn't even punch back at his leather clad breeches.

His grating chuckle at her useless struggles in her ear felt like bugs crawling over her skin, the heat of his triumphant breath searing her neck.

He moved one arm around to hold her taut again and pulled at her skirt, tugging it up so he could get his hand on her bare thigh.

This sent her into a furious hysterical frenzy of resistance- Maratia thrashed, bucking and jerking her body to throw herself out of his clutches and off the horse. He only clamped her writhing body tighter to his.

"Maratia," he cooed. "I just want a small feel, you've always denied me even the tiniest of touches of your precious lady canal." He pushed his hand up- she screamed and threw herself so violently they both almost tumbled off the horse.

"Goddammit Maratia!" Sammel had to jerk his hand out to hold them both steady. His angry breath swatted her hair around her face.

He huffed in fury, "You will pay for that, honey," and he roughly groped her breasts again with his big hard hands, cruelly pinching them just for spite.

He squeezed her viciously then released her. Calming down, he said with a mean chuckle, "I will have to wait until we are alone." His arm around her waist, he hugged her so hard against him she worried he'd crack her ribs.

"I can't wait to strip you." His deep voice quiet, growling tone harsh, he whispered with a malicious smile, "I will start with some nasty smacks on your hot little ass and luscious bare tits with my hand and my belt.

"Then maybe I'll whack you on that pussy that I have yet to see, with my belt, the buckle part, then I'll switch to a whip to pay you back for that escape attempt you just tried.

Are you as excited as I am to reconnect?" His sneer turned back into the mean chuckle when he felt her shudder.

Nuzzling her ear, he murmured, "Oh, and if you're wondering, yes, you will also be punished for leaving me. Greatly. As I was saying, I plan to strip you and bend you forward over the kneeling bench so your naked bottom is high up in the air. Then," he pause, licking his lips thinking about his plans.

"I will pull your arms out and down in front of you and tie them. Once you are immobile, I will spread those beautiful legs of yours and whip the hell out of you with my bullwhip. It will peel slices off your lovely skin."

He licked her neck. "In between whipping your lovely ass, I will fuck you from behind. Again and again and again. Won't you just love that?"

As his sadistic lust built, he snapped the reins to make the tired horse move faster.

"Then I will slam you onto your back while I fuck you so you will see who the man is inside you. The man who owns you. You will quickly learn how to obey your husband."

His gaze lowered to her chest, the corners of his vile mouth curled up. "Yes, we will see how your poor nipples like my bullwhip." He laughed out loud at the color leeching from her rosy cheeks.

Maratia bit her tongue to keep from whimpering. She said nothing, swallowing the bile that rose up her throat. As long as Jashar wasn't hurt, she would learn to tolerate, live with, Sammel's torture.

Like he could read her mind, he said, "I can't imagine that you are still a virgin, if you even were one when you left. That never mattered to me. I just always wanted to have you. Those meager molestations, a grope here and there that

I did as you were growing up were never enough to take the edge off my desire.

"I've never been able to relieve myself of this insane infatuation I have for you. It's endured all these years. It is doubtful I will ever be rid of it, even once I've fucked you and beaten you for not wanting me, until *I* pass out."

He tugged the arm around her so hard with a vicious jerk against him she couldn't stop the cry that tore from her lips.

Sammel smiled at that. "I'm sure you were poked by at least one man while you were gone. I heard the king himself took great interest in you. One certainly can't blame him with that sweet beauty of yours."

He hugged her hard again. "Well, you will soon forget all about him when I am on top of you, pounding between those ivory legs of yours. Eh? You will pay for humiliating me by leaving."

They traveled for days, sleeping in the woods.

Each night, Sammel tied Maratia to a tree sitting up and laid a blanket over her. He had his men sleep in a circle around her, threatening them with instant death should anyone go near her.

He had no desire to fuck her in front of his men; that would have to wait until they were in the privacy of his chambers. Some might chafe at the way he planned on taking her.

Finally, they reached her land, the region of Saorghlanadh. It was another day's ride until they reached her hometown, Ailanthus. But he didn't take her to her home; he took her straight to his estate.

His estate sat on a hill. Made of dark stone the structure looked like a giant black gargoyle perched overlooking the village. Now, at night, lanterns blinked and twinkled like a thousand fireflies down in the dark valley below it.

The hill was more of a wide flat terrace. Sammel had managed to have a moat channeled around his mansion. A thick wooden and steel drawbridge was the only way inside the mansion.

The back side of the hill was so steep it was impossible to climb. Sharp iron posts circled the entire building. Sammel kept most of his men fortified in a semi-circle around the front, with a few guards patrolling the rear.

His home rivaled Jashar's castle in size, with equal modernization, comfort, and glamor.

Sammel's family, his mother, father, two adolescent brothers and a conglomerate of other relatives resided in one side of the estate.

On the other side contained his commands of soldiers, and for those not wedded, the women he brought in to please them.

Sammel's own chambers were central and way in the back. He kept them guarded and no one who wasn't invited came to his rooms. He'd had women brought to him daily, their tortured screams muted by the thick walls.

While he had search parties looking for Maratia, he'd had his rooms refurbished. When he retrieved her, and he always knew he would, she would never leave his home again. She could raise his children without ever stepping outside of the estate.

He had an adjoining room made to keep her in when she wasn't in his bed with him. He'd had locks and chains and pulleys installed, along with a wooden pony and other sexual torture devices made.

Every time he became so enraged at the thought of her leaving him, he had another device installed to appease his fury until he could get his hands on her and get her back to his estate.

In the meantime, he vented his rage on the hapless women he forced on the torture apparatus. Some lived, some died. They were disposed of without thought.

Their families knew better than to come to his door or to the local authorities regarding their missing women. Sammel's reach and wrath made even the fiercest of people afraid to lose their heads.

After so many, he eventually learned how to bring a woman to the brink of death, and stop at the last moment. Many of the *fortunate* females who managed to survive, bare husks of the women they once were, were sent home to convalesce. Not that they ever really did recover, physically or emotionally from the horrendous acts of the savage man.

Last thing he wanted was to have Maratia die from his torture. Sammel Valmyrjr was a rich and powerful blue-blooded sadist. No one was brave enough to speak out against him.

As they came in sight of his estate Maratia spoke for the first time. "My parents…"

"Ah," his voice guttural against her ear, he rubbed his chin in her hair. "Your parents are no longer involved with us. Since you took it upon yourself to run while engaged to me, they gave you over to me to deal with."

He brought his horse to a halt. The other men came to slow stops as they gathered behind him, hooves clomping on the packed dirt.

"Deal with?" She twisted in his arms. "I insist you let me go right now. You have no rights over me. Let me down and I will walk to my home."

He laughed like she had told a funny joke. "Not going to happen, Princess. Your parents will visit you in a few days so they can see that all is well with you. I can't take the chance of them seeing your bruises. Then, when they leave," he grasped her chin, yanked her head up and roughly kissed her, "we will begin our fun."

He smiled at the revulsion on her face.

With her hands bound she couldn't wipe off the wetness he deliberately left smeared over her lips.

"By the time the wedding date arrives, you will have time to heal to look as splendid an angel as you do right now, then," he forced her head up and brutally kissed her, "we will begin our honeymoon and continue on with your penance!"

He held her so she was forced to look him in the eye, with their faces bare inches apart. So close his breath wisped her hair.

"Maratia," he sighed, "since we are separated by 15 years, I had to wait for you to reach adulthood before I could press my suit. Your damned parents kept you under lock and key or I'd have had you long before now. I have wanted you forever.

"When I finally got my hands on you, you slipped away. But I have you now. Your castigation, your punishment will vary, but it will never end. You will never forget what will happen if you ever try to run from me again."

He smiled at the fright that sparked in her eyes. She wrenched from him, but he only laughed, holding her taut.

"Ah, I love that fire in you, my princess. I hope it relates to the bedroom!" He kissed her, tried to push her mouth open but she kept her lips clamped.

"You will learn not to fight me, you willful little bitch," he snarled. Dropping the reins, he jabbed a thumb in her mouth to pry it open, then he put his hand to her neck and squeezed, pushing her head back so her neck arched painfully.

She gasped, her eyes bugged, her mouth opened.

He growled with warning, "Keep it open, and don't even think of biting me, you will lose those pretty pearlies." He lowered his mouth over hers, shoved his tongue in and violently invaded her mouth, sucking her tongue without regard to the pain he dealt.

When Maratia was about to pass out from her neck being stretched, her windpipe forced closed, he finally released her.

The men were fidgeting around them. Sammel sighed and swung down from his horse. Maratia's body slumped right into his arms.

Carrying her, he gave out orders, "See that the perimeter is secured. If that bastard king tries to come after her, I want him dead before he even gets in sight of the mansion."

Half unconscious, Maratia could still hear him. She tensed, tried to struggle, but he held her so tightly she could barely draw a breath.

"Settle down, my princess. There will be no hero coming to save you. We will marry and have children, my heirs. You need to get used to that right now, or you will be miserable."

He glared down at her. Snarling, "Hear me, Maratia, I will brook no other man in your thoughts. If I think your mind wanders from me to another, mark my words," he glared darkly at her, "he will die unpleasantly, and you will be severely disciplined."

A guard opened the door so he could carry her inside his estate. He passed through the main foyer to the east wing where the kitchen areas were.

Before he entered the main kitchen, he stopped at a door. He set her down to open the door. Before her feet hit the ground Maratia ran.

Her legs were stiff and sore from the days of riding the horse, her hands still tied.

Sammel stood with his hands on his hips laughing like a cruel hyena as she stumbled and lurched back through the kitchen.

"Ah, my princess," he chortled at her physical distress. "I see you have learned nothing." He casually strode behind her like a feral beast.

Maratia fell against the wall with a cry; her legs would not do as she ordered. She put her arms against the wall trying to brace herself as she kept working towards escape although she knew it was futile.

With his long legs and muscular physique, he easily caught up, moved directly in front of her and stood just inside the arched door of the main kitchen, his hands back on his lean hips.

He had large hands, surprisingly hard and rough for an aristocrat. He enjoyed doing his own punishing, the beating and flogging of his insubordinates, and captured prisoners.

Her chest rising and falling in rapid pants, pressing her back on the wall to keep upright, Maratia choked back tears of frustration. Her struggle to cease the shaking in her legs was also in vain.

"You always were a sassy willful brat, Maratia, I see you have not changed." Sammel grabbed a handful of her hair, massaged it with his fingers. "Your latest master must have been too lenient on you. He probably fell for that frail beauty."

Exhausted, frightened, and angry, Maratia hovered against the wall to keep from falling and glared at her ex-fiancé.

Well above average height, although aristocratic with an arrogant dictatorial bearing, he kept his dark blond hair neatly combed straight back exposing the widow's peak, but never bothered to try to hide the sick cruelty in his dark blue eyes.

If not for the malevolence that tainted his face, Sammel would be a strikingly handsome man. Sammel Valmyrjr derived enjoyment out of hurting people that were not as strong as him, or as rich, or as titled. Or people he just hated, or simply annoyed him.

As his eyes narrowed on her, his lips edged up in victory. With thoughts of the decadent pleasure he will enjoy while reprimanding Maratia for daring to flee from him, excited heat trilled straight up his legs and surged into his groin.

He lewdly palmed his arousal over the leather breeches and got more trenchant satisfaction at the look of disgust Maratia shot him.

To Sammel, the only hard part that he finally grasped regarding Maratia's pending reprimand was knowing when to stop, how far to punish her, when right at the edge, the precipice where pain shades into death, or permanent mutilation.

He wrapped her hair around his fist to pull her head up.

She glared defiantly at him, but she couldn't prevent the terrified shudder that rifled down her body. His morbid intent to harm her was written all over his gloating face.

"I don't blame you, Princess, for being with that other man, the king, it wasn't your fault." He pulled her face closer, she closed her eyes but he yanked her hair forcing her to open them.

"With your exquisite beauty, you will never escape being made a man's pet. You can't help that; a woman can't elude a man if he desires her enough. And you, my dear, fulfill a man's deepest, and darkest," his mouth creased with hedonistic fervor, "desires. At least you will fulfill mine."

Maratia suddenly pushed from the wall to run past him.

With a delighted snarl, her hair still around his fist, Sammel grasped her shoulder and slammed her back hard against the wall.

Her head banged on the stone almost knocking her out. When she crumpled, he caught her up in his arms.

His nasty laugh hovering over Maratia, he said, "All right, Princess, fun and games are over for this eve. I will take you to your…bed for the night." Sammel looked down at Maratia.

Her head drooped with pained dizziness from banging into the stone wall, her eyes fluttered unfocused, she no longer put up a fight.

Carrying her, Sammel stepped through the door.

Fighting to gain full consciousness, at first Maratia thought she was still out of it because it was dark. She forced her lids half way up.

By the jostling of his steps, he was going down stairs. Goose pumps from the sudden damp cold popped up her arms. Dread filled her belly as they descended the dark stairs into the bowels of the building.

"Ah, you are back with me, I can feel you all rigid and anxious, my lovely soon-to-be-bride. You are right to be scared." The sadistic thrill at her fear resonated in his voice.

When they reached the bottom, he moved from the steps and stopped.

Maratia felt like her skin was going to crawl right off her body.

A few Lanterns placed around faintly lit the horror around her. It was worse than Jashar's dungeon.

Harsh stone walls and floor with tiny windows way up barely let in the paltry cool silver light of the moon.

The room was completely empty except for some wooden contraptions, and spiders the size of Maratia's hand stretched on the webs across the desolate windows.

Already she could hear the skittering of rodent feet running along the walls, hiding in the shadowed corners of the miserable chamber.

Chains attached to walls hung like iron skeletons, the smell was dank cold rock.

As her eyes adjusted to the dark, she looked at the wooden devices, and her heart skipped a beat before it started racing, beating frantically. The hair on the back of her neck literally stood up, her blood ran cold.

She recognized the devices as torture contraptions. Her eyes bounced around the room glancing at a rack, to a pillory that was made to lock a kneeling person's head and hands,

Her gaze moved up to see a bastinado- a bar to hang a person by his ankles, then lowered to a breaking wheel in a dark corner. She had no clue what some of the devices were.

When her eyes lit on the Scold's bridal used to lock over a woman's head, she screamed and jolted in his arms, twisting and jumping in a frenzy to get loose.

"Whoa there, precious," Sammel burst out with laughter at her terror. Letting her drop to her feet he stood behind her and held her arms. He shoved a leg between hers bracing a boot against the inside of one of her feet. If she lifted a leg to kick him she would fall.

Sammel held her inert. His gaze fell to her panting chest rising higher and higher in her panic. The more frantic her breathing the harder his shaft grew.

She tried to wrench from his grasp but he only laughed more. Even if he wasn't bigger and stronger than Maratia, with her wrists tied she was helpless.

He started to drag her further into the harrowing room. She fought harder, he ignored her struggles and dragged her deeper into the dank cellar.

It struck Maratia like a blade in her heart that the further he dragged her into the stone room the less chance of her ever getting away, of ever seeing the light of day again.

So terrified, her lungs turned to stone, she couldn't draw a breath. She knew begging wouldn't help; it would only enhance his sexual thrill at her terror. But she needed to talk to him, get him to see this was wrong.

"Sammel," her voice was too tiny and thin, she inhaled deeply and tried again. "Sammel, listen, it has been a- a- some time since we- we saw each other, let's talk."

He ruthlessly jerked her arm causing her to again cry out in sharp pain.

"You can talk all you want, Princess," he sneered continuing to drag her through the room going deeper into the shadows. "To me, women have one use, make that two, I want heirs. Nothing you can say will make any fucking impression on me, change my treatment of you." His revolting chuckles stung her ears.

"If you talk too much," he snickered wickedly, "look around, I have plenty of ways to shut you up if I feel like it." He motioned his head to steel masks with bars across the mouth opening hanging on the wall, and metal balls to shove into a person's mouth.

Maratia turned her head with a sob. It was useless to try to convince him to let her go.

Sammel brought her to an iron pole that went from floor to ceiling. A chain was hooked to it. At the pole, he pushed her to sit on the cold floor and crouched beside her.

He picked up the end of the chain and clasped it on her ankle. His head cocked merrily when he heard her breath hitch and knew she bit back a cry.

"Here, Maratia," he shuffled behind her. "Here's some good news. I'm going to untie your wrists." He removed the binds and gripped her jaw before she could speak or move her sore arms, and kissed her like a rabid animal.

Then he released her, leaving her lip torn and bleeding, and stood up. Stepping back, he looked down at her and liked what he saw.

Her face was a helix of fear and foreboding and despair. The indigo eyes were blurred with tears; she was gritting her teeth to stall their chattering. The blood smeared on her mouth from his brutal kiss titillated Sammel so much his body vibrated with sexual exhilaration.

He grinned at her. In the dark his handsome face was demonic, alive with barbarous delight at his plans for her, and even better, her awareness of them. She will have all night to think about what he's going to do to her and be at the height of the vivid terror he was shooting for.

"Well, I guess it's goodnight, my princess. You sleep tight, oh wait, I forgot," he hurried over to a stool and lifted a blanket and brought it to her. "I don't want you to be uncomfortable honey."

He dropped the blanket on the floor beside her. She didn't move. He tugged at the hem of his vest pulling the leather down over his big chest then crossed his arms.

"Just think, Maratia, how you will enjoy my luxurious bed after spending some time, a lot of time, here." He grinned at her gasp as he turned and strode to one lantern and turned it off. Then the next.

He reached for the last by the stairs, the light a halo on his dark blond hair, when she finally spoke.

"Sammel," she hated to beg, "please, the light, please don't leave me in the pitch black." When he hesitated, she said, "Please."

He had always known what a sadistic bastard he was, but even he was surprised at the kick he got when he snuffed out the last lantern and trudged heavily up the stairs so she could hear every footstep until he was at the top.

He closed the door, the locked snicked loud, the sound banging down the stairs with its finality.

Maratia climbed unsteadily to her feet.

Sammel had extinguished all of the lights. The skittering grew louder right away, even the spiders in the windows seemed to grow larger, hairier.

She reached down and grabbed the chain and yanked on it. She continued to yank it from the pole and then struggled to get it off her ankle, but she knew it would all be to no avail. Sammel was no amateur to binding people to keep them from escaping.

But she had to do something. She couldn't just sit there petrified, letting the fear build until she went insane, listening to the rats scurry, waiting for Sammel to…return and begin his sadistic fun.

Then, she knew, this would be child's play compared to what he had in store for her.

When a picture of Jashar gazing at her like he did with lust and love blazing from his dark eyes floated in her mind, she cursed, shook her head sharply to dispel the image.

She couldn't dwell on what could have been. Sniffing back the tears sneaking out of her eyes, if she allowed thoughts of the loss of a life with Jashar to sift in, she would lose her mind right now.

Swallowing the sobs clawing up her trembling throat, Maratia jerked and yanked, tugged and pulled, listening to the sounds of life scuttling around her in the lightless room.

Chapter Twenty-Nine

His heart wanted to push his horse, race as fast as he could force the animal to go, but Jashar shut down the uncontrollable urge to go all out to get to her.

His men rode steady with him and he couldn't use up everyone's, human and beasts' energy before they got to the Saorghlanadh region.

As it was, they traveled hard long days and much of the night to get to the land that bordered Thuas sa Spéir province. He couldn't imagine how Maratia had gotten so far from home when she first fled Valmyrjr.

Flanked by his brothers, Kaer and Daron, Jashar felt invincible. But it wasn't for himself he feared, it was Maratia. He had to fight the continuous images of that bastard Valmyrjr beating her, or raping her, or…worse.

He sent a few of his fleetest men and steeds ahead to recon Valmyrjr's estate, his full compound and grounds.

Jashar was already familiar with the Saorghlanadh area that Maratia's village Ailanthus lay in. He has been through it many times while searching for insurgents that had prowled and preyed upon his own region of Thuas sa Spéir.

He was even vaguely familiar with Maratia's particular village, Ailanthus. He has met her father, King Lanaris Araminte.

Most of the kings of their land, at least the peaceful ones, have met to maintain their mutual respect. They meet periodically to keep truces not to invade each other's lands.

King Araminte has seldom had to war, as his lands are not that desirable to others. Which is fine with the king, it kept his people at peace.

Jashar had two messengers sent to the king advising of his presence on Araminte's land. He didn't need Araminte to think they were under attack and gather a coalition of warriors to come up behind Jashar and his troops when they breech Valmyrjr's estate.

Jashar didn't slow until he neared Ailanthus. The village was dark. The teams of well-trained horses became still, not a snort, not a tail swish. The dust didn't even stir beneath their muddy hooves.

Under the stars, Kaer and Daron pulled close to Jashar, and they all stayed still.

It wasn't long before what Jashar was waiting for appeared. His recon.

Two of the six men trotted up to Jashar.

In the background, other animals, farm animals, bayed and grunted and croaked around the night. Curtains at a few thatched houses fluttered as nervous, curious villagers peeked out.

One of the recons gripped his reins to make his horse motionless. He spoke, low and quiet. Jashar and his brothers leaned into listen. "Sire, as suspected, the estate is many leagues long. It is surrounded by a moat."

"A moat?" Kaer repeated bemused. "Are you kidding? What is this, ancient castle country?" He looked at Daron who was trying to keep a straight face and quipped, "Ya think there're serpents in that there swamp?"

Twitters around him were quickly hushed at the severe glare Jashar shot his men.

Jashar asked, "How big is the water?"

The recon whistled quietly. "It's big. Big enough there's no way to get across the lawn and swim the water without the guards seeing you."

Jashar said nothing, nodded for him to go on.

"Anyway," the recon continued, "there is a drawbridge," he paused as Jashar shot Kaer a look to lock it up.

Kaer winked at his brother and turned somber. He feared for Maratia too, but he fought fear with humor. Jashar fought it with action. He strategized and then took action.

"What else?" Jashar asked.

The recon wiped his forehead on his sleeve. They had ridden hard and fast. "Sire, the drawbridge is the only way in. Not good if there's a fire. Anyway, the grounds are heavily guarded."

His hands on his hips, boots akimbo, Jashar said, "Everywhere?"

The recon shook his head. "Nay, Sire. The back of the hill the estate is on is steep, so steep it curves inward like a gigantic shovel scooped out part of it. Because of the inaccessibility it is less heavily guarded. It cannot be climbed."

All eyes were on Jashar as he digested the information. He rubbed his eyes with the pads of his fingers. He squinted at the recon while thinking. "What else? Tell me more about the area surrounding the mansion."

The recon nodded. "Aye. There are the woods that cover miles before opening to the expanse of short grass."

"Are there forests below the house, on the steep side of the hill?"

He nodded again. "Aye. The trees creep right up to the bottom of the hill. Apparently Valmyrjr is unconcerned about the cover since no one can get up the hill. Even our most expert climbers would be unable to scale it. There's not a rock, root or shrub for a climber to utilize, it's all pure dirt."

A slight crisp breeze ruffled the leaves on the nearby trees, several horses stomped their feet albeit silently.

"Officer Smythe," Jashar said to the soldier, "how high is the hill?"

Smythe considered the question, he glanced at the other men that had gone with him. They all shrugged.

"Actually, at the front of the estate, where the road flows up to the house for the horses and wagons to trod, it rolls up grading higher as it goes. The back of the hill is nowhere near as high. The hill the rear of the estate faces, after the scooped out part, it rolls on gently for miles enabling the manor to look over the valley."

"You didn't answer my question." Jashar frowned without looking at the officer.

Smythe's neck turned red. "Aye, sorry Sire. I believe the back is only fifty, maybe sixty feet high?" He looked to the others who all nodded at him.

Jashar's eyes were closed picturing the scene. Without opening them, he said, "What else? What else is near or around the estate?"

Smythe glanced at the others. Brows wrinkled in visualizing the land, but they didn't recall anything else except great expanse of lawn.

"Oh," Smythe snapped his fingers. "There is an iron fence that goes the circumference of the entire back area. It was probably intended to keep people from falling off the steep edge of the hill as much as keeping people like us out."

"Is it outside of the moat?" Kaer asked with a look to Jashar.

"Aye. The fence has sharp spires, but I think you, Sire," he bowed slightly, "have the ability to get over the fence. Also, there are four poles at each corner of the fence, maybe ten feet high?"

Light sparked in Jashar's dark eyes. "How close is the fence to the edge of the back of the hill?" Beside him, Kaer and Daron started slow grins seeing where he was going."

"Sire," not seeing it Smythe was confused, "it goes right up to the edge."

One of the other recons added, "You can see the iron fence from below. There are also very low windows in the building. It's surprising since if there's huge rain that moat is going to fill up and likely seep into those windows.

"Anyway, we had split up, half of us scanned the front and sides, and the others went around the back woods to probe the rear bottom of the hill."

He didn't grin, but some of the worry lines in Jashar's forehead eased. He said to one of the warriors, "*Bine*. Get Jerrison, see if he brought those boomerangs. They came in handy knocking those noisy birds out of the trees that gave away our hiding places last mission."

He turned to another and ordered, "Get Drawlings and tell him to bring his bow and arrow. Kaer," he waited until both men took off.

Kaer asked, "What is your plan, Jash?" as he and Daron moved in closer. The other warriors crowded in as one solid mass. "I can see the wheels turning inside that head. I have an idea, but-"

"Aye," Jashar was pulling up on his reins. "You two take three-quarters, no, take all of the men except for Jerrison and Drawlings. When I give the signal, you storm down the lawn to the front. Cause as much noise and disturbance as possible."

"And you will be?" Daron inquired not sure where Jashar was going.

"Jerrison, Drawlings and I will be at the bottom of the back of the hill. They both are superior with their skills. I'm going to have both attach ropes to the boomerang and also the iron arrows and have them throw and shoot up, hopefully they can get the ropes around those iron poles."

"Uh," Daron was shaking his head, he wasn't sure he liked this plan. He glanced at Kaer who had the same frown on his face.

Moving his horse closer to his brother, Kaer started to speak but Jashar spoke right over him. "If they are successful, I will climb up the rope. Hop the fence, swim the moat and get into one of those low windows." He was already turning his horse around.

"Nay, Jash," Kaer said quickly. "I don't like this at all. The moat? They can easily pick you off from the land before you get a few feet."

"I don't plan on there being anyone there to see me. Once you storm the front, all attention will be on you. Any guards that remain at the back I will take care of."

"Jash," Kaer said loudly, "at least bring more men, and either me or Daron-"

"Nay." Jashar was riding towards the two men he'd called for. "Too many men and we're more likely to be spotted. I am all in black, I will blend into the dark shadows."

He kicked his horse and disappeared into the crowd to pick up his men and headed down through the forest to the back of the hill.

The three warriors trod as quietly as possible through the woods. Fortunately it was dense enough for cover but sparse enough with scant shrubbery and thin groves of trees.

They would have cover but the forest would be fairly easy to get through. They were cloaked by the dark night as they made their way to the hill.

Jashar dismounted then cautiously left the cover of the trees and conscious of leaves crunching underfoot, he moved carefully in one direction, then went a few yards in the other.

After checking the area, he saw there were no guards at the bottom of the hill, and they had passed none as they went through the woods. He waved the two warriors over.

Both men left their horses and promptly joined him at the foot of the hill. They all looked up at the fence.

Spikes around six feet high, spaced only a few inches apart, were visible right at the edge of the hill. As the recon had described, in four corners there were tall iron poles with space on either side of them but not wide enough for a man to pass through.

Jashar turned to the men. "Well?"

Both men grinned and nodded. Jerrison replied, "Easy as the sun sliding into the horizon."

At Jashar's nod, the two men each pulled out their gear.

Jashar had several lengths of rope he'd taken off his horse. He handed one to each man.

Jerrison put on gloves then tied an end of the rope around a large, almost an arm's length long boomerang.

Drawlings tied his rope to one of his huge iron arrows he used to take out big game.

Both men moved closer to the base of the hill. They looked to Jashar. When he nodded, Jerrison flung his boomerang with all his might. It passed close to the fence, but not close enough.

His teeth grit, Jerrison pulled the rope to bring the boomerang in for another try. While he readied, Drawlings put his arrow to his bow and let loose. The thick arrow flew in a silent arc through the air and passed right over the fence.

Drawlings tugged on the rope until the arrow made of iron came up horizontally flush against the fence. He turned to his king with a proud face.

Jashar gave him a sharp nod, "Good job, Drawlings, good job." He turned to Jerrison who was preparing to throw again.

He would prefer if the rope went around a pole and back down. He didn't know if the arrow could slip sideways and slide out from between the pole and the connecting rods. "Go," he said to Jerrison.

Jerrison pulled his arm back and flung the boomerang. It sailed up into the night, swung around a pole and came right back, down the hill, right to Jerrison who caught it with both gloved hands and a hard grunt.

His neck craned, Jashar could see the rope was strung right around one of the tall poles. He clapped Jerrison on the back. "That's perfect."

Jerrison pulled his lips in tight to hold back his grin. He jerked his jaw up indicating he had only done his job.

As soon as the warrior untied the rope from his boomerang, the men took both ends of the rope and wrapped it around a tree knotting it securely.

Jashar moved right to the base of the hill and started his climb. Hand over hand, gripping the rope, he moved swiftly, smoothly, never looking back down the hill at the other men.

When he reached the top, Jashar carefully peered over the edge.

There were ten guards. Most were hanging around near the side of the building talking.

When he made sure he had a good grip on the edge of the hill, Jashar let out a whistle. His signal for his men to strike.

Suddenly there was a roar of noise and chaos coming from the front of the castle. In the rear, the guards all jumped and started for the anterior of the building.

But a few men pushed at some of the others, telling them to stay back.

In all, five disgruntled soldiers remained. Their agitation evident at being kept out of the fray of the fight, they paced the grounds in the dark trying to get a look at what was going on out front.

Jashar climbed over the top of the hill, easily scaled the fence and jumped silently to the ground landing in a crouch.

None of the soldiers saw or heard him. Like the panther he had killed as a child, Jashar raced silent and sleek and deadly across the grass to the closest guard.

The man's back was to him, he was watching his colleagues wandering in front of him squinting into the shrouded night.

It took less than a second for Jashar to kill the man with a sharp snap of his neck. He let him slump to the ground then dragged him towards the moat. Then he slipped stealthily over the grounds to the next closest man and took him down just as quietly and quickly.

His luck ran out when one of the remaining three men turned and saw him.

The soldier let out a shout and the others turned as well. They rushed him bellowing, with swords raised.

Jashar pulled out his sword strung to his back and struck at the first guard who lashed back at him with his own weapon.

While parrying, Jashar snatched a dagger out with his other hand and threw it at the closest warrior. The man let out a tiny scream before he crumpled to the ground.

Infuriated, the other men both came swinging and hacking at Jashar with their swords.

Jashar didn't have the time to fool with them. In a few powerful slashes, so fast there were only silver blurs, he took out both men. It was so loud out front with whoops and hollers, screams, and bellows, no one heard a sound from the back.

Running to the moat, Jashar slipped into the cool water. In a flash he swam the water to the lowest window he could see. When he got to it, he peered inside and let out a held breath.

It was a storeroom of sorts and no one was inside. Using his elbow, he tapped out the glass. It fell, shattering to the floor, with all the noise outside it was soundless.

Jashar put his hands on the sill and pulled himself up, using his feet to scrabble against the stone wall until he was able to slide through the broken window and into the dim room.

Now, all he needed to do was locate where Valmyrjr was keeping Maratia. He crept to the door, opened it slowly and peered out.

There were only a few people in the vast granite halls. Guards were hustling people into rooms. Shouts of, "Get in and lock the door! Put barricades behind it, let no one in but us!" echoed up and down the halls, and much the same could be heard from the above level.

In scant moments the halls were almost completely empty.

Jashar slipped out of the storeroom and moved silently down the corridor. He knew there were too many rooms in the mansion for him to check every door. He stood still and listened.

Around the corner two guards were gabbing excitedly about the attack, they were tossing out theories as to what was going on.

Jashar stepped into the corridor and moved quickly, but not too menacingly towards the guards. Speaking nervously, he babbled, "Hey, there, I'm scared where should I go? Where can I be safe?"

He kept moving, the guards were startled, they stared at him with their mouths open. Jashar kept jabbering in a frightened voice, his arms out asking for help getting closer and closer to the two men.

When he was a couple yards away, one guard looked him over. His eyes popped when he saw that Jashar was soaking wet, then they narrowed. He started to say something to his partner as he reached for his sword-

But by then Jashar was close enough- he leaped into the air and kicked one guard in the head, landed, and punched the other man in the face. Both were stunned, the guard kicked in the head slumped to the floor. Jashar knelt and swiftly broke his neck.

The other guard was reeling from the punch. Seeing his partner killed so quickly, so efficiently, he put a hand to his jaw and turned to run. But Jashar was quicker.

He caught the man, swung him around and slammed him against the wall then pummeled him until he was staggering. Jashar pushed him to the floor, crouched down beside him and drew his knife, and sliced it down the man's arm.

The guard screamed and cupped his hand over the wound to stop the blood.

"*Bine,*" Jashar said and raised his dagger over the man's chest. "I have your attention. I will plunge this knife into your heart in two seconds if you do not tell me where Valmyrjr is keeping the Princessa Maratia."

"Wha- wha-" the man had never been in a real warrior's fight, he started crying. "Please- please-"

"One-" Jashar raised the dagger higher.

"Wait! Please-"

"Two." He brought the dagger down and the man yelled, "The cellar! The cellar! The princess is in the cellar!" He choked; panicked breaths billowed his chest.

Jashar stopped the dagger's route. He grabbed the guard around the collar and jerked him to his feet. "Take me there. Any hesitation and I will cut off your right arm first."

"Uh," the man blanched, his mouth dropped. He held his hand over his bleeding wound. He was so scared he couldn't speak, he just nodded and pointed.

"Fine. Take me there, fast." Jashar let go of his collar and prodded him with his dagger.

Although still reeling from the beating, the man moved quickly down the corridor and then down several more hallways until they neared the kitchen.

They had not come across another soul on the way.

Outside the chaos went on. Screaming, shouting, they were too far inside to hear the clash of swords. His brothers were prime warriors but still some concern for their wellbeing niggled at Jashar.

To lose his brothers in a battle to rescue his beloved would be a horrendous blow. If he could have, he would have ordered them to stay safe at home. But, Kaer and Daron were the most skillful of soldiers and they would have laughed in his face if he had even hinted of them not being by his side on this dangerous quest.

"Th- there, that door, it- it's the cellar, she is being held there!"

Jashar pushed his dagger at the guard's throat. "How do you know she is in there?"

He gulped hard, blood oozed through the fingers clutching his arm and bruises were mushrooming all around his face.

"We all know. He's blabbed nonstop about it to everyone. He's thrilled with his," his Adam's apple bobbed, "torture chamber, and- and- gloated about what he was going to do with the princess when he finds her. He captured her, I was with his retinue that brought her back.

"He carried her through the mansion. There were guards posted in front of the cellar door, they must have fled when they heard the estate coming under attack."

The knife was tight against his throat, a trickle of blood trailed down his neck. The guard gasped for breath, his right eye was almost swollen shut.

"Why was he carrying her?" It might be better if Jashar didn't know, but he waited for the man to speak.

The guard's eyes flashed back and forth as if thinking, would this warrior kill him if he tells him, or will he kill him if he doesn't?

With an impatient growl, the knife carved into his flesh.

The guard gagged, gasped, stammered, "He- he bent her head back as far as he could, it squeezed her throat until she fell unconscious."

"Why was he-"

The guard blurted, spit flew out with his words, "He was kissing her, brutally. He was kissing her viciously like a fucking monster." His tone revealed he was sickened by his superior's actions. "And she's just a wee thing, delicate, fuck," he peered at Jashar out of one eye, the other was swollen shut.

"You," the one eye narrowed, "are you him? Are you her king? The warlord of Thuas sa Spéir?" The one eye widened in awe.

"Aye." Jashar moved the knife and turned his attention to the locked door.

The guard's voice deepened, his tone harsh, "Then get her, my lord, save her. I won't get in your way." He stared hard at Jashar, and bravely.

"Unlock the door," the king commanded.

The guard turned to the door, he shook his head. "I don't have a key to that iron bar."

Jashar moved to stand next to him and studied the lock and realized it wasn't secured." He could see the bar wasn't latched.

"That's good- uh-"

Jashar cracked him in the back of the skull with the dagger's handle, knocking him out. He couldn't trust him, but he didn't want him to be killed for not stopping Jashar, or calling out his presence.

He turned the lever and gingerly opened the door. His thoughts raced as to why the door was unlocked. Had she been moved? Was she dead? He couldn't let his mind go there.

It was dim, but Jashar could see lighted lanterns were strung on the stone walls and lit down the stairs.

As his foot hit the first step he heard voices. His heart started banging- he could hear Maratia, and a man.

He moved silently down step-by-step, preparing for an ambush.

When he reached the bottom of the stairs, he paused to scan the area.

Right away he saw Valmyrjr was right next to Maratia. He had one hand around her neck and the other he gripped the front of her dress in his fist. He was cursing at her.

And she, Jashar's stomach clenched to see her like that, in a dank stone cellar chained by the ankle to a metal pole.

As he continued to scan the room peripherally, his skin crawled. The more he saw, the more his stomach tossed. The chamber was filled with torture contraptions.

Fuck- he knew the man was a sick bastard, but this? The prick meant to use at least some of them on his beautiful Maratia.

"Ah, you did make it here, Warlord Jashar D'Avenant, King of Thuas sa Spéir." There was a bit of admiration underlying the hatred in Valmyrjr's ugly voice.

Jashar only had eyes for Maratia.

Those big indigo eyes radiated such love to him, his knees about buckled. He shifted his gaze to Valmyrjr. "Let her go and I and my men will leave you in peace. If you do not relinquish her, you will die."

A grisly grin smeared Valmyrjr's handsome face turning him as ugly as his voice. "I'm thinking no. You could not have brought enough men to take on my troops, it is you and your men that will die."

The grin sneered as Valmyrjr said brazenly, "But, I think I will wait to kill you. It will be so much fun to have you watch me play with the princess, eh?" He shook Maratia's head with his grip in her hair. "Right, my darling fiancée?"

Jashar moved a few steps towards them.

Valmyrjr whipped out a knife and held it to Maratia's throat. "Back up, *King*," the sneer still present with his every word, "another step and I will slice her."

Jashar hesitated, his brows arched with doubt. "Aye? You wanted her so badly, you would kill her now?"

Valmyrjr's smile tightened with warning. "No. But I will severely injure her. I think it will be enough to stop you in your tracks. Am I right?"

Steel lacing his voice, his face was rock hard and filled will promise of retribution. Jashar demanded, "Let her go."

Valmyrjr looked affronted at Jashar's command. "What the hell, D'Avenant? She was mine, she is mine. She was promised to me by her parents."

"Aye, and she ran from you. She is her own woman. She makes the choice of where she wants to be, and with whom. If she wanted to be with you, I would turn and walk away and pray for her happiness."

Shaking his head, Valmyrjr's grin turned grim. He twisted her head so she was forced to look at him. "No she doesn't have a choice. She is a female. She has no rights in this world. I paid a lot of money to get her back. She is never leaving me again."

"No! I do not want to be with you, you cruel, horrible man! Let me go!" Maratia tried to wrench from his grasp but he released her hair to slam his arm just below her breasts and snapped her back against him.

He moved the knife forcing her to lift her chin and drop her head back to avoid being cut.

"Stop!" Valmyrjr ordered Jashar as he made a move towards them, and pulled Maratia so tight against his chest she struggled to draw a breath. "You have one chance, D'Avenant, to walk away. Go now and live."

"Why don't you let her go you sick fuck and fight me like a man?" Jashar taunted him, motioning for Valmyrjr to come to him.

Shaking his head with a smirk, Valmyrjr slightly lowered the knife and moved his hand to press against the bottom swell of her breast. "I don't need to fight you, King, my men will be here any second and take you out."

Jashar let out a deep resigned sigh. "All right. I don't see how I can get her out of here. I was trying to save face by coming for her, however," his lips bunched in submission, "she is not worth my life."

At Valmyrjr's surprised arched brows, Jashar held his hands up in the air and said, "May I just give her a message from a loved one before I take my leave?" His eyes on Maratia, Jashar's voice was complete sincerity.

Valmyrjr's forehead wrinkled as he considered letting Jashar speak so he would get the hell out. The side of his mouth quirked up in snide superiority. "Huh. I am surprised at your easy defeat. The legends of your bravery and warrior skills are clearly overrated."

"When fighting for my land and power," Jashar nodded with a wry smile, "of course I will battle royal. But, her," he jerked his jaw at Maratia. "A simple female?" He laughed with a toss of his head.

"Women are as plentiful as the sparrows in the fields. Even for one as captivating as this one tis not worth the bloodshed, my friend. As I said, I came half-heartedly really, to reclaim the woman. Makes me look bad, sir, your snagging her from right under my nose."

Sammel nodded, smirking in triumph.

"However," Jashar went on ruefully, "I can see the checkmate. I will cut my losses and move on. She is yours. I will not fight you when tis clear I would suffer great defeat."

297

"Very intelligent of you, my dear warlord king," Sammel replied with a pompous grin.

"So," Jashar sucked in another beleaguered sigh, "before I take my leave, as I requested, may I give her the message from her loved one?"

"Fine. Tell her." Sammel moved the hand with the knife to rest on her shoulder and kept the other around her waist but now not as tightly at Jashar's quick capitulation. He eyed the king with haughty disdain. In Sammel's mind, Jashar was nothing but a blowhard coward.

"Thank you. Maratia," Jashar's words were warm and soft, he stared hard at her.

Her eyes displayed her confusion at his meekness, yet they remained vibrant with her trust.

"Sweetheart," rolling his eyes like a spineless schoolboy, Jashar said timidly, "Tenny wants to bring you his ball. Right *now*."

Valmyrjr scoffed, "What kind of a mess-"

Maratia jabbed her elbow into his belly and dropped to the floor as Jashar had hoped she would like she was accepting a ball from the puppy. At the same moment Jashar threw his dagger-

Valmyrjr happened to move just as the knife reached him so it only grazed his throat. His hand went to his neck and he bellowed, "What the fuck-" he saw Maratia trying to scuttle away on the floor.

Roaring, "Get back here you bitch!" he reached for her.

Jashar raced to them and threw himself at Valmyrjr and the two men rolled to the floor with fists pounding.

The door opened and a guard ran down the stairs with his sword raised, he spotted Jashar and Valmyrjr on the ground fighting.

Jashar didn't see him coming, he had Valmyrjr pinned and his fist raised to deliver the killing blow-

Maratia screamed, "Jashar! Look out!"

The guard was almost upon him, he ignored her not seeing her as a threat.

Maratia ran as far as the ankle chain would allow her- it was enough- she grabbed up the stool nearby, raised it and whacked the guard in the back of the head.

He staggered, but still had his knife ready to plunge in Jashar's back, she swung the stool again and bashed the guard again and again until he dropped to the floor.

Jashar kept pounding his fist into Valmyrjr's already bloody face, until Valmyrjr stopped moving. Jashar jumped to his feet and rushed to Maratia.

He threw his arms around her, hugging her so tightly he feared he'd break her delicate form. He dropped his face into the side of her hair, murmuring in relief, "Baby, Maratia, praise *Dias*, you are safe."

She wrapped her arms around his neck and pulled his head down to kiss him. "You came for me, Jashar," she gushed against his accepting lips.

He smiled. "Aye, did you ever doubt it?" He smoothed her hair back and kissed her again. Then he straightened. "We need to get the hell out of here. Let me see that chain." He bent to look at the clamp around her ankle.

"The key is in his pocket," Maratia told him. "I had hoped at some point that when he was close enough I could do as I did with that guard," she nodded to the man lying on the floor. "Knock him out, get the key and escape."

His hands shaking from such gratitude that she was safe, Jashar cupped her face, smiled down at her. "Aye, and I believe you would have succeeded. But there was a little problem with the guards that protect this place."

"Speaking of, Sammel said his men would kill yours, that they way outnumber your men. I don't want anyone's blood on their hands because of me. I would die if any of your people were injured or killed."

"Hush sweetheart," he said softly, lowering his head to kiss her gently. "His men are basically guards with a little combat training, my men are warriors. There is not a chance his people did anything lethal."

At the relief expressed in her eyes, he told her, "Kaer and Daron were to do their best to quell any fighting, they were to try to just contain the men until I could get in and get you out. Come, let's go."

He slid his arm around her shoulders and they headed for the stairs.

Her head pressed against his chest, Maratia asked, "Jashar, why are you wet?"

He smiled as he led her out of the cellar of hell.

Chapter Thirty

The men Jashar had killed to gain entrance, Valmyrjr and a few of his guards were the only casualties. None of the warriors from Thuas sa Spéir region suffered any major injuries. They encountered no trouble returning home.

When they reached the village of Spiremoor, Jashar pulled Maratia down from his horse and kissed her.

"Sweetheart, I'm going to take care of Daoldubh and I have a few important things I need to do. I'd like a bath and I'm thinking you would like one as well to clean the filth of that man off of you."

He lightly touched her lips. "I should not have kissed you, he has been too brutal with you and your beautiful mouth is already swollen and there's a cut." He caressed her uninjured lip with the gentle pad of a fingertip.

"I'm fine, Jashar, now that I'm…home. With you." Maratia cupped the side of his face, her eyes filled with love. "I want nothing but to kiss you and kiss you, show you how proud I am of you."

"Nothing but kisses?" His brows rose comically, he wiggled them. "Isn't there something else you'd like to do with me?"

She laughed and stood on tiptoe and kissed him. "Yes, there are a lot of things I would like to do with you."

"How about we meet in my chambers after I've taken care of business and we can take that bath together?"

"All right," she replied with a grin. "I'll go there now and wait for you." One more light kiss and they both went in different directions.

Passing around the side of the castle to go in a side door that opened closer to the stairs, Maratia's step was light and happy, she was home with Jashar, she couldn't wait to make love with him and play with Tenny.

Dreaming of sexy time with Jashar, she ran her fingers through her hair trying to get the knots out before they bathed- a hand snaked out and covered her mouth, another wrapped around her waist and snatched her off her feet.

Struggling as she was hauled off her feet and quickly hauled down hallways until they sprung out a rear door.

Eyes wide over the harsh hand at her mouth, Maratia realized she was being carried towards the dungeon! She tried to scream but it was muffled by the hand covering her mouth. Thrashing her body, she kicked and punched at her assailant, she was shocked when she saw who it was!

Her fighting did nothing to slow him down.

As he reached the door to the dungeon, he threw her over his shoulder knocking the wind out of her, then carried her into the dark chambers.

Jashar hurried through his business, he had a beautiful, sweet woman waiting for him in his suite. Thoughts of the last time they bathed together sifted through his mind, bringing his lips up in a smile, and his manhood was already hardening in anticipation.

He had his woman back and he couldn't wait to show her how much he missed her, cherished her, and feared he'd never see her again when that cruel fool took her.

Finally done with grooming his horse and then attending quickly to his meetings, Jashar hurried to the castle.

As he strode across the cool smooth floor of the grand foyer he passed a few people.

They all wanted to stop and talk with him, but he waved them all on with a smile and moved quickly to the stairs. Taking them two at a time, he rushed down the corridors until he reached his room.

He opened the door.

She wasn't in the main room. He smiled, the little vixen must be in the bath waiting for him.

His heart filling with eagerness of soon being with Maratia, Jashar drew off his leather vest dropping it to the floor and headed straight for the bathing room.

When he got there he was puzzled.

She was not there.

Jashar realized the entire area was too quiet. He quickly raced through the rest of his rooms then halted at the front door when he concluded she was not in his lodgings.

He smiled, she must be in her chambers, she could not resist seeing the puppy. Leaving his rooms, he hurried down the hall to hers.

Throwing open the door he stopped dead when he saw McGee sitting in the middle of the floor with the dog.

"Sire!" McGee quickly rose to his feet with a grunt. A wad of dressing was wrapped around his wound, his face was cut and bruised, but his smile was cheerful and welcoming. "You're back! Did you get her?"

The puppy ran to Jashar, jumping up his leg barking and yelping.

Jashar absently bent and picked up the dog. "Aye. The mission was a success." Cradling the tiny Tenny against his massive chest, he frowned at the guard. "Are you saying Maratia has not been here, at all?"

Seeing the troubled look starting to enter Jashar's eyes, McGee grew uneasy. "Nay, Sire. I have not seen her since the day she was taken. Is she...all right?" His concern for her welfare evident on his face, his brows were drawing down as Jashar's were.

"Aye. She is banged up, but she is fine. I don't understand, she was to meet me in my chambers," he trailed off as apprehension took hold. He set the puppy down and headed for the door.

"Sire? Where are you going?" McGee jogged to the king.

Jashar threw the door open and hurried out stating, "I'm going to go look for her. Something is wrong."

McGee closed the door on Tenny's yelps and raced after Jashar.

The two men searched the entire castle questioning people if they'd seen the princessa. No one had.

They went out the main door. Jashar looked to the stables, she couldn't be there, that's where he had come from. He scanned the surrounding land, where could she have gone?

"Sire," McGee panted beside him, they had rushed from room to room and now ran outside. "I don't understand, where could she-" he stopped as Jashar took off running. The guard raced after his king.

Jashar ran to the dungeon. The door was locked from the inside. McGee hurried up to stand beside him.

McGee asked, "It's locked?"

Jashar nodded as he searched the area for something to get the door open. He heard a sound near the first barn, someone was chopping wood.

"Stay here," he instructed then sprinted to the sound. He found a villager chopping wood with an ax. The man was stunned when Jashar ran up and snatched the ax out of his hands and took off without a word.

He rushed to the dungeon.

McGee stood to the side as Jashar brought the ax down on the thick wooden door. He hit it and hit it until he knocked out most of the area around the lock, then the two men kicked at it together until it opened.

Jashar strode inside. He stopped so abruptly on the threshold. McGee almost ran into him.

Footsteps pounded up behind them.

"*Bráthair?*" Kaer popped in right behind McGee, Daron was with him. "What is going on? We heard you've been all over the castle looking for-" he broke off as he took in the scene inside the stone and lime room.

Chapter Thirty-One

In the middle of the cold chamber, Aran was with Maratia. They were kneeling and holding hands. Both of Maratia's hands held both of Aran's.

The couple turned as the four men poured into the room.

Aran's face was twisted with hate and rage, Maratia's was…sad.

Jashar jumped down the couple of steps into the room and strode purposefully towards the couple. His expression inscrutable, he barked, "What the hell is going on?"

The other men gathered beside him.

Maratia looked at Aran and then to Jashar. She shook her head sadly, her beautiful eyes awash with tears. "It was him, Jashar." She cringed as Aran squeezed her hands.

Glowering at Aran, the king commanded, "Explain."

The men around him looked baffled.

Maratia looked to Aran.

His face seethed red with fury, and guilt.

She waited, when he said nothing she took a deep breath and let it out with a pained sound.

Maratia tugged at her hands but Aran held them in a punishing grip. She looked back up to Jashar and pursed her lips.

Jashar took a step closer, his brow drawn down hard, he opened his mouth to demand an answer when Maratia blurted, "It was Aran who killed those girls. Your girls, the young women of **Thuas sa Spéir** that were savagely raped and viciously killed."

Jashar's eyes widened, incredulous, then narrowed with the beginnings of comprehension at the sight of Aran's angry red face.

To deflect her accusations, Aran snarled, "It was Thandie who sicced that guard on you, you bitch. She thought if he assaulted you the king would no longer desire you. Jashar tossed him out a window, but it is Thandie he should be punishing."

Maratia swallowed hard before saying, "But I wasn't murdered like those children. That," wincing, she paled, "that is all on you. Heartless, cruel, a horrendous nightmare of a man. Not even a man, you are the embodiment of the word monster. Pure, unconscionable reprehensible evil, Aran."

Aran gripped her hands so hard, a few tears fell as he hurt her.

Maratia said to Jashar, "He- was afraid you would find out that he was the one who sold me back to Sammel, that Sammel might have told me," she paused as Jashar's eyes shifted to Aran then back to her, his expression unreadable.

"So, he um, grabbed me and brought me here, I guess to kill me so I couldn't tell."

His fist wrapped around one of his daggers, Jashar's gaze dropped to their twined hands. "Why is he holding your hands?"

Maratia turned to Aran, every fiber of her soul wrung with sorrow. Looking at Aran she said quietly, "When he brought me here to kill me, I tried to run and he grabbed my hand to stop me, I struggled and we fell to the floor. That's when," her eyes flit to Jashar, "my gift," she didn't say anything more.

Dawning lit Jashar's rough face, still dirty from the rescue. "You felt his lie? But I don't understand, how did you know about the murders? Don't you need to hold two people's hands to discern who is telling the truth?"

The men beside him shuffled but kept quiet. All expressions were as puzzled as Jashar's.

Maratia shook her head. Her hair still in tangled ringlets from her ordeal with Sammel, the locks swished across her back. "No. I can tell if someone speaks the truth if I hold both their hands, and I can…"

She turned back to Aran who was rigid with his rage, his dark eyes spitting hate at her.

"I can sometimes *feel* uh, an episode in a person's life if it is…extreme enough. He admitted to me he started the rumors about the Princess Butcher to keep suspicion off him."

"Shut up, you bitch," Aran snarled. Fierce sadism ticked in his pitiless eyes. His eyes, polluted with sick cruelty, sociopathic malevolence twisting his face, he pulled her to him.

She resisted, saying quickly, "The- rapes and murders were so- horrible, devastating, and the thrill he got while," she took a breath, sniffed her tears back, "hurting them was so intense it- fairly radiated out of him, his body."

Her blue eyes slid up to Aran's angry face. "He vibrated with an…inferno of…unadulterated evil. I could see, images, some of what he did-" her chest retched with the horror of the visions she bore.

Blinking hard, a film of revulsion rolled over Daron's face, curling his lip and darkening his eyes. He said to Aran, "The look of guilt shrouds your face, half-brother." He nodded to Jashar. "She speaks the truth."

Kaer shouted at Aran, "How could you do that to those children you abominable bastard?"

Aran briefly turned his attention to the men, the evil in him hideously deforming his face. Even as enraged as he was, he smiled with sick delight. "Ah, because they were so young, so sweet, delicious little plump plums, every one of them."

His features pinched with disbelief and abhorrence, McGee declared with anguish, "You killed them, why did you have to take their lives?"

Aran glared at him like he was a moron. "Duh, because they would have told." His eyes hooded in a dreamy smile, he cooed, "Each one was like a blossom ready to be plucked, a fruit ready to be bitten." His eyes turned hard as marbles, he said with a sadistic sneer, "And believe, me, I did bite them."

Kaer whispered under his breath, "Don't kill him, *mi bráthair,* let him suffer the tribunal, the hell that Maratia was to bear.

"And now I've been found out. It's all your fault you bitch!" Aran let go of Maratia's hands and lunged for her shouting, "I'll break your fucking neck!"

Maratia brought her knee up and jammed him under the jaw jarring his head back. When he howled and grabbed his face she slammed both feet into his chest knocking him backwards. She tumbled onto her butt, her hands hitting the floor for bracing.

Aran rolled quickly, leaped to his feet and dove for her but Jashar was already there.

The king strung his big hands around Aran's neck and squeezed.

Aran clawed at his hands while choking, his eyes bugged out. In seconds he fell to his knees but Jashar kept squeezing.

Shouting, "Enough, *bráthair!*" Kaer grabbed one of Jashar's arms and Daron the other.

McGee swung around and grabbed a hold of the back of Aran's collar.

Quietly, firmly, Kaer said, "Stop, Jash, don't kill him. He needs to suffer for what he did. Killing is too quick." The brothers pulled on Jashar's arms wrestling him back from Aran.

Jashar stumbled, his face dark and fierce with fury, eyes like black steel bore into Aran. He fought his brothers' grasp, but the sense of what Kaer said filtered into his enraged brain and he stopped fighting.

His chest pumped with the mighty strain of holding back from murdering Aran and avenging the girls and Maratia. Shoving a hand through his hair, pushing it back off his forehead he panted hard as he tried to gain control of his anger.

Maratia scrambled to her feet and ran over and threw herself at him.

He froze, the rage still burned in him, he didn't want to hurt her.

Softly, she murmured, "I love you, Jashar, I love you, my hero."

Her sweet voice and beautiful words calmed Jashar. He shook off his brothers' hold on him and dropped his arms around her and pulled her into his embrace.

Daron helped McGee take custody of Aran, they shuffled him out of the dungeon. King Allon would want to see him before they locked him in a cell.

Kaer turned to Jashar and slapped him on the back. "Well then, *mi bráthair,* this evil sickness that plagued our people is finally over." He smiled at Maratia. "And, we have the beautiful princessa back. All is good with the world."

Maratia laid her head on Jashar's thick chest, he brought a hand up and stroked her face. She murmured, "Finally, we can all live in peace."

"Aye." Kaer grinned. "So, am I going to be your best man?"

"Yea," Jashar replied lowering his head to Maratia's. "We will put out the wedding banns tomorrow. But right now, we have a date with a bath." He captured her lips, her hands wound around his neck.

Grinning cheerfully, Kaer silently gave the couple their privacy, he whistled as he skipped up the steps and out the door.

Epilogue

Five months later

"Please, stop," Maratia begged the servant, Adella, who was tugging tightly on the bindings of her corset. "I can't draw a breath!"

"I swear," Sheera shook her head with a frown as she watched the two servants trying to dress Maratia in the lace and beaded wedding gown. "You fit in it two weeks ago, what, have you been doubling down on desserts?"

Adella tied off the bindings and with the help of the other maid they held the white gown over Maratia's head then drew it down until it settled on her curvy body.

Adjusting and patting the dress in place around her hips, they smoothed the satin material down until it spooled neatly on the floor around her feet.

"Bend your head, my dear," Adella said. When Maratia complied, the maid set the veil on her curled tresses and pinned it in place, then she stood back with an admiring smile.

"Aye, my soon to be sister," Sheera grinned, "not that you already don't, but you're going to take my brother's breath away. You are absolutely stunning!"

Maratia held still as Adella clipped pearl earrings on her ears and then clasped a matching pearl necklace around her slender throat.

"You-" Sheera broke off in dismay as Maratia suddenly lurched and ran to the bathing room. At the retching sounds, Sheera and the maids shared a knowing, pleased smile.

They had Maratia cleaned up and ready to go when her father entered the room.

King Lanaris smiled ear-to-ear at his lovely daughter. "My darling child," he said as he moved to her. "You are glowing, clearly you are deeply in love with your king."

Maratia smiled happily up at him and he leaned to plant a soft kiss on her cheek. "I am Papa. A dream come true, my warlord king is soon to be my husband."

"And to think that she-bitch Thandie had her designs on my brother!" Sheera grimaced at the thought. Then her eyes danced, she said, "But that witch hadn't a chance with you in the picture, Mara."

"Huh," Adella grunted. "Even without the beautiful princessa around our king never looked twice at that strumpet. He knows trash when he sees it."

"And diamonds when he sees them," the other servant, Nannett lifted her chin at Maratia. The other women laughed and agreed, loudly.

"Anyway," Sheera said cheerfully, "we don't need to worry about that woman. Jashar had charged her an enormous fine and then exiled her to Canthopia for her part in letting that Sammel gain access to the castle to steal Maratia away."

Adella adjusted Maratia's curls to flow in ringlets down her back. "Huh," she grunted again. "Serves her right. There are no creature comforts for the exiled in Canthopia. No shops, no brasseries, no grocers, she'll have to grow her own food, make all her own clothes. She'll be lucky if she has moving water in her bathing room. And it will not be warm water at that!"

Her mouth curved up in a goading smile, Sheera added, "And the hut she'll be living in, alone, is miles from any other people. There will be no handsome farmers for her to lure and take advantage of, seduce to help her."

Maratia's head came up. She said sadly, "That sounds so dreadful. Maybe I should speak to Jashar about not-"

"No!" Everyone shouted in unison.

Sheera set a hand on Maratia's arm. "Don't feel sorry for her. She knew full well how that creep Sammel would have treated you. He would have kept you locked inside his castle forever, beating and torturing you in between using you as a breeder for his spawn."

Maratia blanched at the memory of Sammel's threats of pain and torment. "Still-"

"No!" They all shouted again.

Straightening Maratia's veil, Sheera said, "She's lucky Jashar doesn't believe in flogging women or worse. He didn't want her in a cell because he feared she would seduce some wayward soldier into abetting her."

"And she would start batting her eyes the second the cell door closed on her," Adella said.

"She deserves her punishment," Sheera said with no sympathy. "So does our mother. I don't know if Jashar will ever forgive her. He doesn't speak or look at her. My father begged Jash to let her attend the wedding."

"And? Will she be present?" Maratia asked, not sure if she would be comfortable with the woman who hated her watching the nuptials.

Fluffing her own dark curls, Sheera told her, "Jash relented somewhat. She will be allowed to sit in the last pew at the back, but he doesn't want her at the reception. He doesn't want her to come in contact with you and upset you.

"Her shame will be in watching her first born, and our king, marry and none of the villagers or warriors will acknowledge her presence. She will not be honored at the event as she would have as queen."

"Oh, dear, I'm breaking up your family!" Maratia exclaimed in horror.

"No," Sheera said quickly. "Mother did that, not you. She still treated you dreadfully even after it was proved Aran was the butcher of the little girls. And, she was also complicit in allowing Sammel to be able to get to you. We will have to see how the future unfolds to ascertain her position in the family. Once grandbabies start popping she may change her attitude." She grinned at the blush that swiftly rose over Maratia's face.

Smiling at the soon to be queen, Nannett said to Adella, "I've heard Aran's punishment has begun."

"Aye," Adella grimaced. "His back has been shredded and one of largest, meanest of the warriors will start the next part. You know," she lowered her voice, "the mirror penalty for raping the girls." The two maids shared a gruesome shudder.

Lanaris cleared his throat. "Ahem. We must set up a time soon for you to visit home."

Maratia's head tilted with her warm smile. "This is now my home, Papa. Wherever Jashar is will be my home. He is my home." Her mouth twitched at the collective romantic, "Ah's" from the women in the room.

"Of course, of course," Lanaris said in agreement. "But your family and old friends still reside in Ailanthus therefore you must break away on occasion to see us."

"We will come, Papa, I promise. But, it may be a while because I-"

"Well!" Sheera said quickly, interrupting Maratia's about to be confession. "I'm sure your guests are all waiting, dear sister-in-law, we should get going!"

Lanaris turned to Maratia. Tugging on his jacket sleeves, he held his curved arm to his daughter to take. "Of course. We should head downstairs. One of Jashar's brothers has escorted your mother to her seat. Ladies," he bowed to Sheera and the two maids.

The chapel at the far end of the castle was stuffed with villagers and warriors all chatting amicably. Pink peonies and violets filled baskets throughout, their sweet scent permeating the air under pink and white ribbons that wreathed the room.

The vast chamber immediately became quiet when the organist started playing and the harpist plucked the musical strings. All turned as Sheera started down the aisle carrying a bouquet of pink and white peonies and violets.

When she reached the altar, she moved to stand next to Daron who winked at her.

Jashar stood on the altar with Kaer as his witness.

Kaer was grinning like a trussed peacock but Jashar looked as cold and grim as usual.

Then, Lanaris started up the rose petal strewn aisle with Maratia on his arm, and the brooding coldness in Jashar's eyes warmed to soft dark chocolate as he gazed at his bride.

Carrying a bouquet of calla lilies and violets, Maratia smiled at villagers and family as she passed them, then her step stuttered when her eyes connected with Jashar's.

Lanaris grinned at the sharp change in Jashar's cold expression and urged Maratia forward.

Jashar moved down the few steps to meet them. Sheera took Maratia's bouquet from her.

At the altar, Lanaris handed his daughter to Jashar's keeping and bowed to the king of Thuas sa Spéir. "Take care of her, son, she is precious."

His eyes on Maratia, Jashar said solemnly, "Aye, she is that, sir."

Jashar held his arm out and Maratia slid her hand inside and he drew her close to him. "My bride," he whispered with a grin. He led her up to the altar where the priest awaited with the Holy Book open in his palms.

The priest said his words and Jashar and Maratia repeated their vows, and they were now joined as husband and wife.

Lifting her veil, Jashar pushed it back off her face and kissed her. He sighed with longing for more when he separated their lips and Maratia's misty eyes beamed up at him.

Jashar raised their clasped hands and turned them to face their guests. His smile grew wide as the crowd cheered the new couple.

"Onto the party! Kaer shouted as Jashar and Maratia started walking hand-in-hand back down the aisle now duly wedded.

Sheera batted Kaer's arm as they followed the new couple through the chapel. "Behave yourself, brother," she playfully admonished.

Daron trotted up behind them. "As if he could ever act with proper decorum," Daron teased his brother. The siblings joked and giggled all the way to the grand room in the castle set up for the reception.

In the grand room, music played joyfully and loudly, the crowd was happily boisterous. Couples were already dancing in the open space in front of the musicians.

A great buffet was spread out over several tables and guests were heaping plates high with colorful rich food.

Jashar drew his bride to the side and kissed her. Cheers and randy suggestions rang up around them, but the lovers were oblivious to the attention.

"I love you, my wife," Jashar whispered as he set his forehead against hers.

"And I love you, my wonderful husband," Maratia whispered back.

"Can't wait for the honeymoon," Jashar whispered with a sly grin.

"Huh," she snorted a laugh. "We haven't stopped honeymooning since you brought me back here!"

He chuckled. "And that isn't going to end, my love, not ever. Even when we start having the wee ones, I plan on ravishing you day and night."

Her lips bunched, she cocked her head and smiled an uncertain secret smile. "Um, there's something I need to tell you, Husband." Suddenly Maratia wasn't so sure.

Maybe he didn't want children, maybe he did but not for a long, long time. She bit her lip in trepidation.

"What is it, darling?" Jashar asked, concerned at her sudden worried expression.

"I," she looked down demurely.

"What?" Now he was worried. "Are you ill? Please tell me you are all right, my love. I-" he swallowed and cupped her cheek. "I could not live without you. Tell me, tell me you are okay."

Her long lashes swept over round pink cheeks as she gazed lovingly up at him. "I, um, do have something to tell you. I, well, I pray that you are not angry with me."

His brows daggered down. "Never. I will never be angry with you, my beloved bride." A soft bliss filled his eyes as he gazed at her. "Now, tell me, what is it that has you so wrought in nerves."

She pulled his head down and whispered in his ear.

Jashar froze.

Maratia held her breath.

Then the partying throng suddenly stilled at the roaring "Whoopee!" that bellowed from the king.

Sheera and her brothers, whom she had told the secret to all grinned with glee at the adoring way Jashar gazed at Maratia.

As Jashar splayed his big palm tenderly on Maratia's belly and smiled at her so broadly it had to hurt, Kaer called out, "Blessings to my brother, his bride, and our soon to be princess niece or prince nephew!"

The newly wedded couple didn't hear them, they were too busy engulfed in their embrace and scorching kiss!

The End

Dear Reader, thank you for purchasing The Butcher Princess! *I know you could have picked any number of books to read, but you picked this book and for that I am extremely grateful.*

I hope you enjoyed this novel, and if you did, **please leave a review** *where you purchased it, and look for other exciting titles in my name!*

Please look for my other historical romances as well as my contemporary romance/suspense stories.